ISBN: 978-1-965714-01-0

This series of books is based on historical figures, locations, and events. However, all physical descriptions of these persons and locations, characters' personal behavior, and dialogue and conversations are fictitious. Some characters are purely fictional, and any similarities these characters have to real people are only coincidental.

The storyline is based on real people who lived at the time this series is set and follows many of the historical events that occurred during their lifetime. The dialogue and connections between characters and storyline are solely the imagination of the author. The political and personal views portrayed in this historical series are strictly those of the author.

This series is the culmination of many years of work. The research and writing of this series involved the reading of many documentary books by renowned authors. Any resemblance to those author's writing is coincidental.

This historical fiction series is licensed for your personal reading pleasure. Your copy should not be gifted or re-sold. If you enjoyed this series, please purchase additional copies and present them to people you feel would appreciate this historical novel series. Writing a series such as this takes a lot of time and effort, so I ask you to respect the efforts of this author.

Chapter 1

Redwood Agency, Minnesota

August 18th, 1862

AN IRRITATE MAN tosses and turns on his not-so-comfortable goose feather under-stuffed mattress.

A canine stands snarling by the door.

Joe asks, "What is it, boy?"

The dog acknowledges the question with a turn of his head but turns his attention to the door again, growls, and lies down in front of it.

Unable to sleep soundly the entire night, 29-year-old Joe Carsoulle throws back the covers and gets out of bed again.

'Damn, another night of little sleep. I'm going to be regretting it at work soon.'

Joe, a fur trader and teamster at the Redwood agency, is a mixed-blood. His young French Dakota wife, Jane, also lies awake, also frustrated by the interruption of her slumber.

Joe whispers, "Sorry, I can't sleep."

"That makes two of us. Just lay down and try."

On his way to the window, he passes their hound dog. It continues to growl.

A tired smile gives way to an obvious question, "I will as soon as I check on what is bothering him."

Jane rolls over and pulls the covers over her shoulder.

Joe recalls the meaning of his Dakota name, Hinhankaga, which was given to him at birth. It ironically means 'The Owl'. At the window, he parts the bed sheet curtains that hang from square nails. He stares out at the 'full moon' lit night.

'Nothing to see out there but those few clouds drifting over our modest log cabin.'

His three children, two daughters, Elizabeth, six, Minnie, four, and his nine-month-old baby boy, Little Joe, are sound asleep.

Joe's parents died at a young age. He was adopted and raised by a wealthy man from Mendota. A trader turned Indian Agent who eventually became the first governor of the Minnesota Territory, Henry Sibley.

In frustration, Joe turns away from the window and runs his hands through his long black hair. He slides back under the covers in another attempt to get some sleep. Moments later, he is surprised as a cool hand touches his shoulder. His sudden alarm awakens his wife, who begins to scream but is cautioned by the female voice speaking in Dakota.

The woman speaks softly, "Be calm."

Joe sighs.

Jane attempts to scream.

He comforts his wife by holding her in his arms.

The visitor says, "Shhhh, Hinhankaga, be still. I am here to warn you. Today, warriors will come to kill all whites."

"But?"

"And those that help the whites."

Joe acknowledges the statement and unwraps his arms from around his wife. He throws back the covers.

The messenger continues, "Hurry, you must go. There is little time."

Jane regains her composure and protests to the unannounced visitor, "What do you mean? And how did you get in here?"

"Never mind the questions. There is no time to waste. Don't tell anyone who warned you. I have taken a great risk. If they find out, they will kill me too."

As quietly as she entered, the Dakota woman vanishes. Their watchdog chews ravenously on fresh meat by the door.

Joe and his wife don't hesitate. They gather the children, leave the dog that is prone to barking in the log cabin, and flee down the hill to the banks of the Minnesota River. The only light, a few stars scattered between the thin clouds and the full moon. The family of five creeps through the sharp reeds. There, in those reeds of the river bank, lies a small dug-out canoe, Joe's personal vessel. He uses it to cross the river to get to work at the trading post. Joe readies his canoe as his family huddles together to stay warm. Increasing cloudiness has brought almost total darkness a few hours before sunrise.

Joe whispers, "Girls, I will take Mother and little Joe to the other side first. I'll be right back for the two of you."

Elizabeth pleads, "Don't leave us!"

Minnie asks, "Why can't you take us with you?"

"Because the canoe is not big enough for us all."

Joe kisses both on their foreheads and gives them a blanket. Then tells them, "Hide in these reeds, don't make a sound. I'll be right back."

The two girls do as they are told.

Joe whispers one last instruction, "Be quiet. No talking."

He paddles as quickly and quietly as he can in the darkness. Joe spots movement on the shore, where he has left his two daughters. He stops paddling abruptly. Four Dakota braves in war paint have emerged from the woods and are walking along the path beside the river.

Jane notices and turns. In a hushed call, "The girls!"

Joe whispers to his beloved wife, "Be quiet."

The mother, father, and infant child drift downriver farther and farther. Joe waits until the four warriors are out of sight and earshot. He resumes paddling silently but only as quickly as he can risk. Reaching the far shore, he beaches his dug-out canoe. Joe helps his wife and child out while standing in the shallow water of the river's edge.

Joe ensures them, "I'll be right back. Stay out of sight."

Jane and her infant child huddle between two trees on the dew-covered muddy bank of the river.

Joe hastily paddles, turning often to see if the coast is still clear. Finally, he beaches his craft again on the other side of the river.

He wades through the reeds softly, calling, "Girls… Elizabeth, Minnie, come out!"

There is no answer or any sign of movement. Joe continues searching the reeds and tall grass. He finds nothing.

'Maybe they went back to the cabin.'

Joe retraces his steps back to the family's cabin. All the while, he keeps an eye out for his two precious daughters. The other eye searches for more warriors. On his way back to the log cabin, he smells smoke. He sees the flickering of light between the tree trunks and the many low-hanging branches. He continues to creep closer. As he approaches the last bend in the footpath, he can hear the crackling and roar of a fire. His log cabin, their home, is engulfed in flames.

In the distance, he hears gunfire and screams to terrorize and screams of terror. Smoke rolls above the treetops from the flames of the agency buildings set ablaze.

He returns to his wife Jane. She sees he is alone.

She almost screams, "No! Are the dead?"

"Shhh, I don't know. They were not there."

"Did you look?"

Joe, "Of course, I went back to our cabin. I went to the agency. I didn't see any women dead. So, I believe they are alive."

"What do you mean you didn't see any dead women? You mean you saw men dead?"

"Yes, many bodies, some gruesome deaths."

Jane trembles with the cold of the night and fright, "I didn't see anyone while you were away. But I heard many gunshots and much screaming."

"I heard that too. Enough. We must make our way to the fort."

"That is over twelve miles."

Joe insists, , "We'll make it." But worries, "If we stay out of sight."

***

THE SAME MORNING, just before 6:00 am, an hour or so before sunrise, George Spencer, a heavy-set clerk at the Forbes Trading Post on the lower agency, gets ready to open for business. Outside the front window on the dew-covered dirt street, he notices several natives gathering. All carrying various armaments of war while also dressed and painted for the same. The Dakota dressed for war isn't anything out of the ordinary. The Dakota have regularly engaged with their sworn enemy, the Ojibway, usually over territory and other grievances of honor.

George opens the trading door and takes a few steps outside, "What is it this time?"

A warrior responds, "Nothing to be worried about. We have word the Ojibway are in the area."

"Well, if you need anything, I'll be open soon."

George shakes his head with a laugh, reenters his store, leaves the door open, and returns to his morning routine.

A short while later, four of Spencer's co-workers wander outside to take a coffee break. They sit on wooden chairs on the porch to watch the parade of Dakota warriors gathering in the streets. Without any warning, the shooting starts. All four clerks are shot and killed almost immediately. At hearing the musket fire, Spencer rushes to the door. Shot three times before he can close and bar the door. He bleeds profusely from his wounds.

Spencer, in pain and agony, shouts, "Get upstairs!"

He, another white clerk, and Billy Findley, a mixed-blood young boy, climb up a rickety wooden ladder and hide in the attic.

The Dakota warriors break down the door. Some begin taking what they want from the trading post. Others gather at the bottom of the ladder.

First warrior at bottom of ladder, "Send the boy down. We will not hurt him."

George whispers to the clerk in the attic, "We can't trust them."

The clerk responds, “There is no way out of here.”

“I’m going to bleed to death, but you might be able to escape.”

“How? You seen how many of them there are!”

George rationalizes, “They don’t want the boy, it is you they want, … you!”

“That is not helping.”

“When you get to the bottom of the ladder, look for your chance.”

Billy looks puzzled at the two discussing his fate. He blurts out, “They’ll kill me too.”

George insists, “No, you are of mixed blood. You, they will let live."

“Are you sure?”

There is no answer.

The white clerk to the boy, “You go first.”

Little Billy Findley cowers behind George and whines, “Why me?”

George, “Just go.”

The clerk and young boy gingerly descend the ladder with their backs turned to the warriors. The young boy steps off the last rung and turns to the Dakota braves. When the clerk steps off the ladder, he turns to his tormentors and pushes the mixed-blood boy into them. In the confusion, the white clerk runs for the back door. He doesn't get far.

Warriors quickly tackle him outside and strip him of all of his clothes. A wood pile is nearby, so they begin to pile firewood on top of him.

Standing bewildered nearby is the half-breed boy who asks, "Why are you doing this?"

There is no answer.

Gunfire from the other agency buildings distracts these warriors. They also hear screaming coming from the rest of the lower agency. Two of the attackers leave with the child.

Trapped under the weight of the logs, the clerk pleads, "Don't kill me!"

Second warrior, "We will burn you alive for cheating us. For killing our families."

"Please don't. I didn't cheat you or kill your families."

"But you did."

More of the attackers hear the commotion not far away. Two more leave.

A Dakota brave carrying more logs approaches the firewood-covered clerk. Screams and gunfire come from all around. The brave drops the logs and disappears.

Now, only one warrior remains.

Standing over the clerk, the last warrior says, "Don't you leave. We'll be back." He drops the wood..

The dumbfounded clerk tries to peek through the pile of logs. Then begins to call for help and then stops.

'That is not a good idea.'

No one is there. He begins to wiggle and squirm slowly at first. The logs start to roll off of him one by one, then more. Finally, he is free. Scanning his surroundings, he spots his clothing, quickly grabs them, and hobbles to a nearby stand of trees for cover.

***

GEORGE SPENCER REMAINS in the attic until he, too, feels the coast is clear. Unaware of the fate of the other two, but believes the worst. He climbs down from the same rickety ladder, blood oozing from his wounds.

He mutters to himself, "I'm going to die." He limps to his living quarters in the back of the trading post, lifts the covers, and climbs into his bed.

An hour passes as he listens to the commotion from all over the Redwood Agency. Screams, then gunfire, then silence. Whoops and hollers repeat until Spencer hears footsteps in the store. In great pain, unable to move, in a vain attempt to conceal himself, he pulls the covers over his head.

A single set of footsteps comes closer and closer. The bedroom door opens with a long creak. Spencer remains still. One of Little Crow's most trusted warriors, Wakinyatawa, stands alone in the doorway. Dressed and painted for war, he notices the outline of the potbellied trader under the homemade quilt. He smiles as he sees the cover rise and fall and hears a moan of pain.

He approaches the bed, "George, is that you?"

Spencer does not answer.

The inquisitive friend of ten years pulls back the covers.

Spencer hands over his face, "Don't kill me!"

"I am not going to kill you, but judging by the amount of blood you've lost, you may die if we don't get you some help."

The shocked look on Spencer's face turns to a sigh.

The warrior friend, "Here, let me get you out of that bed. I'll have my woman take care of your wounds."

Wakinyatawa helps Spencer to the front door. They both step over the bodies of his employees, who lay in front of the doorway. They meet fellow warriors outside in the street.

One of the braves, "There is to be no mercy!"

Wakinyatawa, "He is my friend. If you want to kill him, you'll have to kill me first."

The warriors don't hesitate to leave.

***

AROUND 6:00 AM the same horrific morning, a 60-year-old, Philander Prescott, opens the door of his home when he sees Little Crow outside.

Little Crow, "Stay in your house."

Throughout the agency, Dakota warriors swarm around every building, all painted and armed for war.

Not taking that advice, Philander hitches up his wagon, gathers his wife, and flees toward Fort Ridgely. Prescott is married to a Dakota woman and instructs the natives, who are willing to learn how to farm and interpret for the traders. He makes it a few miles before a band of Dakota warriors stops him. He pleads for his life, but he is shown no mercy. They take his wife captive.

***

THE DAKOTA BRAVES silently surrounded every building in the Redwood agency village that fateful morning. Every building, whether or not it is associated with or supports the agency, is encircled. The stone warehouse, the sawmill, the boarding school, the mess hall, the stable, all of the houses for the agents and superintendents, and the four trading posts.

Little Crow and many of his loyal Dakota braves gather specifically around one trading post, the one owned by Andrew Myrick.

Myrick, a late sleeper, is still under the covers in his upstairs bedroom. His clerk, James Lynd, sits in the doorway of the trading post, drinking coffee. Lynd has three children by two Dakota women. He is the first to die at Myrick's trading post. Shot where he sat. A second clerk, George Washington Divoll, hears the gunshot and comes to see what has happened. He is also shot and killed. Even ole man Fritz, his German cook, was not spared.

When Andrew Myrick hears the shooting start, he peers out his upstairs window to see the streets filled with painted warriors. He tries to hide in a large cedar chest in his second-floor bedroom. Then, he hears the frustrated warriors searching downstairs.

Unable to find him, one Dakota warrior declares, "Myrick! We will burn the building down with you in it."

Another yells, "Wachinco… Spunky!"

The warriors all laugh.

Myrick doesn't see the humor in his nickname at this time.

He immediately flips open the lid on the wooden box, climbs out, and scurries as silently as possible to the back window. But the creaking wooden floorboards betray him. Myrick understands he has been discovered. So, he scampers out the window, reaches for a nearby flag pole, swings himself over to a lower porch roof, and jumps to the ground from there. He runs for cover in a grove of trees that has a groundwater spring inside. But he is quickly surrounded by a horde of warriors and forcefully pinned down to the ground. A warrior to each limb. He lies prone on his back.

"Don't kill me."

There is no response from Little Crow or the Dakota braves surrounding him.

Myrick notices those holding him down have turned to look at something. A Dakota warrior approaches.

Myrick asks, "What is it?"

The warrior comes to a halt over him.

"It is for you." Little Crow informs the prone man on the ground.

"What is it?" Myrick asks again.

Laughter by all who have pinned him to the ground.

Little Crow, "If you are hungry, you can eat it."

The warrior carries a hand full of fresh horse dung.

Myrick furiously tries to shake free. He wiggles and squirms to no avail. The brave with the smelly dung in hand kneels next to him. He recalls what he said just days before.

“I didn’t mean it.”

Little Crow adamantly disagrees, "Oh, yes, you did."

Myrick clinches his teeth, refusing to open his mouth. A Dakota bravely reaches in, puts his fingers on both sides of Myrick's mouth, and squeezes viciously. Myrick continues to resist until he feels the sharp point of a knife penetrate his chest. Immediately, the brave forces the horse manure into his mouth. Myrick gags and writhes in pain and humiliation. He tries to spit it out. But the warrior forces his mouth closed.

Myrick hears a familiar voice state, “No, it is you who can eat shit.”

After they all laugh hysterically, Little Crow states, "Enough."

Little Crow motions for the assailants to stand. All those pinning Myrick to the ground get up and look at each other.

Myrick remains defeated now sitting on the ground. He spits, wipes his mouth, and tries to speak.

Little Crow pulls his arrow from his sheath and places it across his bow.

Myrick looks up, “Don’t kill me.”

The rest of the six warriors surrounding Myrick also pull arrows across their bows.

“Please don’t kill me. I didn’t mean it!”

Little Crow, “Oh, yes, you did!"

One after another, each warrior sends an arrow piercing Myrick’s chest.

***

LITTLE CROW AND his followers pass by Reverend Samuel Hinman's church and parsonage. Little Crow had attended the preacher's service the day before. The reluctant warrior chief even complimented Hinman on his sermon. But today, a crowd of warriors has the minister outside his home, secured to a tree and ready to be killed.

Hinman sees Little Crow approach, "Please have mercy on me. Please?"

A disgusted Little Crow announces, "Let him live."

The surprised warriors release the urine-soaked preacher.

Hinman collapses to the ground, "Thank you, thank you."

***

THE ATTACK ON the Redwood agency is complete, but the carnage spreads to the surrounding countryside. Desperate refugees begin to arrive at Fort Ridgely around ten that dreadful morning. At first, the officers didn't believe the stories until the wounded arrive.

Captain John Marsh commands the two companies of troops stationed at Fort Ridgely. He had previously fought as a private at the battle of Bull Run in the war back east. Now, he faces the responsibility of decision-making.

He gives the order, "Assemble the troops!"

Sergeant Bishop to the bugler, "You heard him!"

A bugler sends out the appropriate signal.

Men come running from all corners of the wide-open garrison. What is called a fort is actually a mix of buildings scattered haphazardly with no barricades or fortifications.

Marsh to his sergeant, "This can only be the work of a small group of drunken renegades."

"But Sir, the wounded are saying."

"I know. They are scared and hysterical civilians."

A few minutes later, seventy-five soldiers are standing at attention.

Captain Marsh finishes his directives to the men, "We have a job to do. Let's get this done quickly."

He instructs Sergeant Bishop, "I want one company. Have them gather one day's provisions, ammunition, and gear. Be ready in a half hour."

"One day, Sir?"

"Yes, we will be back by nightfall."

Sergeant Bishop, "You sure?"

Marsh dismisses the question.

Marsh to Peter Quinn, an evacuee, "You are coming with us. We'll probably need you as an interpreter." Then to his Lieutenant, "Gere, you are in charge here."

Nineteen-year-old Lieutenant Thomas Gere takes command of the twenty-nine men left to defend this spread-out group of buildings.

Lt. Gere asks, "Yes, Sir. Should I send word to Lt. Sheehan?"

Just the day before, Lt. Sheehan was sent to Fort Ripley on the Mississippi River with a company of fresh recruits. These fifty men had signed up to fight back east.

Captain Marsh, "Yes, that is a good idea, even though this is probably nothing to be concerned about."

Marsh to a private, "I need you to take a message to Lt. Sheehan."

The captain quickly writes, then seals a note and hands it to the private.

> The note reads
>
> You are to return to the fort immediately. Some of the natives are raising hell at the Lower Agency.

Captain Marsh leads his forty-seven men along the river toward the Redwood Agency. Only six miles out, they discover the first evidence of what they are up against. The column of soldiers sees from a distance a cabin engulfed in flames.

Bugler, "This is where Doctor Humphrey and his family live.

A private yells, "There is a survivor."

A boy emerges from hiding, petrified by what he has witnessed.

Captain Marsh dismounts and approaches the young boy, "Are you alright?"

Unable to talk, the boy stands there stone-faced.

Marsh continues to ask, "What happened here?"

Sergeant Bishop suggests, "Give him some water, that might help."

Captain Marsh is handed a canteen. Opening it, he places it up to the boy's lips.

The boy's eyes glance at Marsh's. He takes a drink of water and responds, "My father sent me for water."

"Did you see who did this?"

He shakes his head yes.

"What can you tell us? How many were there?"

He shrugs his shoulders and begins to cry uncontrollably.

Captain Marsh tells Bishop, "Have some men check for other survivors."

The boy utters under his breath, "They killed my family, they killed my pa. Right over there."

He points to the body, which is not far away.

Sgt. Bishop, "You three go check."

Captain Marsh to the boy, "Are you able to walk?"

The boy shakes his head yes.

"Do you know where the fort is?"

The lad shakes his head yes.

"Good. I'll have this private take you to the fort. They'll take care of you there."

Both the private and young boy nod yes.

Captain Marsh pats the boy on the shoulders.

Bishop reports, "No other survivors, Sir."

Marsh announces to his men, “Mount up.”

The column of forty-six men proceeds toward the Redwood Agency. With each turn in the road, over every hill, they encountered more and more refugees. Reverend Hinman is among the refugees.

The reverend announces, "Captain, you should not go any further. You don't have enough men."

Captain Marsh, “We'll see.”

"Do not go to the Redwood agency. They are everywhere, hundreds of them. They're mad… They are crazy!"

“What started this?”

Hinman shakes his head violently and thrashes his arms, "I don't know, but they surrounded every last building in the Lower agency. When the order came down, they began killing everyone."

“Who gave the order?”

"I don't know. It all happened so fast. I don't know, but it was not a random act. It was planned."

Captain Marsh, “How many of them are there?”

“All of them… hundreds of them. From every tribe near the Redwood agency.”

“Serg, have the men get ready to move out!”

Bishop relays that message to the bugler, and he sounds off.

Horses and men begin to assemble into formation.

Reverend Hinman recommends, “If you must go, go no further than the ferry landing.”

Marsh, “Why?”

“You don't have enough men.”

Captain Marsh, “We'll see for ourselves.”

The column moves out again toward the ferry landing across from Lower Agency.

Sergeant Bishop, "Captain, maybe we should listen to the Reverend after what we have already seen?"

"We'll see for ourselves. I've seen it before. These civilians exaggerate. This can't be more than a few out-of-control savages."

The column of less than fifty men arrives at the ferry landing opposite the Redwood Agency by noon. All is quiet. In the distance, smoke from the Lower Agency rises above the treetops. The ferry secured to the post.

Bishop states, "It looks ready for use."

"Yes, it does. But there is no ferry operator."

"That is understandable given the circumstances."

Marsh confidently asks, "Where is everyone? See, it is not as bad as they said."

The location is tranquil, with tall reeds along the bank fluttering in the light breeze. Brush and thickets of young trees surround the landing. On the other side of the river, a lone Dakota Brave approaches the landing.

White Dog yells in his native language, "Captain, come across. We have no quarrel with the army. We only have issues with the traders. We want to council with you to help settle our differences."

Quinn, the interpreter, tells Captain Marsh what he said.

Marsh to his sergeant, "See, it isn't anywhere as bad as the Reverend and those people said."

Bishop doesn't respond but continues to scan the surroundings.

A corporal next to Sergeant Bishop mentions, "I'm out of water."

Bishop, “Me too. Captain?”

Marsh, “Go ahead, but be quick about it.”

The two soldiers dismount to fill their canteens from the river.

Captain Marsh to Quinn, “Ask him what started all of this?”

After receiving White Dog's response, Quinn translates to Marsh, "He wants us to come across so he can explain."

"Tell him, sure. Give us a minute to get the ferry set up." Then, to the closest two privates, "Ready the ferry."

The privates dismount and begin to secure the ferry.

***

SERGEANT BISHOP AND the corporal squat down along the river bank and open their canteens.

Bishop, in a whisper, "Over there, don't turn. To your right."

“I see em.”

"Don't let them know you see them. Not yet!"

They see on the other side of the fifty-yard-wide river several natives hiding among the reeds.

The Corporal whispers, “Look there.”

“What?”

"In the water. It's muddy and filled with leaves and debris."

Bishop, “What of it?”

“That means they are on this side too! That debris means they have crossed upstream.”

“Stay calm, don’t let them know we know.”

The two men finish filling their canteens, stand up, and casually wander further downriver. On the other bank, they spot many Dakota ponies hidden in the distant trees.

Bishop doesn’t wait any longer. He yells, “Captain, I think we are surrounded. There are a lot of Indian ponies in those trees.”

Captain Marsh urgently instructs Quinn to ask White Dog, "If everyone is waiting at the agency, why are all those horses hidden over there?"

White Dog didn’t wait to hear the translation. He casually raises his rifle and fires into the air. All at once, the trees and brush erupt with musket fire. Black powder smoke billows up and over the reeds. Peter

Quinn is shot and killed before he can finish his question, along with almost a dozen other soldiers. Arrows follow.

Captain Marsh yells emphatically, “Fall back, away from the river.”

There is no need for the order. The men are already scurrying for cover in nearby trees away from the river, only to discover that more Dakota await them there.

In the confusion, Marsh takes cover behind his fallen horse and points, “Bishop, get the men to those trees along the river. Get your men to those trees.”

"Yes, Sir."

Marsh orders, “Sergeant, have them stay along the river in the reeds and avoid open ground."

Again, there is no need for these orders. The men are already scampering for cover. In the chaos of musket balls and arrows whizzing past their heads, only twenty of the forty-seven men reach the river.

Marsh to a private nearby, “We’ll work our way south back to the fort along the river. Tell the men to keep low and stay in the brush for cover.”

“Yes, Sir.”

For three hours, the men snake their way along the river. They defend themselves when they can from menacing warriors following their every move. Up until their only cover, the reeds and brush, come to an end. A large number of renegades have taken up positions, waiting for the dwindling number of soldiers to emerge on the open ground.

Bishop to Marsh, “The men say they are almost out of ammunition.”

Marsh scans his surroundings and smiles when he notices no Dakota on the other side of the river.

He suggests, “There is no way to go except to try to cross the river. There is cover over there.”

“We’ll be sitting ducks.”

Marsh, “Maybe on horseback.”

“That would be worse.”

Marsh reasons, “I understand, but the river is crossable here.”

Bishop states, “All of our horses have been lost. Even if they were available, that would be suicide.”

A private, “What can we do?”

Marsh, "We can swim for it. Have the men stay low, belly crawl out to where it is deep, and then swim downriver. Give them as small a target as possible."

Sgt Bishop, “But some of the men can’t swim.”

“They will have to figure it out right quick.”

Bishop, “Sir?”

“We have run out of options. As commanding officer, I’ll go first.”

Marsh crouches low while still secluded in the reeds. He pulls his sword and pistol out of their sheaths. He holds both over his head and wades out into the river. Men begin to follow, one at a time.

The warriors continue to send arrows and occasionally musket balls at the wading soldiers.

Captain Marsh ducks lower and lower. He walks deep into the river with his weapons still over his head, which is barely above water. The captain loses his footing and begins to drift downriver. He drops his weapons and attempts to swim but is visibly struggling.

Bishop calls out, “I need two strong swimmers.”

Two men scamper through the reeds and dive into the river’s current in a failed attempt to rescue Captain Marsh.

The two men return, “We tried, Serg… we did.”

"Yes, I know you did. Now rest. We need to get out of here.”

Sergeant Bishop to whoever was closest, "Take a count of our strength and condition. Get back to me as soon as possible.”

"Yes, Sir."

One of the swimmers asks, "How far do you figure to the fort?"

“We can only be a few miles from the ferry, so maybe ten miles."

The dire look on the private's face needs no words.

Soon, sloshing through the muck of reeds is heard.

A private exclaims, "Fourteen remain, two wounded."

Bishop, "How serious are the wounded?"

"They say they can make it, Sir."

"Good!"

***

DAKOTA RUNNERS BRING word of the uprising to Yellow Medicine, the Upper Agency, around noon the first day. The Upper Agency Dakota Chiefs do not believe an outright war has broken out.

Dr. Wakefield is among the first whites at the Yellow Medicine Agency to get word of the atrocities. But to ward off suspicion, he makes light of the news as an exaggeration. Doc and his wife have been at odds long before this incident occurred. His wife has already made plans to leave with the children and go back east. These recent events around the Yellow Medicine agency made his decision much easier. Doc now has a plan to be rid of his wife for good.

***

THE SUN IS beginning to set over the ridge. Streams of frightened refugees continued to arrive at Fort Ridgely.

Reverend Hinman to Lt. Gere, "The Redwood agency is in ruins. They set fire to everything. If anyone is left, they are most certainly dead if they didn't get out."

First refugee, "There are hundreds of them bastards, and they are everywhere."

Lt. Gere to his sergeant, "I am concerned for Marsh and his men."

"Didn't the Captain say he would be back by now?"

“Yes, and there is no word among these last refugees of seeing them along the way.”

A sergeant asks, "What are we going to do if they attack here?"

“We’ll fight. Lt. Sheehan and his fifty men might be back later this evening.”

“If we are lucky.”

“Yes, if we are lucky.”

Fort Ridgely’s Dr. Muller and his wife have set up a treatment area in their residence. The fort's small hospital is already full. The fort sutler, Benjamin Randall, is put in charge of gathering water. There is no well inside the scattered buildings of this so-called fort. He recruits volunteers to fill and carry buckets of water from a small spring located out in the open field.

Joe Carsoulle arrives at the fort with his wife and baby boy.

He approaches and asks Lt. Gere, “Have you heard anything about two young girls?”

“Two girls?”

“Yes, my daughters. They were taken.”

Lt. Gere, “No, but you should ask around. These two hundred settlers may have seen something.”

“I will.”

Lt. Gere, “And more refugees are coming in all the time. I’m sure someone will know something.”

Carsoulle turns away disheartened and takes his wife by the arm, "We'll find them. We'll find them."

Lt. Gere looks on with little hope.

The sun has set, and darkness has invaded the fort. One of the picket guards sees two uniformed men walking slowly up the ridge. He sends word to Lt. Gere.

Two of Marsh’s men arrive with the news Lt. Gere didn’t want to hear.

Lt. Gere, “I need a volunteer.”

He begins to write a note.

Young Private William Sturgis steps up, "Here, Sir."

“I’m sending you to Fort Snelling. Do you know the way?”

"Yes, Sir."

Lt. Gere, “You will go alone. We can't spare any more men."

"Yes, Sir."

"You are to avoid all hostile Indians. Your mission is too important. Don't try to be a hero."

Sturgis, "Yes, Sir."

“If you reach the fort.”

"I will reach the fort, Sir! I promise."

Lt. Gere, “If you get to the fort by the day after tomorrow, say around this same time. Let them know we need reinforcements quickly.”

"Yes, Sir."

“It is all in the note, but you’ll need to convince them it is urgent.”

Sturgis, "I will, Sir."

“If we are lucky, they can get here in a few days.”

"I better get going then, Sir!"

Lt. Gere, “Right, be off!”

***

AROUND 10:00 PM, one of Fort Ridgely’s civilian pickets fires his weapon to signal he has heard or seen something. Then turns and runs into the fort.

The entire population of the non-fortress is in a panic. Already loaded muskets are aimed toward the darkness surrounding them.

Sergeant Bishop yells as loud as he can, “Don’t shoot! It’s us!”

A few of his men stagger up the slope from the Minnesota River toward Fort Ridgely.

Bishop informs those coming to assist, "There are more behind us. Send out a wagon to get them. There are several wounded among them."

Two men run back to the fort, and a group of men run toward eight wounded soldiers, hobbling slowly in the darkness.

Lt. Gere asks Bishop, “Captain Marsh?”

Bishop shakes his head from side to side. Then explains to Gere, "We waited till there was total darkness so we would have some cover."

“You were lucky.”

A dismissive, “Right!”

Lt. Gere, “I mean.”

“I know what you meant. We were at least lucky enough to evade detection.”

“Yes, that is what I meant.”

The young Lt. Gere is both pleased and concerned. He sends another messenger to Lt. Sheehan, "Force march your men."

Lt. Gere to Sergeant Bishop, “We are all that stands between here and Fort Snelling.”

***

HUNDREDS OF TEPEES surround Little Crow’s two-story brick home. Warriors bring captive women and children to all of the native villages near the Lower Agency. Little Crow’s village is no different.

Some of the warriors ride through the villages with the scalps of their oppressors dangling from their waists. Still, other combatants bring their captives tied, walking behind their horses.

Little Crow is not happy with what he sees. He had given orders that morning not to kill indiscriminately. He wanted to take the women and children as captives to hold for ransom. Many of the warriors didn't follow those orders. Instead, vengeance took over. And the rallying cry, "All Whites Must Die," was the rule.

The captive adult women are forced into servitude, ordered to pick corn, make fires, and prepare food for their captors. All of this was in retaliation for years of abuse and ridicule they had endured from the arrogant white settlers, their wives, and the traders.

Little Crow wanders his village in disbelief at the day's events. Braves return with wagons full of food, medicine, blankets, and clothing. The items secured from the warehouses are piling up next to the village tepees. His people would eat well for a time, but that would come to an end, and he knew it.

He is happy that many of the crooked traders who had cheated on his people had met what he considered a just end. But he is not pleased with learning many others he had considered friends were killed before he could reach them.

A couple of the peace-seeking chiefs, Wabasha and Wacouta, wander Little Crow's camp.

Wabasha, on his horse, to a returning brave carrying scalps as trophies, "You are not a Dakota warrior. You are not fit to be called a Dakota warrior."

"What do you know, old man!"

"I know Dakota do not kill women and children. We fight men, like men, not like cowards."

One brave restrains the first warrior, who then adds, "The whites don't have any problem killing our children and our women with their diseases or starving our families. But you don't care because you are well fed, you and your family, but not ours."

Wabasha, "I will not stand for this. I am a chief."

"Then go, seek your peace, old man."

***

AS HE WANDERED on foot in his village, Little Crow spots Chief Wabasha approaching on horseback. He had great respect for Wabasha before all of this transpired. But they don't see eye to eye on this situation. Wabasha is against the uprising and, during the tribal council, pleads for a peaceful solution.

Wabasha rides up close to Little Crow, wearing a full headdress of eagle feathers and fringed buckskin over his arms and legs. He has a new musket in the saddle's sleeve and a pistol on each hip. He stops to talk.

Little Crow, "Did you lead your warriors in battle today looking like that?"

"No. I will not participate in this. This is not a battle. This is not war. It is the senseless slaughter of innocent men, women, and children."

"The braves would not listen to reason. They only want revenge."

Wabasha, "This is not what Dakota warriors do. It is a disgrace. We will pay a great price for this outrage."

"They won't listen."

"They listened to you. That is why they are in this situation."

Little Crow, "That again… Our only hope is to negotiate. But if they keep killing every white they see, they will not want to negotiate."

"At least you admit you were wrong."

"I was right to stand up for our people. If you would have joined us. If Wacouta had joined us. They would have listened to me, but no, you are too much of a coward to stand with us. You'd rather our people die of starvation than fight to keep them alive."

Unnerved by the insult, he responds, "You are right, you will have to negotiate. You are good at that."

Little Crow looks at Wabasha with hate-filled eyes, "You blame me for this? You know we had no choice. They lied to us over and over again, but you are willing to trust them, still?"

"I know you sold them our land. You negotiated away our land."

"Yes, and now we will take it back. You were there. They lied to us, and now we will make them pay for those lies."

Wabasha scoffs at Little Crow.

Little Crow continues, "I did not order any of this. I made it clear our grievance was with the thieving traders, not the settlers, but they wouldn't listen."

"You are responsible for this. You gave into the Soldiers Lodge demands. You could have stopped them, but you gave into their anger."

Little Crow dismissively waves his arms at Wabasha and walks away, leaving his village to inspect the remains of the Redwood Agency.

Not much is left but the smoldering burnt-out shells of once-solid buildings. Smoke floats calmly to the night sky. Ironically, the stone chimneys are the only thing not billowing smoke and are all that is left standing.

Intermittent caravans of warriors on horseback stream through the carnage, followed by groups of young men on foot, who search through the remains of the Lower Agency.

A young son of Chief Wacouta is one of those men who is on foot.

Little Crow stops him and says, "You were against this?"

"I was, now my father is unhappy with me since I participated."

"You let the anger of others rule your wisdom."

Wacouta's son, "But we have taken back our land. The white settlers are all gone. They fled like scared deer on the prairie."

"There will be more to replace them. They will not flee again as easily."

"It was so easy. We can win this."

Little Crow, "We can only keep our land if the braves listen to reason. We need to fight like the white man."

"How do you mean?"

"We need to take Fort Ridgely, but now there will be no element of surprise. They will be ready for us."

Chief Wacouta's son, "The fort? You want to take the fort, and keep it? You think we can do that?"

"Yes, we will need to take it and then get their cannons. Then, we will seek a truce on the grounds of strength. We will not be successful unless the braves begin to listen to me."

“I am sure we can. We are Dakota. We will drive the whites from our land.”

Little Crow cautions the young braves' enthusiasm, "Only if we can get the help of all the tribes. The Sisseton, the Wahpeton, and even Winnebago. All of the tribes… And even our enemies, the Ojibway.”

“I don’t know. Will all of those bands join us?”

“They must if we want to keep our lands.”

The young man remains silent, contemplating what has never been tried before. Uniting all of the tribes, enemies, and friends alike.

Little Crow, "You go home, get some rest. We will have a long day tomorrow.”

“Can I stay with you? My father will not have me in his lodge.”

“Yes, if you help me convince the others to do as I say.”

Chief Wacouta’s son, “I will, I promise.”

Chapter 2

Chaska's village

Spring of 1862

CHASKA APPROACHES HIS father, Black Elk. His father is sharpening a skinning knife, with a spear sitting nearby that is next.

Chaska blurts out what is on his mind, "Father, how do I get out of this marriage arrangement?"

A bit startled by this comment, he puts down the sandstone and knife, "Why? Why are you against it?"

"She is intolerable. She doesn't listen to me. She talks constantly. She always tells me what she wants and what she expects. It never ends."

Black Elk laughs, "Welcome to adulthood and to women."

"It is not funny, father. I am serious. How do I end this?"

"There are many things you need to learn about a woman."

Chaska, "What do you mean?"

"She wasn't always like this. Women change just like we do. I am not the same as I was just a few years ago."

"How have you changed? I don't see any difference."

Black Elk, "I have matured. Just as you have. Over the years, we learn and adapt."

"I understand, but I don't want to learn or adapt to her."

"I will talk to her father. This may take time."

Chaska, "How long?"

"Does she know you are unhappy?"

"She doesn't listen to me at all, so I don't think she sees it at all."

Black Elk shakes his head and enlightens his son, "Well, first, I will talk to her father. Your mother will talk to her mother. They will then have to discuss it. That may not go well."

"Really? This is going to be complicated!"

"Quite complicated. Your mother and I thought you two were a good match. You were good friends growing up. You know her father and I are friends? He is very well respected in our village. He may not want to end this."

Chaska exclaims, "Father!"

"You don't think the two of you could work it out?

"Father!"

Black Elk sighs and continues, "Alright, but don't expect this to be quick. Your mother may not want to change this either."

"Why?

"She is close to Little Thunder's mother, too."

Chaska, "What if I offer to pay them?"

"Son, that is not always the solution."

"But I have paid her parents myself. I will buy my way out also."

Black Elk, "It may not be as simple as that."

"I will repay them myself."

"It doesn't work that way, even if we agree. It may have to go to the tribal council."

Chaska asks in an annoyed tone, "Really? The village council will get involved?"

"Yes, it is difficult to explain."

***

BLACK ELK DISCUSSES the problem with his wife, Shining Moon.

Chaska's mother says, "I thought they were good together."

"Me too, but I guess he has his mind made up."

"Her mother will be quite upset."

Black Elk: "Her father will be, too. I'll talk to him if you break it to her."

"I wonder if they will offer to give back what Chaska has paid them?"

"I don't know, you could ask."

Shining Moon, “You never had second thoughts about us, did you?”

“Never! Not one second.”

He pulls her close and kisses her.

***

LITTLE THUNDER TO a girlfriend, Bird Song, “Chaska always ignores me.”

Little Thunder continues to scrub rawhide-tanned leggings vigorously. Satisfied, she hands the dripping deer skin to her friend.

Bird Song begins wringing the clothing by hand, saying, "He is just nervous."

“I hope you are right, but he won’t talk to me.”

Little Thunder dunks the next piece of clothing to wash in the tub in front of her.

“Do you let him talk?”

Bird Song drapes the wet leggings over the taut string line, then pins the leggings in place. Little Thunder, again, begins scrubbing furiously.

"Of course I do, but he is so quiet."

Bird Song awaits the next piece and states, “Men like to talk about themselves. Ask him about what he is interested in.”

“That is so boring.”

Little Thunder hands the next dripping-wet shirt to her assistant.

Bird Song shakes her head and then begins the same routine.

Little Thunder, “All I do is plan our life together.”

“Like what?”

“How many children we’ll have.”

Bird Song, “Wow, how many do you plan on having?”

“Lots!”

Bird Song laughs and takes the next piece of clothing from Little Thunder.

Little Thunder continues, “He will be a good provider. I told him I think he could be chief someday.”

A stunned look comes over Bird Song’s face.

“Well, he could be!”

Bird Song says, “But his father is not a chief, nor in line to become a chief.”

"It doesn't matter. Chaska is a good hunter, a good leader."

“You have high expectations for Chaska.”

Little Thunder blusters, "That's another thing. I hate his name. Junior. He needs to change his name."

"Really? You want him to change his name."

“Yes, to something more manly.”

Bird Song responds, “Oh, my. Like what?”

“Something powerful. I don’t know, but anything but Chaska.”

“You have told him you don’t like his name?”

Little Thunder, “Not in so many words.”

“Really?”

“He is named after his father, Black Elk, so something like that would be much better. But he keeps Chaska.”

Bird Song shakes her head in disbelief.

Little Thunder continues, “He is so handsome. He could do anything he wants.”

“Chiefs are not elected on their looks.”

Little Thunder, “I know, but …”

“There is a lot you don’t understand about the traditions of the village.”

"I know a lot depends on his possessions. He already has many horses, almost more than any other brave in the village."

Bird Song comments, “Yes, that helps, but that is not all there is to it.”

“But it is a good start.”

***

BLACK ELK'S WIFE approaches Red Dove, Little Thunder's mother's tepee.

Shining Moon "Red Dove, are you there?"

"Yes, come in." Red Dove motions for her to enter, "How are you?"

"I am fine." Then continues, "I have something to discuss with you."

Red Dove, "Come in, sit. Can I get you anything?"

She motions for her friend to sit on a buffalo hide blanket.

Shining Moon settles in and replies, "No, thank you."

"What is it?"

"We have been friends a long time. ... I'll just say it. Chaska doesn't want to marry Little Thunder."

Red Dove, "What?"

"I know this is a shock to us also. We both thought they would be happy together."

"Well, he will have to change his mind. This will not do."

Shining Moon, "He has made up his mind."

"So have I. There will be no going back on the arrangements."

"We'll let you keep half of everything he has offered."

Red Dove, not listening, states, "What will everyone think."

"They won't think anything."

"She will never be able to find a husband if this happens."

Shining Moon, "It is not like that. You will find someone who will be a good match for her."

"She will be chastised. Little Thunder will be looked down upon. We'll be outcasts."

"We'll let you keep all Chaska has given for her."

Red Dove, "Yes, you will. Because they will be getting married."

***

BLACK ELK APPROACHES Little Thunder's father, Roaring Cloud, who is building a cooking fire.

He asks hesitantly, "What are you cooking tonight?"

"We'll be having fresh catfish."

Black Elk, "Your Red Dove is a fine cook."

"Yes, she is. My Little Thunder has much to learn, but she'll learn."

"About that, I have some bad news."

Roaring Cloud asks, "What is it now?"

"Our Chaska wants out of the marriage arrangement."

Roaring Cloud laughs, "I was wondering about that. My daughter can be very difficult."

"Then you have no objection to nullifying the arrangement?"

"I didn't say that. My wife can be very difficult also. They are like two peas in a pod."

Black Elk almost laughs but thinks twice, "Shining Moon is talking to Red Dove as we speak."

"Oh no, I better get over there."

"But the fire."

"Can you watch it?"

"Sure."

Roaring Cloud drops everything, begins walking, and then starts to run to his tepee.

Black Elk picks up the wood scattered on the ground. Then, he removes a few logs from the potential fire.

***

ROARING CLOUD IS out of breath as he arrives at his tepee. He can hear crying coming from inside. He throws back the flap to find Little

Thunder and Red Dove embracing. His daughter is in tears, his wife scowling at him.

Red Dove, "You are going to fix this."

"Me!"

***

BLACK ELK TO Shining Moon, "How did it go?"

"Not good. Red Dove won't listen to reason."

"Then it must go to the council."

Shining Moon, "Unless Chaska changes his mind."

"I believe it is too late for that."

Chapter 3

Second Day of the Uprising

August 19th 1862

THE YELLOW MEDICINE Agency, the Upper Agency, hasn't seen any signs of the uprising until the early morning hours of the second day. The news has prompted the agents to take cover in the stone-walled warehouse with their employees, mixed and full-bloods alike.

Forty-two-year-old John Other Day, a full-blood with a violent reputation, stands guard along with his employers. He has converted to Christianity, but that hasn't satisfied many of the white traders he is hunkered down with now. In his younger days, he had proven himself a great warrior by defeating one of the most feared warriors of the Dakota by biting off the tip of his nose. That defeated warrior has forever after been known as Cut Nose.

Both sides now watch Other Day with caution. The men he helps protect and the warriors who want to harm those same men. His reputation is all that is needed for their concern.

He makes it clear who he is to the Dakota attackers. He yells out the window to the braves surrounding the warehouse. Other Day fires his first shot, nearly missing a brave's head. The Dakota warriors immediately rush off for easier pickings.

Most of the Indian Agents have stores in both the Yellow Medicine and Redwood agencies, as do Myrick and Forbes.

One of the men hold up here is Steve Garvie, one of Myrick's clerks at the Upper Agency. One of the first shots fired earlier that morning found Garvie's midsection. He retreated to the upstairs of his trading post and out the back window, running for the safety of this stone-walled warehouse.

Constans, one of Forbes' clerks, a Frenchman, is killed outright.

Two other clerks from another store race to the warehouse also, narrowly avoiding a band of warriors.

At Francis Patoile's store, his nephew has been shot in the chest. His attackers left him for dead, but the boy manages to survive and has made his way to this same shelter.

John Other Day continues to survey the situation.

He announces to anyone who will listen, “We have a window of opportunity!”

Dr. Wakefield responds, “What do you mean?”

“They are distracted. They have moved on to the other stores. They are not anywhere near us.”

Garvie asks, “What are you suggesting?”

“We can make a run for it.”

Dr. Wakefield, “Are you crazy or trying to get us all killed?”

“If we load up the women and children and few provisions. We can make the woods before they come back. They will come back.”

Garvie grimaces in pain, "I trust John. Let’s get a move on.”

It is agreed. They load the wagons and head for the woods. Most of the able-bodied men are armed and walk alongside the wagons to guard their progress. Steve Garvie reluctantly accepts a spot in a wagon.

Once far enough away from the agency, they stop to discuss their options.

Garvie suggests, “I think we should head toward Fort Ridgely?”

Other Day disagrees, “No. All of the villages involved in this uprising are between here and the fort. That would take us right through the heart of it.”

Dr. Wakefield states, “I agree with John.”

Garvie looks peculiarly at the Doctor, “Where then?”

Other Day offers an idea, “We have enough provisions, and what we don’t have, we can find. We can avoid all danger by heading to St Paul.”

Garvie exclaims, “That has to be over 120 miles!”

Another man states affirmatively, “Yes, at least.”

Dr. Wakefield states the obvious, “We’d have to go through the big woods.”

"Yes, my people will be attacking settlers and towns near their villages, returning each night with their plunder. They will not raid that far."

Dr. Wakefield, “Your people! I knew we couldn’t trust him.”

“I am the only one you can trust. If you go to Fort Ridgely, you go without me.”

The decision is made. They will follow Other Day's advice and head to St Paul.

***

ANOTHER GROUP OF refugees, including Reverend Stephen Riggs, Dr. Williamson, and forty-two others, make their way past all the native village encampments. They take a circuitous path on the north side of the Minnesota River to the town of Henderson. Traveling a long meandering route, they bypass Fort Ridgely, New Ulm, and St Peter. It takes them a week to arrive.

***

The day before

August 17th, 1862

EARLY MORNING AT a shady boarding house at the lower agency, a Dakota working girl speaks up, “Mr. Dickinson.”

The irritated owner, J. C. Dickinson, asks, "What is it, young lady?"

“The men from my village are not going out to fight the Ojibway.”

Dickinson is even more angry, "If they aren't preparing to do battle with the Ojibway then what is this all about?"

"They intend to kill all whites."

"What in god's name? Why would they do that?"

The woman hesitates to answer, "Because they want to take back the valley."

"That is just crazy."

The young woman explains, "There was an incident yesterday at the Jones store and at Howard Baker's farm. Dakota hunters killed three men and two women."

Dickinson is bewildered, "I haven't heard anything about this. You must be wrong."

"I'm not. You and your family will be killed. You must flee."

"You are serious."

The young lady affirms her position and asks, "Can you take me with you?"

"Well, you are sure about this?"

"Yes, and they will kill all whites, women too. So, you should take the girls, too."

Dickinson: "Of course. Tell the girls to gather only what they can carry, and I'll prepare the wagon."

The young woman rushes up the stairs and wakes the other working girls. In a hurried rush, the half-dressed women scramble from room to room, gathering personal belongings.

One lady of the night reminds the others, "Don't forget the candles."

A new working girl responds, "For god's sake, why?"

"No matter where we end up, we'll need to make money. Don't forget your candles."

The girls gather what clothes and personal items they can carry. An unorganized procession of scared young ladies rumbles one by one down the stairs. The scantily dressed women scramble inside the covered wagon, where Dickinson's wife and children await them. They flee the Redwood agency with a snap of the reins before the fighting breaks out.

On his way past Fort Ridgely, Dickinson stops to inform Captain Marsh of the uprising before they continue on to St Peters. His warning was one of the first the captain ignores.

***

August 18th, 1862

DICKINSON NOW INFORMS Major Galbraith of the same news.

Major Galbraith to thirty-year-old Charles Flandrau, an attorney from St. Peters, "From the sound of it, they are going to need a lot more help. I'm going to head back with these men I have. Can you gather as many volunteers as possible and follow me as soon as you are ready?"

Charles replies, "Sure, I will put out the word for volunteers. But they will need ammunition and supplies."

"Yes, gather what you can, and don't wait. Bring what you have starting tomorrow."

Flandrau laments at the task ahead of him, "I'll bring as many as I can."

He is able to organize a would-be fighting force of 115 men, but it is taking too long for some. The sheriff of St Peters, Mr. Boardman, and a small group of men decide to go ahead of Flandrau's ragtag group. They set out for New Ulm in an attempt to assist in defending it. As word spread across the countryside, refugees flood the small villages like St Peter, tripling their size overnight.

***

First Attack on New Ulm

AT A COUNCIL in Little Crow's village, he attempts to reason with the enraged warriors.

"We need a plan of attack if we are going to take New Ulm."

A revenge-filled warrior says, "We don't need a plan. The whites run at the sight of our war parties."

"The town will be much different than the agency or the settlements."

"It will be the same. They are all cowards and scatter like deer into the forests."

Laughter follows.

"If you go without a plan. You will not be successful. You do not have the element of surprise like we did yesterday."

"We plan to attack. They flee. We run them down. And we take back our valley."

Boisterous shouting and war cries fill the council lodge and all around the outside.

Little Crow is frustrated and bewildered, "If you will not listen, I will not be a part of this."

"Then stay here with your women."

After his leadership is dismissed, Little Crow leaves for his two-story house.

***

DISCUSSIONS ARE HELD between the different village's Soldier Lodges. Some join the group that wants to attack New Ulm. Others, a hundred or more warriors, decide to venture out on their own, attacking settlers all over the countryside. Some heed Little Crow's pleas not to kill women and children, but not all.

***

Fort Ridgely

A CORPORAL AT one of Fort Ridgely's lookout posts exclaims, "What the hell!"

Lt. Gere asks, "What is it, corporal?"

"They are on the move."

"Then we should sound the alarm. Bugler."

"No, Lt. Come see for yourself. They are passing us by. They are not going to attack us."

Grabbing the telescope, Lt. Gere confirms the corporal's report.

Gere hands back the telescope and suggests, "They might be trying to surround us?"

"I don't think so, Sir., It looks like they are continuing on. They are staying on the road along the river."

"That only means they are going to New Ulm. If they take the town, we will be surrounded. They will have braves on both sides of us now."

Sergeant Bishop offers his opinion, "That is a good thing then. They have split their forces."

Gere explains, "If they take New Ulm. We will be cut off from any of the reinforcements we have sent for."

Corporal asks, "How many people live in and around New Ulm?"

A private nearby answers, "Maybe 900 men, women, and children. Almost all of those are farmers."

Gere solemnly replies, "If they succeed in taking New Ulm, we will be next."

***

AT AROUND MIDAFTERNOON, the leaderless warriors advance on the town of New Ulm.

An ambitious 1st brave, “They are better defended than I expected.”

2nd warrior states, “How is that possible?”

“They have had two days to prepare.”

"We can still take this town of businessmen and farmers."

1st brave, “They have wagons turned on their sides.”

“Yes, and barrels and wooden crates stacked and shoved together.”

“They have made a barricade.”

2nd warrior, “We can still do this.”

Another brave announces, “Our scouts say that most of their women and children of New Ulm have fled.”

1st brave, “That means they have probably gone east to their neighboring villages.”

2nd warrior, “That would mean mostly the men have stayed.”

3rd brave, “Little Crow told us they would be ready.”

1st brave says, "Yes, he did. But if we surround the village, we can take them.”

2nd warrior, “Without a plan of attack?”

1st brave, “If we attack, they will run.”

“But they had two days to run. They have built barricades instead. They don’t look like they are going to run.”

“You will see.”

***

AFTER HOURS OF ineffective assaults, the 2nd warrior proclaims, "Each of our many attempts have failed."

3rd brave, “They are not running. They are staying.”

1st brave, “If we attacked all at the same time, we might be able to overwhelm them.”

3rd brave states emphatically, “Or our brothers will be all killed.”

2nd warrior, "Each time we attack, our warriors are easily repelled.”

1st brave, "That is because when one group of warriors charge, the others wait to see if they are successful."

2nd warrior, "They wait because there is no plan. They are without a leader. So, they send in the next group. Another ill-fated attempt from another direction."

3rd brave, "We need a plan."

1st brave concludes, "We need a leader with a plan. Someone that they will listen to."

They all look at each other and remember what Little Crow said at the council.

3rd brave, "Look."

1st brave, "What is it?"

"A cloud of dust. Over there. It floats above the trees coming from the east."

"Their army."

2nd warrior, "We should see for sure."

1st brave, "No, I am certain it is their army."

3rd brave, "Me too. We have not been successful against the townspeople. We sure can't take on their army."

The Dakota attackers leave the New Ulm battlefield for their villages.

***

L.M. BOARDMAN HAS arrived with just fifteen volunteers.

Boardman to the first men he sees, "Well, I guess we saved your fair village."

Jacob Nix, self-proclaimed leader of New Ulm defenders, "You saved it. We saved it. They were hightailing it before you arrived."

A townsperson, "Enough already. They will be back with more warriors and a better plan."

Charles Flandrau arrives on foot with over a hundred men, mostly farmers and ranchers, about sunset. A disagreement erupts among the townspeople about who should command New Ulm's defense. Flandrau's name is volunteered. After a vote, he is unofficially named Colonel of the town's defenders.

***

THE SECOND NIGHT of the conflict, Little Crow's village again has the peace seeking chiefs, Wabasha and Wacouta wandering his camp.

Wabasha again chastises Little Crow, "They couldn't take a small town, smaller than your village."

"No, they wouldn't listen to me again. They had no plan."

"Many of our people see what is happening. They are leaving and heading west."

Little Crow responds, "They will return when we take the fort."

Wabasha laughs and says, "You intend to attack the fort? Are you crazy?"

"No, we have over 400 warriors. It can be done."

"And you are going to lead them?"

Little Crow replies, "Yes. I have a plan."

Wabasha has no response, just a forlorn look on his face.

Little Crow, "We shall call for another council. Hopefully, they will listen this time."

***

At the Council Lodge

LITTLE CROW TO those gathered, "We need to stop killing the women and children. We need fewer scalps and more white captives. They can be held as ransom."

Rdainyanka, "Then you intend to negotiate with the white liars?"

"Eventually, we will have to negotiate, but if we do it from a position of strength, we have a better chance of regaining our territory."

Rdainyanka, "A position of strength. We can't even take a town of farmers."

Chief Big Eagle, "At least we tried."

The chief looks directly at Little Crow.

Little Crow begins to respond, but Big Eagle continues, "As you said, they would be waiting for us; there was no surprise. They were barricaded in and ready."

"Will you listen now?"

The warrior chiefs who had attacked New Ulm nod affirmatively.

"Because you did not listen to me before, our scouts tell us we now face over 180 defenders at Fort Ridgely. Not the 29 they had the previous day."

Big Eagle, "We will listen."

Little Crow, "We still have over 400 braves, do we not?"

Rdainyanka, "Yes, we have those numbers and more if Red Middle Voice and Shakopee join us."

Little Crow, "We will send word to them. Maybe they will join us."

Rdainyanka, "What about Wabasha's and Wacouta's people? Will they stand and fight with us?"

Big Eagle, "I have talked with Wabasha, and he has not changed his mind."

Rdainyanka adds, "We won't need them. If they are unwilling to fight, they will not help us. They would only hinder us."

Little Crow, "What we need is a plan. A plan that will work."

They debate strategy almost all night.

***

Little Crow enters his tepee in a solemn and tired mood.

His wife, Saiceyewin Makatowin, asks, "Are you hungry?"

"Yes, what do we have?"

"A lot to choose from now."

Little Crow, "That won't last long, then we'll be back to nothing to eat."

"What are you going to do?"

"We have been debating that all night."

His son, Wowinape, wakes up.

"Son, you can go back to sleep."

"What did they decide, father?"

Little Crow, "We will be attacking the fort tomorrow."

Saiceyewin, "Are you crazy?"

"No, I am not. We need to take the fort to have any chance of getting our land back."

Wowinape, "Can I come with you?"

"Yes, I want you by my side, son."

His son is overjoyed. His wife, not so much.

Saiceyewin, "I'm not liking this one bit."

Little Crow, "I understand, but if he wants to lead our people, he will need to learn."

Saiceyewin, "Yes, whatever will be left of our people when this is over."

Little Crow dismisses the comment, then responds, "If we did nothing, we will all perish. They will attack us to avenge the four hunter's actions. At least if we fight, we will have a chance at survival."

Saiceyewin hands Little Crow some pemmican.

"Eat. Before you lay down to get some sleep. So, you will be able to fight tomorrow."

Little Crow looks at it and smiles.

"With all the food the braves have brought in, I still prefer this over that."

Wowinape, "What shall I bring, Father?"

"Your bow, plenty of arrows, and the sacred medicine bundle."

"But that is for…"

Little Crow, "We, you should take that sacred medicine bundle with us always. This is war, son. We may need it."

Saiceyewin, "We will take the other children west."

"Why?"

"To be safe."

Little Crow, "That is probably a good idea. We don't know when or where the Army will arrive. Yes, that is a good idea."

Saiceyewin, "I could stay and let the other wives take the other children west."

"You would do that, risk your life and stay here?"

Saiceyewin smiles slyly and shakes her head.

"Who else is going to take care of you when you are done fighting?"

She laughs but then grimaces at the thought of what is to come.

***

The next morning, they make preparations for battle.

Chapter 4

The Journey home

August 4th, 1863

HENSON STOPS AT the top of a low hill. The Missouri River surrounds two-thirds of his lofty perch. The Mighty Mo has eroded its way around the base of a rocky outcropping. Sweat runs down his nose as he squints into the midday glare coming off the river before him. Wildfire has done her job, bringing him to the top of this shortcut. He pats her on her neck.

"Good job, girl. I'll give you a break."

Henson dismounts with a thud. He stretches his legs for a few moments and then checks his canteen.

“Nearly half empty.”

Wildfire glances back at him.

"You must be thirsty too. Here, girl, you need this more than I do."

Henson pours some water onto a rawhide pouch he made just for this purpose.

“Those yahoos thought I was nuts making this pouch.”

Wildfire sucks up the water quickly.

“That is enough girl. I’ll refill it when we get down to the river.”

She responds with a head nod as if she understands.

"Okay, now, which way do you think is the best way down this slope?"

Wildfire searches for anything edible nearby. Spying a tasty weed, she wraps her lips around it and snaps it from its root.

“Okay, we’ll wait to make our way down. You get what you can find to eat. I’ll return some feeling to my backside.”

Henson wanders back and forth, looking for the best path. He spots what looks like a game trail.

"That will do. Deer and antelope have been in this area a long time, and they'd know the best way down."

His mind is free of the task at hand. It goes back to a year or so earlier. That smell of bacon sizzling in the frying pan for breakfast in the morning.

***

Summer of 1862

A ROOSTER CROWS as the unseen sun begins to brighten the morning sky.

Pheobe is already up with an empty coffee pot in hand. She dips a ladle in the thirty-gallon crock pot of drinking water. She fills the tin pot to just the right amount, slips the coffee basket full of fresh grounds onto the metal stem in the pot, closes the lid, and sets the pot on the warming cast iron cook stove.

Henson puts his pants on while sitting on the edge of the bed, "Morning, sweetheart!"

"Morning, dear."

"What's for breakfast?"

Pheobe, "I haven't decided yet."

"Eggs and bacon sound good."

"I don't have any eggs."

Henson, "I'll send Hannah."

He stands and pulls his suspenders up over his shoulders. He makes his way to the other cabin.

"Hannah, Ma needs eggs for breakfast."

A groggy young girl replies, "Why can't one of the boys do it? I always have to fetch the eggs."

Henson replies, "Because I asked you."

"But you didn't ask."

Pheobe from the other cabin, "Hannah, enough out of you."

Hannah, "Alright, but it isn't right."

The other three boys listen silently and hold their giggles to themselves.

Henson shakes his head, snickers, and turns to go back to the main cabin.

Loren to Hannah, "I'll come with you."

Hannah ruffles his hair, "Ok, get dressed quick."

Pheobe says to Henson as he enters the main cabin, "The chamber pot is almost full. Have one of the boys take that out."

Henson, instead of going back to the other cabin, turns and yells, "Andrew, I have a chore for you."

There was no answer.

A minute or so later, a sleepy Andrew finally emerges in his pajamas.

Pheobe notices him first, "Get dressed, son. We need you to take the chamber pot to the outhouse."

"Ah, Ma, why do I have to do that?"

Henson replies, "No need for all the questions. Just get dressed and get it done. We don't need to smell that while we have breakfast."

"What about Arthur? He is bigger."

Henson insists, "Enough, young man. We all have to pull our weight around here. We will all take turns doing the chores. Now do as you are told."

"But Pa!"

Henson just stares at the sleepy youngster. A bit of pity flows through his veins.

"Okay." Andrew turns slowly.

Pheobe adds, "It isn't going to go anywhere. Get a move on, son."

Andrew hears William and Arthur laughing as he enters the door of the second cabin.

Henson hears the ruckus and announces, "Enough out of you two. Wipe those smiles off your face. Or one of you two can take his turn at this chore."

Both stopped teasing Andrew.

***

SQUAWKING CHICKENS flop their wings in protest as Hannah and Loren gather the fresh eggs in a neat reed basket. A cloud of fine dust fills the coop from the flustered birds dashing from roost to roost. A few minutes later, their basket is filled with over a dozen still-warm eggs.

Loren holds Hannah's hand as they walk back to the cabin.

They meet Andrew, who is tilted sideways and has one arm stretched out for balance as he carefully carries the bucket of urine and feces so as not to spill.

Hannah tells Andrew, "You should carry another bucket in the other arm for better balance. It makes it easier."

"Right, adding more weight, that would be easier."

"It is. When I carry water, I always take two buckets."

"Well, this ain't water."

Hannah laughs, "Okay, don't listen to me. I tried to tell you!"

The two egg carriers entered the cabin. Loren exclaims, "We got the eggs, Ma."

Pheobe informs Henson, "I thought we had enough bacon, but we are a bit short."

Henson looks across the table, then yells toward the front door, "Arthur ..."

From the other cabin, "I know, Pa. How much you want, Ma?"

The last two boys begin to dress.

"A couple of pounds, ... oh, on second thought, we'll need some grease for later, too, so maybe three pounds or so."

"Ok,".

He turns to William, "You want to help?"

"Nah."

Moments later Arthur enters the main cabin followed by William.

Henson, “William you going to help Arthur?”

A groggy William begins to shake his head no but sees his father's look, "Okay.”

Arthur, "You can hold the belly flap while I cut it."

“Sure, I can do that.”

These two errand boys pass Andrew as he returns from the outhouse.

Arthur asks, “What took you so long?”

“I had to go!”

Arthur nods affirmatively, “Ok, looks like you’ll get to eat first.”

Andrew grins at the news.

Arthur adds, “Don’t forget to rinse it out first.”

“Right.”

“And wash your hands.”

Andrew responds with, “Shut up, I know that.”

Arthur and William open the smokehouse door, and the scent of hickory smoke and bacon wafts past them. The coals are almost cold under the hog carcass. A light green mold grows on the surface.

“William, can you grab some kindling? I’ll start the coals again once we are done here.”

“Ok.”

Arthur gathers the larger chunks of wood while William brings the rolled-up kindling of leaves and small twigs.

Arthur begins to slice sections of the hog's belly, then carefully hands each slice to William, who places each slice in a tablecloth-lined basket.

William asks, “What’s that green stuff?”

“Mold.”

Arthur skillfully scraps the green fuzz off the carcass, and flicks to the ground.

“Why do you remove it first?”

Arthur, “Because it isn’t good for you.”

"Then we shouldn't be eating meat that has mold on it?"

Arthur hands another slice to him, but it slips through William's fingers and hits the sawdust-covered wooden floor.

"No, it will be fine. Put the basket down, wipe it off, and it will be fine."

"Ok. You sure?"

"Yes, the bacon will be fine. That is why I scrap it off first. It only grows on the surface. The fat and meat are fine."

William, "Are you sure?"

"Yes, Pa told me when I was your age that if the meat begins to smell rotten, we don't eat it."

"It kinda smells bad now!"

"No, that is not bad. When it goes rancid, you'll know, trust me."

William, "How do you know when you have enough?"

"After a while, you know. I have been doing this for quite some time now."

"Why do we burn hickory wood instead of all the other wood we have cut?"

Arthur, "It helps with the flavor."

"Oh."

"And the heat helps cure the meat so it lasts longer."

William suggests, "I think we have enough."

"Almost done." A few slices later, "There, that is enough."

***

PHEOBE TO HANNAH, "You know what to do next, young lady."

"Yes, Ma. Loren, you want to help?"

Loren asks, "With what?"

"We need to candle the eggs."

"Why?"

Hannah begins to reply, “So, we know they don’t have …”

Pheobe cautions, “Hannah.”

“So, we know they are good to eat.”

Loren, “They look alright to me.”

"We need to candle them first just to be sure."

Pheobe smiles and nods at Hannah.

“How do we do that?”

"First, we need a couple of candles."

“Okay.”

Loren looks around quickly and spots a couple of unlit beeswax candles.

“Will these two work?”

Pheobe answers as she flips thick slices of bacon in the sizzling cast iron fry pan on the wood-burning stove, “Yes, those will do just fine.”

Hannah, “Now we light them.”

Loren watches intently.

Hannah holds an egg up, “Now we check to see if they are clear.”

"This one isn't. It has some yellow stuff inside."

Henson and Andrew begin to giggle.

Hannah explains, "That is the yoke. We are looking for any dark stuff."

“Oh.”

Loren holds another egg in front of the flame, “Nothing dark in this one.”

"Good. Hand those good ones to Mom."

"Here, Mom." He stretches his tiny little arm as far as he can.

“Thank you, son.”

Hannah exclaims, “This is what we don’t want to see.”

“What is it?”

“Blood.”

Loren asks, “Oh, how did that get in there?”

Henson submits, "You're gonna have to tell him eventually."

Pheobe warns, “He is too young for all of that.”

Hannah says, “It comes from the mother hen. She lays the egg, and sometimes it has blood inside."

“Oh!”

Hannah turns to Pheobe, "See, no problem."

Loren, “Was it going to be a baby chick?”

Everyone laughs hysterically.

Pheobe, “How did you know?”

“I listen!”

Chapter 5

St Paul, Minnesota

August 20th, 1862

ON THE THIRD day of the uprising, word has made it to the governor of Minnesota, Alexander Ramsey. He heads across the river to Fort Snelling to assess the situation.

Ramsey arrives at the fort with his entourage, steps out of his official carriage, and makes his way to the commander's office.

Ramsey enters without warning, "What have you heard?"

"About what?"

"The Indians. For god's sake, man, haven't you heard?"

Commander Colonel answers, "No, Sir. You are the first to bring any news of a problem."

"I received word this morning that the Indians are killing settlers all across the Minnesota River valley."

A corporal enters the room.

Commander Crooks, "What is it?"

"Colonel, we have a rider approaching."

"And?"

"Military uniform. At a distance, he seems quite distressed."

Colonel to Ramsey, "This may be our first word from the area."

Colonel to the corporal, "Bring him to me."

The corporal salutes and exits quickly.

Ramsey questions, "It must be from Fort Ridgely."

"But that is over a hundred and seventy miles."

"He must have been dispatched at the onset.'

Crooks, "Then it is not going to be of much use."

"They say it started three days ago."

"And you just received the news this morning."

Ramsey, “You are probably right. We need to begin making plans…”

A Sergeant enters, salutes, and presents a weary traveler.

Private William Sturgis is covered in dust from the trail and exhausted.

Ramsey to the corporal, “Get him some water.”

Colonel to Sturgis, “Have a seat.”

“No Sir, with all due respect. I would prefer to stand.”

Ramsey responds, "Understood." Then he asks, "What can you tell us, soldier?"

“Here it is in the letter from Lt. Gere.” Sturgis hands an envelope first to the Colonel. But then Ramsey steps forward and snatches it.

A miffed Commander Colonel William Crooks asks, "Gere? What happened to Captain Marsh?”

Too fatigued to talk, "It's in the message, Sir."

A Corporal arrives with water and some jerky.

Sturgis takes both and says, “Thanks.”

Ramsey to Sturgis, “When were you given this message?”

"Yesterday, Sir."

Colonel asks, “Yesterday morning?”

"No Sir, yesterday evening around dark, seven or eight, I think."

“But how did you make it here in … eighteen hours?”

Sturgis catches his breath and explains, “I was told it was urgent. To make sure you understood it was urgent when I got here, I didn't follow the river. I rode straight as the crow flies, taking shortcuts where I could, and rode all night."

“Your horse?”

"She is a good horse, Sir.”

Ramsey questions, “I mean, you didn’t stop?”

“No Sir, I mean only enough to rest the beast. They told me it was vital you received this message as soon as possible.”

Ramsey to the commander of Fort Snelling, “You will promote this man.”

Crooks, "Sir?"

"This man has gone over and above the call of duty. He deserves a promotion."

Colonel Crooks to Sturgis, "Private, you are now a Corporal."

Ramsey interjects, "Sergeant! Young man, you are a sergeant."

Sturgis, "Thank you, Sir. Thank both of you, Sirs. But they need help back there. We, you need to send reinforcements."

Colonel, "Yes, you are right."

Sturgis' legs begin to wobble under him, "I think I'll have a seat now."

The corporal catches him before he falls to the floor and helps him to a chair.

Ramsey to the Colonel, "How many men do you have here?"

"Eight companies of mostly green recruits. Some haven't even been sworn yet. They were promised to the federal government for Union service."

"Well, we need them more than Lincoln does. Screw his foolish war over them worthless slaves... How many can you spare?"

Crooks answers, "It depends if the uprising spreads to other tribes."

"Send half!"

"Yes, Sir."

Ramsey, "We'll raise more. I'll send out a proclamation for every able-bodied man to join up. ... I need to get word to Sibley."

"Sibley? The ex-governor?"

"Yes, he knows these savages better than anyone I know."

Ramsey also has hatched a plan of his own.

He sends a messenger to ex-Governor Henry Sibley.

***

Sibley's Palatial Home

RAMSEY SAYS TO Sibley, "Well, this is just the type of adventure you told me you were looking for when you left Detroit."

The governor pours his predecessor a shot glass of whiskey.

Sibley picks up the glass, "That was a long time ago, and no, this is not quite what I was hoping for."

"How old were you when you left home?"

Ramsey raises his glass.

Sibley mimics the governor's action, "Eighteen."

After a clink of their glasses, they both toss back the shot.

"Interesting."

"What is interesting about that?"

Ramsey, "With your experience working at all of those different jobs, especially the American Fur Company. You are well suited for this."

"I don't know. There has to be someone else. Why not a general?"

"I have no authority over a general."

Sibley asks, "That is what this is about having authority over me?"

"No, that is not what I mean. I mean, I need someone I can trust. That understands the Sioux Chiefs. Someone who has had dealings with them."

"Yes, my time with John Astor's company may have prepared me for this unwanted opportunity."

Ramsey, "Besides, you know a few different languages, so you can bridge almost any language barrier you will come across out there."

"I'd be better suited to remain back here. To use my experience in procuring and trading with local businesses and the federal government. I could be useful in securing the provisions needed to quell this uprising."

"Yes, but no. You were a Sutler before you took that job with the American Fur Company."

Sibley responds, "I was a Sutler's clerk... So, you agree."

"No. You are best suited for this."

“You should find someone else to lead this ragtag army. If you even want to call it that.”

Ramsey, "We will get volunteers. Don't you worry?"

"But what type of volunteers? Greenhorns, rabble-rousers, gamblers, farmers and ranchers?"

Ramsey, “They can be trained.”

"You don't seem to understand. That all takes time. We don't have time. From what you have told me, the Sioux are waging war as we speak."

“We have the recruits at Fort Snelling… “

Sibley, "All fresh off of the farm. Or worse yet, half-breeds that will stab our men in the back the first chance they get."

“You are worrying about nothing. You will be fine. Didn’t you tell me you get bored easily?”

“This is not what I was thinking of for excitement.”

Ramsey, “I will put out a proclamation to secure the necessary supplies. The federal government will come through. We’ll make good on this also.”

“There you go again. It is always about getting over on the government.”

"Don't you go off high and mighty. You are in this up to your neck, too."

Sibley, "But it will be my neck that is on the line with the Sioux."

“You will be a general. You will be sending those farmers and ranchers out to take care of those Sioux.”

“You have this all thought out. You are hoping I fail. Then you will have all of those coins for yourself.”

Ramsey, “Not at all. You will take care of this in a week or so and be back here counting the government subsidies with me. Just like last time.”

“Did you take care of the newspapers?”

“What do you mean?”

Sibley asks again, “Did you have your journalist friend write an article explaining what happened to the Annuities?”

"Not yet. It is too soon. But once this is over. No, I'll have him state the annuities arrived the same day of the uprising."

“That is too…”

Ramsey, "Trust me, I'll take care of it. Yes, I know. We'll say the chests arrived at Fort Ridgely the day the Redwood Agency was attacked."

“And what happened to them after that?”

"Ohhh, yeah… I know. I'll have them write they were brought back to Fort Snelling."

Sibley continues to inquire, “What happened to them after that?”

"I have an idea. We'll tell the newspapers that the money will be handed out to the survivors of this uprising. That will give us the goodwill of the people. They'll never know the difference."

"That might work. There is no one to oversee such a process. We'll just make the statement, and people will forget all about it once this is all over."

Ramsey, “Another shot?”

“I don’t mind if I do.”

“You have to have a stash put away somewhere.”

Sibley gets defensive, “I do. But I am not telling you where it is.”

“You must have made a ton of money selling trinkets to the Sioux for their buffalo hides.”

"I did alright. I made partner with the American Fur Company in just five years."

Ramsey, “That is impressive.”

“Did I tell you they had me overseeing all of Michigan, Wisconsin, and eventually Minnesota territories?”

“I think you might have, but I didn’t remember that. How old were you when you ran for Congress the first time? Another shot?”

Sibley, "Yes, I was thirty-eight."

"In Wisconsin first, right?"

"Yes, they made my district a part of the new Minnesota Territory. That is how I got out here."

Ramsey hands him a shot, "When you returned, you ran for the territorial legislature?"

"Yes, thank you… Yes, that was a few years ago."

"Then you ran for governor of the territory."

Sibley, "Yes, and now you are the governor of the State of Minnesota."

"To Minnesota!"

"To Minnesota!"

Ramsey mulls over his thought process, "You have done a lot of different things, so this is just another career opportunity."

"This is not what I would say is a great opportunity. Now, staying back here and staking out the best properties would be a great opportunity."

"I'll take care of that."

Sibley replies in haste, "That is what I am concerned about."

"Trust me, I'll take care of your funds as if they were my own."

Sibley shakes his head in disgust, "I'd like a say in how my funds are used."

"You have nothing to worry about. I have some men in mind who will make the arrangements to secure the best locations for both of us."

Sibley becomes serious and incessant, "I will not tolerate any interference with my decisions. I will be the one calling the shots."

Ramsey, "Understandable, I agree. I have already told the Major at Fort Snelling to make anything you need available to you as quickly as possible."

"Thank you. Now, remember when I told you we shouldn't …"

"Don't worry about that now. We have more important things to take care of now."

***

Little Crow's village

AN HOUR BEFORE sunrise, the village begins to stir. Warriors begin to gather weapons and supplies for their next assault. By noon, their preparations are complete. While they eat, they discuss the fine points of their strategy.

Little Crow announces, "We will need to work together if we are to be successful."

Big Eagle, "Yes, after New Ulm, we realize this."

"I believe the best way is for multiple attacks."

Wowinape asks, "Not an all-out assault?"

Little Crow paces as he replies, "No, at first, we'll attempt to draw the cannon fire away from the main assault."

Big Eagle agrees, "That may work."

Wowinape nods in agreement.

"It will work if we work together."

An hour past high noon, they break camp en route to Fort Ridgely.

***

Outskirts of Fort Ridgely

OUT OF RANGE of musket fire, Little Crow is with his son, Wowinape, and two of his best braves. They ride back and forth in clear view of the fort's defenses.

Lt. Sheehan peers through his telescope and asks Lt. Gere, "What the hell is he doing?"

Lt. Gere, "Beats me, maybe they are working up the courage to fight?"

Lt. Sheehan hands his telescope to Sergeant Bishop,

Lt. Gere to Sergeant Bishop, "What do you think he wants?"

Bishop continues to watch Little Crow, "I think he wants to talk."

Lt. Gere laughs under his breath, "Then have him come closer." He then nods to his best shot to get ready.

***

ONE OF HIS braves to Little Crow, "They want us to come closer."

"Right… No way!"

The brave waves his recognition of the request and shakes his head no at the same time.

***

FORT RIDGELY WAS set up years before when the thought of attack was not even a consideration. There is no barrier wall surrounding it. It is only a loose array of buildings haphazardly arranged for fur traders and businesses to trade with the Dakota and the ever-increasing number of settlers. The so-called fort is almost a mile from the river and sits on a flat plain, high enough to avoid catastrophic flooding in the spring rainy season. This bench of level land is on an open treeless field, with natural ravines nearby. The ravines provide drainage of the seasonal rainfall to flow away from the fort. Now, the ravines offer excellent cover for the Dakota warriors. They are within arrow and certainly musket range of most of the buildings. Most of the buildings making up the fort are constructed from logs or milled lumber. There is a real danger of those buildings being set on fire. This is understood by both sides. Even the two stone-built structures are vulnerable to flaming arrows, the roofing material being wood shingles.

With limited material, the defenders have attempted to set up barricades between the most likely targets of an assault. This arrangement leaves many of the outer laying buildings susceptible to attack.

***

LITTLE CROW, "It is time. The others should be in place."

One of his two closest warriors draws his musket and fires. The signal is given. Immediately, the ravine erupts with whoops and hollers as hundreds of Dakota warriors advance on the distant parade ground.

Lt. Sheehan has nearly fifty men divided into two lines behind the makeshift barricades. The first line knells, weapons loaded and ready. The second line stands behind the first line, muskets at their sides, ready to fire when called upon.

A nervous Sergeant Bishop insists, "Wait."

The screaming is getting louder and closer.

"Wait till they are closer."

Bows are loaded, and the string lines are taut.

"Wait."

The bows are raised and aimed.

"Fire!"

Immediately, the first line fires and black powder smoke fills the air. The first line falls back, and the second line steps up. The citizen onlookers watch the attacking warriors fall to the ground or take cover. The second line is ready to fire on command while the first line reloads.

The attackers, not wounded, seek shelter behind anything they can find. Rocks, fence posts, the corners of the outer buildings, and even bushes are used. The attackers advance now with stealth instead of a full outright suicidal charge.

Lt. Gere, "Swing one of those cannons around to face this attack."

The artillery crew do as they are told.

Bishop, "Let me know when you are ready."

Arrows become lodged in crates and the bottoms of wagons. Musket fire continues with random irregularity.

Artillery corporal, "Ready, Sir."

Bishop, "Fire!"

Silence follows. Nothing happens.

The attackers scream and yell as they continue to make their way closer.

Bishop insists, "Light the fuse."

First artillery private, "I did!"

Time is of the essence.

Second artillery private, "But nothing is happening."

The third man working the artillery reports, "There are rags stuffed in the charge port."

Bishop, "Remove the rags. It is undoubtedly the work of mixed blood who have since joined the rebellion."

"I would assume so."

"Hurry, they are getting closer."

"Yes, Sir."

Lt. Gere, "Commence firing when ready."

Moments later, "Fire in the hole."

A tremendous blast occurs.

Bishop exclaims, "Good work men. It is working."

Lt. Gere, "Reload."

"Yes, Sir." The artillery crew begins their work.

Sergeant Bishop, "That'll stop 'em."

Lt. Gere, "Once that cannon fire begins, they will turn run."

First private, "I'm not so sure, Lieutenant."

Lt. Gere ignores the 1st private, "They are not advancing anymore." He pauses and surveys the fight. "Aim at that building over there. Let me know when you are ready to fire."

Second private, "Yes, Sir."

Moments later someone along the front-line yells, "Fire!"

The artillerymen turn and look bewildered, "We are not ready, Sir."

Lt. Gere asks, "Who made that call?"

A farmer from behind the barricade said, "I did, Sir. That building is on fire. It was hit by a flaming arrow."

Joe Carsoulle calls out, "I got it."

He climbs a nearby ladder, one of many placed alongside as many buildings as possible. He rolls onto the roof and begins stomping out the flames while arrows and lead shot fly by him.

He exclaims while dancing on the flames, "Damn it to hell."

Once the fire is out, he jumps to the other side of the roof's peak and rolls off to a lower porch overhang. Not wanting to climb down the ladder, he jumps to the ground.

***

LITTLE CROW, "Send in the second wave from the opposite direction."

The signal is given, and Dakota warriors come out of the ravines and begin approaching the fort, screaming and yelling.

The first cannon fires again.

A frantic Lt. Gere, "Get that other cannon over on that side."

The cannon is inspected, and debris is removed before firing the second gun.

"Ready, Sir."

Lt. Sheehan yells, "Fire!"

The attackers scatter for cover. The combatants remain a safe distance apart for the next five hours. Both sides firing indiscriminately at anything that moves.

Bishop, "Over there."

A private, "What is it?"

"A few of the Sioux have taken cover behind that stack of hay near the livery."

"What should we do?"

Sergeant Bishop, "Set the stack ablaze."

"How can we do that? We don't have flaming arrows."

"Get a cannon over here. Red hot cannon ball will do just fine."

Private, "Yes, Sir."

The ensuing battle quickly goes through the little ammunition the soldiers and settlers have on them.

Settler announces, "I'm almost out of power and lead."

Lt. Sheehan, "Damn, the reserve ammunition is out there in that building."

He points to a depot building located forty yards beyond the barricades.

Lt. Sheehan to Bishop, "If Little Crow finds out what is in that building. We are in trouble."

Bishop asks, "What do you want to do?"

"If they capture it, they could hold a siege."

"Or they could burn it down. Either way, we'd still run out of ammunition soon."

Sheehan concludes, "He must not know what is in it then."

"What do you want to do?"

"I need a crew of at least four men."

Sergeant Bishop, "Yes, Sir."

Bishop calls for volunteers. Four men quickly show up.

First man to Bishop, "You didn't say what it was."

Bishop, "He didn't tell me either."

Sheehan, "Men, we need more lead and black powder."

First private, "Where is it?"

Lt. Sheehan points to the building.

Second private, "Oh, for Christ's sake. Why didn't you think of that before they got here? Oh, hell no."

Bishop, "We'll cover you. It is still a good distance away from any attackers."

Second private asks, "What is a good distance out in the open?"

Third soldier standing near first man, "Lt, when do we go?"

Sheehan, "As soon as you are ready."

A fifth man replaces the one not willing to go. The four gather together in a huddle as Sergeant Bishop pulls a few boards away from the barricade.

Bishop to the four volunteers, "We need two kegs of powder and two boxes of shot and caps."

Fourth private to the other three, "Any of you know where they are in the building?"

Both officers shake their heads no.

Second private standing nearby exclaims, "Oh, for Christ's sake, they don't even know where it is."

Third private to Bishop, "Don't worry about him, he is always like this."

Bishop nods and then asks, "You all ready?"

Fifth private, "Hell, no, but let's get this over with."

The four men dash from behind the barricades and enter open ground. Muskets erupt from both directions, and arrows begin to fly past them.

***

A DAKOTA WARRIOR declares upon seeing the four soldiers scamper out into the open, "They are not armed."

Another brave announces, "There is something important in that building."

Another warrior suggests, "Ammunition!"

A few Dakota warriors leave their ravine to advance on the ammo building.

***

LT. SHEEHAN YELLS, "The howitzers."

Bishop understands, "Fire over the top of them and on those advancing towards the depot."

The third soldier hears the cannon go off and jumps two feet in the air. "What the hell? Now they are firing at us, too?"

The Dakota warriors quickly do an about-face and hurry back into the ravine.

The four soldiers reach the depot, open the door, and dash inside.

Fifth private, "Damn, we made it!"

First private, "Shut up and find the boxes."

Third private, "I got mine, I'm out of here."

First private, "No, wait. We'll all go together."

Third private, "Who put you in charge?"

Arrows can be heard striking the wood siding. One breaks a window.

First private, "Everyone ready?"

Third private states emphatically, "Hell, no, I am not ready."

"We'll go when they fire the cannon again."

Glass shatters. A window breaks as a lead shot barely misses the complainer.

Fourth private, "I am now! Let's get the hell out of here."

The four men lumber their way back with the heavy boxes in their arms. Musket fire explodes again from behind and in front of them.

Bishop to his artillery men, "Aim over their heads and fire at will. Don't stop until I give the order."

The cannon fires again. Each of the runners' hearts skip a beat as they race toward the distant barricades.

Fourth private, "I didn't sign up for this shit."

Musket fire continues as they run. Arrows fly by them. Musket balls whistle past their ears.

Third private screams, "Damn, I'm hit."

First private yells back to him, "Can you make it?"

Third private limping, "Damned right, I'll make it. I ain't dying out here."

The first three hunched-over runners scurry through the narrow gap in the barricade with their cargo in arms.

Bishop, "You made it."

"Sir, there is still one coming in."

The last soldier limps through the barricade opening.

Bishop orders the men, "Close it up."

Bishop to the four runners, "That wasn't so bad, was it?"

"I've been hit. And you say it wasn't so bad!?"

"Let me see?"

Bishop pulls the pant leg up to expose the wound. ... It is just a scratch."

Wounded soldier, "It went clean through."

"You'll live. You can still shoot."

The private looks up in bewildered amazement.

***

A FEW BRAVES make it to the stables and use the corral and structure to fire on nearby buildings and defenders in sight.

Sergeant Jones, "Aim for the stable."

"Sir?"

"Aim for the broad side of the building."

Artillery corporal, "Yes, Sir."

The artillery piece is moved and adjusted.

Sergeant Jones, “Fire when ready!”

The men without the ignition torch cover their ears. An incredible explosion erupts. A flash of flames, then a cloud of smoke, rolls up around the men.

The cannonball crashes through the roof of the stable.

Private to private, “I knew you couldn’t hit the broadside of a barn.”

Sgt. Jones, "The roof will do just fine. Good job, soldier."

***

FIRST WARRIOR INSIDE the that same stable, “That was close.”

Second warrior, “This will be a good spot to fire from.”

Third warrior, “Smoke!”

The attackers look up to the loft. All they see at first is light smoke, then flames.

“Let’s get out of here.”

***

LITTLE CROW SEES a dark cloud bank closing in from the Northwest.

To his first warrior, "Send runners. We end the attack now.”

He turns, to Rdainyanka, one of his most trusted warriors, “If we wait any longer, it will rain soon and be even darker."

Rdainyanka , “Ok, I understand.”

Little Crow to no one specific, “If they had only listened to me at the previous council, the fort would have been ours.”

Rdainyanka sends two warriors on the detail and then says to Little Crow, “We can try again.”

Little Crow dismisses the comment outright, “Damn those cannons.”

They both shake their heads in rage.

***

AT THE FORT, Lt. Sheehan to Lt. Gere, “Thank god for those cannons.”
They both shake their heads affirmatively.

***

FRUSTRATION HAS SET in on the Dakota combatants. They are greeted in their village by questions they don't want to answer.

An angry warrior yells, "All whites must die! We should kill the white and mixed-blood captives."

Little Crow, “No, we will not do that. We need them.”

“They should all die.”

“Listen to me. If we can't take the fort or even a small town. We will need the captives when the soldiers come. They will come. Sooner than later. I guarantee you.”

The warrior refuses to acknowledge Little Crow is right. He strolls away, muttering over and over again, "They should all die."

***

LT. SHEEHAN, “I need an assessment of our losses.”

Bishop, "Yes, Sir."

***

LITTLE CROW TO his first warrior, “Find out what you can of our losses.”

“Ok, but they are all spread out to all of the other villages.”

“Send runners to each village. Do the best you can. Tell the runners to keep an ear open for the willingness to continue.”

***

BISHOP RETURNS WITH his assessment, “Two men killed, there are nine more wounded.”

Sheehan, “The wounded condition? How many seriously?”

"Seriously, Sir?"

"Can they hold, aim, and reload a musket?”

Bishop, "I'll find out, Sir."

“Anything else?”

"Yes, Sir. A dozen buildings have been burnt or are still burning… Most of the horses and livestock have been either run off, killed, or taken."

Sheehan exclaims, "Damn, that is not good."

"Yes Sir, I mean no Sir, that is not good."

“If this siege continues for very long, the loss of those creatures will become more crucial.”

Bishop asks, “Do you have any orders for me? Sir.”

“Yes… Order half rations until further notice.” The Lieutenant drifts into his thoughts, then quickly returns to the situation at hand, “Is there anything else?”

"Yes, Sir, it has begun to rain."

Sheehan smiles briefly, “Well, there is good news.”

The settlers and soldiers alike take that as a good sign. They no longer have to fear flaming arrows in the middle of the night setting fire to their shelters.

After enjoying a brief walk in the rain, Sheehan makes another decision, "Bishop, those buildings can be of use to us."

"How so, Sir?"

"Get as many men as you can spare and begin to salvage anything they can from those buildings."

"Sir? In the rain?"

"Yes, in the rain. We don't have time to wait. We can use the timber, siding, or anything else to strengthen or expand our defenses."

Lt. Sheehan thinks, *'We need reinforcements and supplies as soon as possible.'*

He asks Bishop, "Who's our best scout? Who can be trusted? … Someone who could evade detection from the Sioux and make it to Fort Snelling the quickest?"

Without hesitation, "Well, that would be Iron Face."

"Get him for me!"

***

SIBLEY HAS LEFT Fort Snelling, but is stuck ironically near a town called Shakopee, a village named after one of the warring chiefs' fathers. His camp is still over 150 miles from Fort Ridgely. A steamer has arrived, as Governor Ramsey promised.

Sibley asks, "What do we have to work with?"

"Not much, Sir. Most of the provisions you had requested were not on board."

"With little ammunition, not enough muskets. What are we supposed to do?"

Lieutenant, "There were no tents either. And the other necessary military equipment hasn't arrived."

"No cooking utensils?"

"No, Sir. Not even enough food supplies."

Sibley, "How many cattle?"

"Only a few head."

"How am I supposed to feed this growing number of men?"

There is no answer.

"I guess I'll need to do this myself."

Sibley begins to draw upon his life experiences as a trader.

Lieutenant, "What do you mean?"

"Being a trader, I was required to travel to remote outposts. These travels gave me a unique understanding of the difficulties a person would have to endure to survive out here in this wilderness. Surviving without the basic provisions most people would need in this harsh environment was difficult for just one man."

Lieutenant, "But we are now responsible for hundreds."

"The Governor owes me. He and anyone that he can get to listen will come through."

"But when?"

Sibley makes his decision, "We'll send out details to hunt for anything that has four legs."

"But the Sioux are out there."

"Yes, and we need to feed these men."

Lieutenant, "Yes, Sir."

"There has to be farms around here with cattle, pigs, chickens even."

"I'll send out details to forage."

Sibley, "Thank you, Lieutenant. I will not lead these men into that wilderness unprepared. They will be facing a well-seasoned enemy. One experienced at living off the land. An enemy that is in their own element."

Chapter 6

Wiseman place

Early Summer of 1862

SWEAT ROLLS DOWNS Arthur's face as he guides the two-row cultivator, pulled by Wildfire's mother, through a field of young corn. The bright sunshine beats down on man and beast while a cool breeze makes the work almost tolerable. They reach the end of the row.

Arthur directs his beast of burden, "Whoa, Whoa now."

He picks up the back of the till, tugs on the reins, and steps carefully between rows of fledgling corn stalks. They harmoniously make their turn. Arthur decides to pause for a break and wipes his brow. He unhooks his canteen from the side of the mare's harnesses, takes a quick swig, checks the feed sack, and positions it for his plow horse to access. Satisfied, Arthur takes a seat in the minimal shade on the ground against a wooden fence post. In the distance, back toward the log cabins, he sees his family all at work.

***

ANDREW SCRAPS HIS long-handled hoe against the dry dirt, severing the grass and weed stems from their roots in and around the fledgling tomato plants. On the other side of the large rectangular patch, William hoes between the rows of potatoes. Pheobe pulls weeds from the cucumber hills with Loren's help.

Pheobe states, "Boys, you need to dig down. Open the soil. The hoe needs to get under the roots, not just cut them off at the surface."

Andrew protests, "Why, they are gone."

"No, they aren't. The root is left, and they will grow back even stronger."

“Uh uh.”

Pheobe insists, "Yes, uh. Now do it the right way, or you'll be out here again tomorrow doing it right."

Hannah hangs shirts and sheets on the clotheslines stretched tight between two ‘T’ shaped wooden posts.

Pheobe, “Loren, be careful not to step on the leaves, dear."

"I will, Ma.”

William wearily asks, "How much longer do we have to do this, Ma?"

She sighs, “Till we are done, son.”

Andrew suggests, "When I'm done with the tomatoes, can I go?"

William chimes in, “No way. That’s not fair. They were almost done when he started.”

"No, Andrew. We need to get this done. These weeds are going to take over if we don't stay with it. So, when you get done there, you can help William finish. When we are all done, you can go play."

Back at the two cabins, Hannah pulls the last damp item from her laundry basket, quickly finds a corner, and wraps it over the sagging line. She skillfully pulls a wooden pin from her apron pooch and fastens the bed sheet to the clothesline. A light breeze wafts the sheets and garments back and forth. Finished, she picks up the basket and clothespins and heads back to the cabin. Moments later, she reemerges with a basket and runs towards the barn.

Andrew complains, “Isn’t Hannah going to help?”

Pheobe, “She has been up since dawn cooking and cleaning in the cabin. I told her that when she got the laundry done, she was free to go."

William responds dejected, “But we have to stay here and slave in the garden?”

"Yes, because we are not done. If you two would spend half as much time complaining and more of your time working, you would be done by now and free to go also.”

The two middle boys begin with new vigor to attack the stubborn weeds.

Pheobe, "Do it right, or you will have to go back over it!"

Each of the brothers glances up in frustration. They watch enviously as Hannah rides off toward the river on Wildfire.

***

CHASKA AND HANNAH lay in the shade on a well-used, tattered quilt under a giant weeping willow. The remnants of their lunch spread about them. A cool breeze floats off the river.

Hannah looks up at his chiseled chin, with her head in Chaska's lap, his long dark hair flowing down his bare chest. Innocently, she glances at his smiling eyes.

Out of nowhere, she asks, "How did we get here?"

Chaska, "Huh? We rode our horses!" He smirks with an unsure, questioning tone.

"No, I mean, how did we get here on Earth?"

"Wow, now that is a question."

An unease seeps into his consciousness.

She quickly continues, "We have been taught that God created the world in seven days… What do you believe?"

"That is a difficult question to answer, even harder to explain."

Chaska pulls her closer to him.

She replies, "I know. The thought of anyone making all of this, the grass, the trees, the flowers, the hills and mountains from nothing seems so unbelievable."

"Well, I agree, but we have been taught all of this." He raises his right arm and swings it from side to side. "The world is so huge, it isn't meant to be understood."

Hannah states, "I am confused already! So, you don't even think about it?"

"Oh yes, we give it great thought. See, the way we see it. There are many mysteries in this life and what happens after death. But we don't try to explain them all because they are too complicated to understand."

"Then what do you explain?"

"The elders have told us the world we live in has existed as it is today since the beginning of time. They believe it will remain as it is into the future."

Her thoughts immediately go to the ending of so many prayers, '*As it was in the beginning, it is now and ever shall be, forever. Amen.*' Then she asks, "Is that what you believe?"

"I believe the world is a pretty stable place. Night will follow the day, the seasons come and go in cycles, but all in all, the world will remain the same."

"I see what you mean."

"For as long as any of our elders can remember and their elders before them, our world has remained as it is. It has never changed. Life is good. There is no need to change it."

"But what about before us, before humans?"

"Before humans?" Chaska asks.

Hannah sits up and turns to Chaska, looking into his deep brown eyes.

"Yes, before us."

Chaska touches her on both shoulders firmly.

"That is one of those mysteries. The world is a mystery. A mystery we do not feel we need to understand completely. The stars and the moon are there. No need to explain it. We don't worry about those things that don't affect our lives."

"But don't you just sometimes lay back and wonder?"

Hannah lays back on the blanket, stretching her arms out as if to hug the world.

"Yes, I do. I wonder about it all. Especially you."

Chaska rolls to her side, leaning on his left elbow, and hovers over her, his eyes staring into her light hazel blue eyes.

He says, "But it is difficult to explain." He stops to consider examples, then continues, "But we do have stories, many stories. Yes, some explain where we come from?"

She adds, "Not who are our parents, or where did they come from, but where did man come from? Or woman?"

Chaska rolls on his back. Hannah rolls to his side. She snickers as she shyly looks at him.

"The story that explains where we come from involves what we call Wakan."

Hannah, "Wakan?"

"Yes, Wakan!

"Tell me, who is Wakan?"

Chaska, "Wakan is not a person. It is a spirit."

"A spirit?" Thinking to herself, *'Like our holy spirit, … Interesting!'*

Chaska confirms with a "Yes."

He tries to figure out where to begin, then states affirmatively, "The center of all things is Wakan Tanka."

He pulls Hannah close to him. Hannah listens intently, with her arm over his torso, her head on his chest at the shoulder, his arm around her.

"Wakan Tanka is the spirit of all things of the world. Not really even a spirit, but more of a mystery, an unknown. Wakan is a spiritual force that is in everything. Those rocks, these trees, the grass, these pebbles." He scoops up a handful of gravel with his free hand, then slowly lets the pebbles sift through his fingers. Chaska adds, "All things of the world, that is Wakan Tanka."

"We say that about our God also, but we say he lives in heaven and has a son and a spirit form, too!"

"Yes, I have heard the missionaries teach that, but we believe that Wakan exists in all creation. The earth, for example, is just one part of all things. Therefore, to us, it has a spirit. We call her Mother Earth." Chaska contemplates his thoughts.

"Really?" Hannah listens intently. She smiles, waiting for Chaska to continue.

"Wakan Tanka brought all things into being, much like your God in Genesis. But what we have been taught is slightly different. When we speak of all things, we mean being a part of any one of the Six Grandfathers."

"The six grandfathers?"

"Wakan is essentially all of the six grandfathers."

Hannah, "What are the six grandfathers?"

"They are the four directions," Chaska sits up, raises his arms, and points, "North… East… South and... West!" Then he points up, "The sky." Then down, "And the earth below… All things!"

"Oh, All things."

They lay back down into each other's arms.

Hannah, "Interesting. Wow, that covers it!"

"You asked!"

"Yes, I did, tell me more!"

"A kinship has developed between my people and these spirits because we have observed them to have human-like characteristics. When we are born, we receive a Takuskanskan,

"Ta cu kan can, what?"

"Just checking to see if you were paying attention. Tak-us-kans-kan is a guardian-type spirit, much like your guardian angel. It is a breath of life that comes from the stars. When we die, this spirit returns to the stars."

"Heaven?"

"Kinda, but not the same."

"There are some similarities, aren't there?"

"Yes, a few. All things have their individual spirit. Yet, they all share the same spiritual 'essence' of Wakan Tanka. All things are one. This spirituality is a part of everything in the world."

Chaska pauses, takes her left hand off his chest, holds it, and raises his right hand to hers.

"Do you feel the heat?"

"Yes! You are always so warm."

They both smile.

"All living beings can share their knowledge, experiences, and understanding through this exchange of energy, through the spirituality that is within us all."

Hannah rests her head against his bare chest, then pulls his arms around her, "Hmmmm!"

Chaska smiles and continues, "Especially in times of crisis. Since we can feel this kinship, this bond, this 'essence' has been described as having a human-like quality, it has come to be known as the 'people'."

"So, it is human?"

"No, not really, but it is human-like. This 'essence' can best be described as being like the breath of life. Like I said, it is difficult to explain."

She giggles. "Ok, I understand." Then she admits, "Not really, but continue."

"My people believe humans are born of the womb of Mother Earth, as are all living things, the buffalo, deer, cows, horses. Everything."

Chaska points to their respective steeds grazing nearby.

"They have their own individual spirit. But all things are connected to Wakan Tanka. All things are one. This spirituality is shared by everything, even the non-living things in the world, like the water in the river, the dirt we walk on."

"Amazing, so even those rocks have a spirit?"

She points to the bluff nearby.

“Yes, the hills and the mountains all have a spirit, and they can teach us many things. All living beings and all things not living can share their knowledge through this spirituality. Especially in times of crisis. As I mentioned, this kinship, this bond came to be known as the 'people.'"

Hannah turns and looks into his eyes, “How can you tell if they are telling you anything?”

"In time, you will understand if you allow it." He touches her gently on the nose.

Hannah smiles and returns to her comfy resting place, awaiting his next word.

"Our rituals seek to calm the Wakan spirits, which may be either good or evil. Much like your Angels and Devils.”

"Really? Your religious beliefs and mine are not that different!”

"I know."

Chaska leans over and gently kisses her lips. "These rituals reveal Wakan's essence and how all things share the wisdom to our people."

“What kind of rituals?”

"Let's see. First, there is the Vision Quest. When a young boy has earned the privilege, they go on a vision quest."

Hannah, “Have you been on yours?

“Yes, I have!”

“What did you see or hear?”

“Someday, maybe. I will tell you about it!”

“Ahh? … Did you have to go all alone?”

Chaska, “Yes.”

“That must have been scary.”

“Not as bad as you might think. We have to earn the right to go. We must prove we are ready."

“Still!”

He smiles at her concern, then continues, "When we return from a vision quest, we have to perform in front of the whole tribe."

"Perform?"

"Yes, we tell of our experience through dance and song. We act out what we have experienced as best we can. My father and his father before him, and so forth, have shared their vision quest experiences in this way. It is through this ritual that we gain a better collective understanding."

"Understanding of what?"

"Of what is necessary to maintain a balance between us and all other forms of life. This unity among all things living and non-living. This Vision Quest provides a strong, cohesive force through this ritual. As young warriors, we become teachers by sharing our newly acquired knowledge. Everyone in the village learns because we share with the young and the old alike."

Hannah hangs on Chaska's every word.

"The Black Hills are sacred to the us. Remember when I told you all living, breathing things were born of Mother Earth? We believe the Black Hills are the mother of all of us. That is where the Lakota people come from, the many Lakota people. We believe that Wakan first told our people the sacred instructions at Bear Butte."

"Bear Butte, where is that?"

"It is very far way, on the north side of the Black Hills. It is where I made my Vision Quest. It is where many of the warriors go to Bear Butte. It is one of the most sacred of all places. We call it in our language, "Mathǒ Pahá." We also believe that the spirits of the Lakota people, will go to rest in the Black Hills after death."

"But didn't you say they went back to the stars?"

"No, that was the guardian spirits."

Hannah, "Oh, that's right, sorry!"

"It is ok. I said it was difficult to explain but even harder to understand."

"Go on! I love listening to your voice."

"I love telling you these things. All right, the buffalo are an extremely important life force for our people. Wakan Tanka's essence, through these visions, is relayed through the buffalo most often. Besides that, most of our life's necessities come from the buffalo. For example, we use the hide to make most of our clothing and tepees. We use the extra hide to make ropes, moccasins, and even snowshoes."

"Really?"

"The buffalo horns and large bones are made into spoons, ladles, and other useful tools, even into weapons and ritual articles. The sinew is used for our bowstrings, to fasten arrow points to the shafts, and to sew clothing and hides together for our tepees. Our braves use the rest of the buffalo's bones to make various useful instruments."

"Amazing."

"The Buffalo also has a spiritual connection with the Sun."

"Really?"

Chaska looks to the sky. Puffy white clouds slowly pass overhead, momentarily obscuring the sun's warm rays.

"It sounds as if the buffalo is your god."

"No, but its spirit is associated with the affairs of the heart."

Hannah asks, "Really?"

Chaska leans in to gently kiss her lips. "Yes, really."

"I like that!"

He laughs, "Me too." Then he continues, "The life essence of the buffalo cares for all of our people, our young, our old, our families, and our tribe and all other tribes and all other people. The buffalo connects us to the spirits of all growing things."

Chaska mentally pauses as his words take on even more heartfelt meaning.

“The Buffalo is the 'center' in the life and thought of the Lakota.”

Smiling, Hannah squeezes Chaska firmly.

"Then there are the other sacred rituals, such as the Sun Dance, Yuwipi, and Purification ritual."

“What is a purification ritual?”

“It is a Sweat lodge. I'll explain in a little bit. All of these rituals acknowledge, celebrate, and enrich our kinship with the Earth, with Wakan Tanka."

Hannah, “You mentioned something called Uyipee?”

"Yes, close. The Yuwipi prayer is an offering to the spirit of the stones."

“You pray to stones?”

“I did say it was difficult to explain!”

“Yes, and even harder to understand!”

They both laugh, and then Chaska returns to his explanation.

"See, a Spirit Stone offers protection against danger or illness. The Spirit Stone represents our belief in Wakan's spiritual force, which exists in all forms of creation. Both living and what other people consider non-living things. Then there is the Sacred Pipe, which was given to our people by the White Buffalo Calf Woman."

“White Buffalo Calf Woman?”

"Yes, don't ask. I'll get there! Our ancestors handed down the Spirit Stone ritual through the generations as a symbol of unity for all Lakota people. The Sacred Pipe is the center of this unity. All the other pipes are like the roots."

Hannah asks, “So when different tribes or different villages smoke from their pipes, those are the roots you just mentioned?”

"Yes, that was good. You are beginning to understand. When our people pray with the Sacred Pipe, the spirits come. The Sacred Pipe is the mediator between Wakan Tanka and all things. The ritual is a way of expressing our beliefs to all in the village. These rites reinforce the understanding that we have a relationship between all Lakota people and all of creation."

Chaska spreads his arms out as wide as he can and then brings them back to a tender embrace wrapped around her.

With a kiss on her forehead, he continues, "Another ritual is The Sun Dance. Only a select few can participate. One must be chosen to participate."

"Have you been chosen?"

"No, not yet. This ceremony brings about a sense of unity and kinship."

Chaska pauses to think about what he knows of this ritual.

"Not everyone understands it. Those who have been chosen say it is very intense. They describe the dance as being like a sacred ecstasy. Those who have participated in the dance describe it as enlightening and an 'awakening.' They say they can see and feel the wholeness and unity of all things."

The thoughts roll through Chaska's mind rapidly as he ponders the unknown.

"Through these rituals, each warrior discovers and then shares his experiences with everyone in the village. This shared knowledge is what we know of this life in this world. Through this ritual, they are taken spiritually to a new spirit world, a place of new knowledge."

Hannah, "It sounds a little like our heaven."

"Yes, it does, doesn't it? Like your religion, all of these rituals teach us how to live our lives in harmony with all things. These rituals define our place between the human and non-human creatures, even with the land itself."

A puzzled look on Hannah's face shows she is overwhelmed.

"I understand this is a lot to take in. Let's see, how can I explain it?" After a brief pause, Chaska continues, "Think of 'Wakan' as our religion's center or main 'symbol'.

He pauses to find a way to explain it better.

"I know. It is similar to your belief that God is everywhere."

"Ok, that makes sense."

"Like your crucifix or the cross, we use symbols also. The circle is one symbol we use in everyday life."

"How?"

"I'll get to that!"

He touches her nose gently.

"Then there is the Sacred Pipe I mentioned before and a few sacred numbers."

Hannah settles in next to Chaska. She leans her back against his waist and bent legs while he lies on his left side. Her left arm rests on his torso, her legs curled between them. They face each other.

"The 'circle' represents life itself and is thus held to be sacred. In many ways, it represents Wakan. Everything in this world tries to be round in one form or another. For example, the earth is round."

"I see!"

"Other things that are round, the human body. Your head, our necks, our torsos, legs, fingers, eyes, all are round."

He points to the trees.

"A tree trunk, the branches are round, the roots are round."

Chaska pauses again briefly.

"Time itself revolves. A day is circular. Morning follows night, night follows day, and the moon orbits the Earth. The seasons revolve again and again. Years… The most basic of nature, for example, a bird's nest, is circular."

"I get it. I never thought of it like that. Everything is round, amazing when you think about it!"

"So, we imitate this natural order by arranging our villages in circles. We sit in circles for ceremonial occasions. We construct our tepees in the shape of a circle."

"Wow! … Kind of like how we are laying here."

Hannah draws an invisible circle starting at Chaska's abdomen, up and over his shoulders, then his head, up her legs to her torso, and back to his hips.

"Yes, just like that!"

Chaska touches her face gently.

"Symbolically, our camp circle is the 'sacred hoop'. Once inside, all is safe, knowledge is shared, and all is good. The circle represents wholeness, which helps us remember that the center of all things is Wakan Tanka. Who, like the circle, has no end."

Hannah, "Very interesting!"

"Then there is the Sacred Pipe."

"My father has a pipe!"

Chaska acts amazed, "Really?"

"Yes. Sorry. Continue."

"Don't be, the Sacred Pipe was brought to our people by the White Buffalo Calf Woman. She is one with Wakan Tanka."

"She is Wakan Tanka?"

"No, she represents and is one 'with' Wakan Tanka, no different than any living creature. White Buffalo Calf Woman is the representative, a symbol of all creation. There is a story about White Buffalo Calf Woman, but not today."

Hannah inquires, "Why not?"

"Because it is a long story."

"Ok, another day."

"Yes, but I wanted to tell you about the other symbols."

"Ok, sorry."

Chaska, "Don't be sorry. I am glad you are interested... See, all forms of 'creation' are understood to be our relatives. When we participate in the ritual of the Sacred Pipe, it binds us to all things, to our relatives. So, by smoking from the pipe, we accept our responsibility toward all of our relatives, all of Wakan's creation. The pipe bowl is traditionally made of red stone, symbolizing the Earth and one of the Six Grandfathers. Our artisans carve an image of a buffalo into the red pipe bowl stone. The four legs of the buffalo image represent the four directions. The smoke that floats from the bowl rises to the sky, the final Grandfather."

"It all comes together!"

"And I am not even finished. See, the Sacred Pipe's stem, the wooden part we smoke from, symbolizes everything that grows."

"Interesting."

"There are eagle feathers attached to the Sacred Pipe's stem. These represent the eagles and all creatures that fly. All of these symbols represent the spirits, the essence of all creation, the 'peoples'. These 'peoples' collectively send their voices to Wakan Tanka, the Great Spirit. When we smoke from the Sacred Pipe, we pray for and with everything, all things. The Sacred Pipe symbolizes the essence of the 'peoples' - these 'peoples' are the Lakota religion."

Hannah is mesmerized. She doesn't want him to stop. She waits for him to continue.

"We also have Sacred numbers, four and seven. The structure of the world around us and all things within it reflect a four-fold division. There are four divisions of time: Day, Night, Moon, or months and Year. There are four seasons: There is Spring, then Summer, Fall, and Winter. There are four parts to all growing things: The Roots, Stem, Foliage, and Fruit or seed. There are four stages of human life: Infants, Childhood, Adulthood, and the Elderly. To represent what the Great Spirit has created in fours, we should do everything that is possible in fours. So, we plan our ceremonies to span four days or divided into four separate sessions."

"WOW!"

"There is more. You asked about the Purification Lodge, the sweat lodge. Our braves construct them from sixteen willow branches. Sixteen, equally divided by four, equals four. They place each sweat lodge according to the four directions. The Sun Dance I told you about earlier, the Lodge for the Sun Dance, is built with twenty-eight poles, four times seven, both of our sacred numbers. When completed, the lodge appears round, which returns to the circle symbol. The central pole of the lodge symbolizes Wakan Tanka. Again, the center of the spirit world, holding up all of the spirit world. Everything we construct, our tepees, the Sweat Lodge and Sun Dance, and how we lay out our villages. All of this represents the whole world. So, all of these rituals are intertwined and woven together.

One of the other reasons for the sacred numbers is the legend of the White Buffalo Calf Woman. The story tells us she brought seven sacred rites to our people and stayed with us for four days. The Dakota people are known as the 'Seven Fire Places' long before our people first encountered white men.

Seeing she is again overwhelmed, Chaska stops.

Chaska, "Enough for today!"

"That is a lot to take in!"

"I understand!"

Hannah, "It seems so simple, but yet so complicated, all at the same time."

"Agreed!"

Chapter 7

Fourth Day of the Minnesota Uprising

August 21st, 1862

DESPITE THE RUMOR that Fort Ridgely has been burned, Sibley continues to move slowly up the Minnesota River, cautious to a fault.

In a letter to Governor Ramsey, he makes excuses.

"The roads are terrible. We have very little in the ways of provisions to take care of so many men. Unless we can get supplies to us via Steamboat or wagon train, we will be stuck here indefinitely."

Stage coaches and ordinary wagons have used the same roads in the same condition, covering the same distance in one day. It has taken Sibley two and a half days to get just halfway.

Iron Face, the scout Lt Sheehan had dispatched to Fort Snelling, arrives at Sibley's camp.

He dismounts and asks, "Who is in charge here?"

A soldier points in the general direction of the officer's tent.

"Thanks."

Iron Face approaches the tent with two guards on either side of the flap.

First guard, "What is your business?

"I have been sent to inform the General."

"Wait here. I'll see if he will see you." To the other guard, "Watch him."

Iron Face can hear the guard inside the tent inform Sibley.

Sibley responds with a question, "Is he armed?"

"Yes."

"Have him leave it with you and send him in."

Guard, "Yes. Sir."

He turns and exits the tent.

Guard to Iron Face, "Leave your weapons with us. You will receive them back when you leave."

Iron Face removes his revolver and motions to his rifle, which is still on his mount.

First guard, “You may enter.”

Sibley notices the soldier’s ethnicity and asks, “Who sent you?”

“Lt. Gere. Commander of Fort Ridgely. Sir.”

“What can you tell me of the situation? How many… Sioux are involved?

Iron Face suggests, “There must have been 1500 Indians involved.”

Sibley, "Oh my god, that means more could join in."

"Then we need to hurry, Sir. We need to get to Ft Ridgely."

"We? Private, this means we need to be cautious. Between the two agencies, there must be over 6000 savages. I mean Sioux."

"I know what you meant."

"Certainly, they trusted you to deliver this message. You must be on our side."

"Yes, Sir."

"Well, that only means there could be nearly 2500 warriors."

Iron Face questions, “Yes, that is possible. But Sir.”

"Quiet. While I think. You say at least five villages of braves are on the warpath. By now, they probably have overrun Fort Ridgely. And they can be advancing as we speak.”

Again, Iron Face protests, “But sir!”

“No buts, we only have a little over 200 men. Most are just farmers and ranchers, with a few tin horns and a few nearly worthless businessmen."

"I might have exaggerated a bit, Sir."

“No, I believe you are correct. Little Crow and the other chiefs could gather all the tribes on both ends of the reservation. We need to be careful.”

“But we need to get reinforcements to the fort as soon as possible.”

Sibley, “Precisely why you are a scout… That and being half Sioux." He pauses realizing his insult. He continues, "If Little Crow is as cunning as I think he is, he'll be waiting for us to make our way through the thick woods along the bluffs. If he has all of the tribes involved. There could be over 2500 warriors waiting to ambush us.”

“The Lieutenant told me to make sure you got there as soon as possible.”

"If the Fort has fallen, the Sioux will have captured all of their weapons, ammunition, at least two cannons, and other supplies at Fort Ridgely."

“But Sir!” Iron Face objects again.

"With those armaments, they would be a much more deadly force to contend with."

“I was only trying to…”

Sibley interrupts, "I know what you were told. But I need to make my decision based on all the possibilities." He turns to his Sergeant. "Get this man some food and drink. He has had a long ride."

Iron Face protests, “But Sir.”

Sibley waves Iron Face's last objection off and turns to his Lieutenant, "Those savages could be anywhere. Even if this half-breed was only partially correct. Little Crow could have his warriors in any of a dozen places along the road to the fort."

The lieutenant waves for his sergeant come over to the table.

A sergeant brings a map and rolls it out over the small folding table.

Sibley points with his middle finger to locations on the map, "This road is flanked by thick forest here and along the high bluffs here and many other areas like here and here. These can be potential ambushes."

Lt, “What will we do?”

“We need more men and supplies.”

"What do you want me to do, Sir?"

Sibley, “Send a courier to Captain Hiram Grant.”

"Yes, Sir,"

Lt. to his Sergeant, “Find a reliable rider.”

"Yes, Sir."

Lt. to Sibley, "What are you thinking, Sir?"

“We need Captain Grant and his men back here to St Peters.”

“But they are already on their way to Fort Ridgely.”

Sibley, "We need to pull them back before they are lost too. Didn't you hear how they ambushed Captain Marsh and his men?"

“Of course.”

"We only have maybe 225 men, mostly of which are green, untrained, and ill-equipped."

Sibley pauses momentarily and then states, "Send for another courier."

The Lieutenant turns to another Sergeant.

"In it, Sir."

The young sergeant skedaddles out of the tent.

"Where am I sending this one, Sir?"

“To the Governor.”

He pulls up a folding chair, takes a seat, slides a piece of paper in front of him, and finds a quill pen.

“What would you like to say to the Governor?”

Sibley begins to dictate, "Something short and to the point.” He scratches the side of his face. “How about this? We needed supplies and military equipment yesterday. I would respectfully suggest if there is any red tape, that you cut it with a bayonet.’”

Sibley waits for a response for another four days, using the time to drill and prepare his men. Frustration is beginning to set in with Sibley and his men.

***

Little Crow’s War Council Lodge.

TWO CHIEFS SIT face to face, separated by the flames of an open fire in the large council teepee.

Little Crow's thoughts are interrupted by his closest ally's question. "What do we do now?"

Each solemn face stares through the leaping flames.

Little Crow, "We try again. We must take the fort."

"But how?"

"That is what we need to figure out. Those damn cannons."

Gray Bird suggests, "Many of our warriors don't believe it is possible."

Little Crow stands quickly, "It is possible. If they fight like Dakota warriors."

Gray Bird remains seated but follows the pacing Chief with his eyes and asks the obvious question, "How can we take the Fort then?"

"We are too few in number. We need more warriors."

"Yes, what about Red Middle Voice and Shakopee?"

Little Crow scoffs at their names being mentioned, "Yes, those two. The chiefs that spoke so forcefully about wanting to fight a war. Where are they now?"

"Fighting in the Big Woods, I hear."

"Hiding in the woods is more like it. They certainly are not here where they are needed."

Gray Bird meekly asks, "What can we do?"

"We will send runners to convince them to join us."

"How will runners ... find them in time... since they are scattered in the Big Woods?"

Little Crow, "We'll send our runners to the Rice Creek's Soldier Lodge. Tell them to have their people find their own Chiefs and give them this message. Have them and their warriors meet me here in my village!"

"Will that be enough?"

"Send other braves to the Yellow Medicine villages. The Sisseton and the Wahpeton may join us. Tell them we need them to join us in this fight. The time is now to rid our valley and the rest of our ancestral homelands of the whites."

***

Second Attack on Fort Ridgely

LITTLE CROW LOOKS on with pride. His decision to send runners has paid off. The number of braves has swelled to twice what they attacked with the first time. The council has decided on a simpler plan of attack this time. They will surround the complex of buildings just like last time, but they will attack from all directions all at once. No trickery, just overwhelming numbers. The only thing specific is to go after the big guns, those damn cannons.

Still, Red Middle Voice and Shakopee, two chiefs that pressed for war, are again absent, but many of their braves have answered the call.

***

Defenders of Fort Ridgely

AROUND NOON, THE first picket reports, "Let Lt Sheehan know they are back. Tell him they are spreading out on our perimeter."

Private, “Ok, any idea how many?”

“No, not really, but it looks like a lot more than last time.”

Upon hearing the report Lt Sheehan gives the order, “Bugler, sound everyone to their stations.”

As the bugler plays his screeching noise, men and women scatter in every direction. The cannons are ready and waiting, both strategically placed. Men take their positions behind the barricades. Women continue with their support positions and making improvised ammunition.

Crouched behind a wagon, one soldier to another, “Will these barricades hold?”

“Whether they hold or not, we will need to make every shot count.”

"I hope all of this preparation to strengthen and expand the barricades wasn't a waste of time."

Much of the material was scrap from the demolished buildings from the first attack.

"We'll know soon enough."

***

THERE IS NO signal this time. There was only silence until the first horrific screams began to roll around the besieged fort. Revenge-thirsty Dakota charge from their hiding places. Their assault has begun. The arrows quickly darken the gray afternoon sky. The din of lead shot striking the sides of barricades and shelters sounds like hail without the thunder. Flaming arrows find their mark on the still-damp shingles, but the results are only smoldering fires. The soldiers and settlers return fire, and the cloud of black powder smoke obscures the vision of both sides. The initial charge successfully takes over a few of the outer buildings. Given up as unimportant are the empty ice house, a recently emptied root cellar, and the distant grain storage building. The now-empty warehouse of the fort's Sutler is the only building outside the perimeter that the Dakota hasn't overtaken.

Chief Mankato to a warrior, “Have some of our men set fire to any building they can reach that is not close to the fight."

He notices and now begins to watch as the thick smoke hangs in the air.

Mankato, "Have them burn everything they don't need for protection. We'll use the smoke to cause an even bigger diversion and, better yet, more cover.

***

ONCE THOSE BUILDINGS within range of the barricades have been overtaken by the Dakota, Sheehan gives his sergeant an order, “Destroy all of those outer buildings.”

The artillery crews fire red hot cannonballs into those buildings.

Sheehan assesses the situation, "That worked. They have nowhere to hide now."

Sergeant agrees, "The warriors will have to seek shelter elsewhere soon.”

"Yes, now they are forced to run back into the open."

The give-and-take battle continues for hours. Many attempts to reach the center of the compound have failed. The cannon fire again has devasted the attackers' ranks. After six hours of fruitless attempts with no significant results, the Dakota withdraw.

***

The defenders are jubilant!

***

A SOLEMN PROCESSION of the defeated makes its way along the Minnesota River. They stop at a small creek to camp. Little Crow calls another council. The chiefs gather around a fire in the center of the camp.

Little Crow begins, "We must try again. If we are to be successful in driving out the whites, we need to take this fort."

Gray Bird offers his opinion, "It is too well defended."

Red Leg, “Those cannons are too powerful.”

Mankato, “There is too much open field to attack the fort.”

Little Crow, “There must be two or three hundred people held up in that fort. They have to be running out of ammunition and powder."

Gray Bird, "What about food? They don't have any cattle to eat. They will starve soon enough."

Red Leg, “We should attack New Ulm again. They don’t have the big guns. They don’t have any army.”

Gray Bird, "I agree we can leave some warriors here, and the rest of us attack New Ulm. That will prevent any reinforcements from getting any further upriver."

Red Leg, "There are only old settlers, their wives, and little children at New Ulm."

Little Crow, “We are Dakota warriors. We don’t pick our fights because they are weak. We fight because it is right.”

Gray Bird explains, “Our scouts tell us the women and children have left for Fort Snelling. Not many stayed behind.”

Little Crow, “Good. It does not matter who is there. Better the women and children are gone. But we need to take that village.”

Gray Bird to Little Crow, “Shall we have a vote?”

“Yes, vote!”

The votes are tallied. The next attack will be on New Ulm. Again.

Chapter 8

Henson on his way home

August 4th, 1863

HENSON BRUSHES OFF the bugs and leaves after a short rest under a boxelder tree. A cool breeze floats along the banks of the Missouri. He makes his way back to Wildfire. Rubbing his hand across her reddish back, he checks her condition. She is breathing easier, and the sweat has dried to a light white powder.

His thoughts go back to his family.

'It was your family.'

Then he remembers the day he left for training.

William Henry pleading, "Don't go papa."

The memories flow back into his mind. His children beg him to stay, especially his youngest, Loren. "Papa, the Indians will come if you leave."

Tears well up in his eyes as he remembers hugging and kissing each of them goodbye. He wipes away the tears with his sleeve and rests his head on his mount's back.

Moments later, he shakes off the sorrow, and a fit of rage takes over. He throws the saddle over Wildfire, cinches it good and tight, climbs aboard, and resumes his trek south.

His thoughts go back to a story his youngest told him one day after supper, not more than a year earlier.

Loren and Boots

A year earlier.

"PAPA, I CLIMBED a tree today." The four-year-old announces.

Henson replies, "You did. You shouldn't be climbing trees, young man."

"Why?"

"Because you could get hurt."

Loren states affirmatively, "But I didn't."

Henson remembers patting his youngest on the head and recalls the rest of Loren's story.

***

LOREN RUNS AT a boxelder tree behind the two Wiseman log cabins. The tree haD fallen over many years ago and grew at an angle above the ground. Resilient, it continues to grow but has an upward curve to its trunk.

He scrambles up the leaning tree as far as his little legs can take him. His arms stretch as far as he can reach. His fingers grasp the branch, but he is unable to hold on.

As he tumbles to the ground, "Darn it!" He brushes off his clothes and gets ready for another try.

Boots barks his concern.

"I will be alright, boy. All I need to do is reach that first limb."

Still worried, Boots barks again.

The determined tike makes another run up the leaning boxelder trunk. With a big stretch, he catches one hand on a branch. Now hanging perilously by one hand, he swings, trying to catch the branch with his other.

"Help!"

Boots barks insistently.

After a few short moments, Loren drops two feet to the ground, rolls, and sits up.

"That was fun. I'm gunna do that again."

Boots nudges Loren and then gets between the child and the tree. His bushy tail isn't wagging.

"Ok, Ok, but what else is there to do?"

Loren looks up at his goal. Further up the tree, Loren's brothers have nailed in a few pieces of scrap lumber across some higher branches. His two older brothers call it 'their' tree house.

Hannah has left for a ride on Wildfire along the river.

Andrew and William have wandered off somewhere without including Loren again.

His pa is down by the river unloading another wagon load of split firewood.

Pheobe is doing laundry.

Arthur is chopping more wood.

Loren has already been down by the corral, wishing for the day to come when he can have a horse of his own. But like everything else, he keeps hearing the same thing over and over again. "You are too little."

"I know. Let's go check out the hay loft in the barn!"

Boots turns his head slightly.

"Come on, boy!"

With tail wagging, Boots tags along.

The double-wide doors are propped open. The multiple harnesses hang on pegs on both sides of the alleyway down the middle of the barn.

As Loren steps inside the barn, he notices the ground change under his feet. Holding pens are on both sides. Horses are on the right, and the enclosure for Bessey's calf is on the left. Halfway down the alley, on the center post, the rungs of a wooden ladder are nailed.

Loren to Boots, "I can climb this!"

He barks his concern.

"You don't think so. Just watch."

One rung at a time, slow and meticulously, he edges his way up, a grunt here and there, and he is in the loft. The field hay and straw are stored up here. More feed hay than straw. Pitch forks lean against the center post that supports the roof. The loose field hay lies scattered on the wooden flooring in a semi-circle around the hatch openings above each pen below. During the winter months and rainy season, the older boys and pa pitch hay through these openings to feed the livestock. The other side of the loft is where the straw is stored. Another opening on that side has another trap door to deliver straw to the calves for bedding.

Loren looks toward the far end of the loft, where a large opening exists. Through this door his pa and brothers lift the hay and straw, and bring it through this large barn door. Above him, pully attached to a large beam. A rope over the pulley is attached to a center buckle with four ropes running to the corners of a raft-like platform. That raft-like platform dangles before Loren. A pole with a hook hangs on a long nail next to the open door.

Loren walks over to the open door. He shuffles his feet slowly, getting closer and closer. He hears his father and his big brothers tell him, *'Get back. You are too little to help. Go, stand over there out of the way.'*

No one is here to tell him now. Loren ventures closer and closer to the edge. The tips of his tiny shoes pass over the last board of the loft floor. Looking down to his right, he sees the mud and muck of the cattle pen. He steps back. Out the loft door, he sees the farmland his family owns. The river runs slowly along the east side of the property to the southeast. The garden he is allowed to help in is to the left of the corral. This corral is for the workhorses when they are brought in from the pasture. Starting at the end of the corral, the tall and green cornfield goes back as far as he can see. The hay fields are further off to the right, all the way back to the distant tree-covered bluffs. Stacks of dried golden-brown cut alfalfa sit scattered in the field, dotting the new growth green landscape. The grazing land used to pasture the livestock lies just beyond the hay field.

From below, Boots barks again.

"Ok, ok!"

Loren descends down the ladder carefully, "Let's go check on the little pigs."

The hog house is set off to the west side of the home place, lower than the rest of the farm buildings. The adjacent pig pen is even lower. Inside the hog barn, most of the pens are empty. All of the medium-sized hogs are put out to rut during the day. In the evening, they come in to be fed grain and watered. Pitchforks are placed upside down on pegs, ready for the worst job on the farm. Cleaning the pig pens. Straw bedding is spread in a more confined space for the sows to lay on when they are about to have piglets. Inevitably, the bedding becomes saturated in dung and piss. Removing this smelling mess is dreaded by all.

Loren, "I'm glad he is not old enough to do that job."

Boots doesn't respond but stares admiringly, panting and wagging his tail.

Loren hears squealing in the far corner of the hog house.

"Let's go see the little pigs."

Boots pants heavily and follows.

Laying on her side, a large sow grunts a loud, throaty, guttural sound. Tiny piglets scurry to find a nipple. Some try to push their siblings out of the way. The bigger piglets suckle and don't give up their spot. A smaller one nudges another off a teat and quickly takes his place. Squills of frustration occasionally erupt. Loren smiles as he watches the feasting.

"They are so cute!"

One piglet wanders close to the edge of the pen near Loren. He reaches through an opening in the pen fence to pet the tiny thing. Loren hears a loud grunt, and the mama sow twitches. She begins to get up. A few suckling piglets lose their hold on their nipples but quickly regain them.

Loren stretches his arm between the rails, which he has been told not to do.

With a loud squeal from the angry sow, she is on her feet. A piglet momentarily dangles, then drops to the ground as the sow charges.

A startled Loren jumps back and falls on his behind in the dry dirt of the alleyway.

***

HENSON REMEMBERS HIS son's excitement as he told his story.

"That is when Boots began barking. He sure told that sow."

"Did the sow stop?" Henson smiles and asks.

Loren adds, "Oh yeah. But it continued to grunt at me."

"She was only trying to protect her babies. …"

Henson remembers his words over a year earlier. A tear wells up in his eye at the thought, *'She was only trying to protect her babies.'*

Wildfire stops in her tracks. Henson has tugged on the reins.

He hears the sound of his youngest imploring him to stay.

"Don't go, Papa. If you leave, the Indians will come."

Henson's head rests in both of his hands as he begins to weep.

Chapter 9

St Paul, Minnesota

May of 1862

A FANCY EAST coast-style stagecoach arrives at the Governor's residence in the burgeoning young town of St Paul, Minnesota. The four uniformed men on horseback escort an elaborate decked-out carriage. Two bearded, unkept men ride on top. One drives the carriage. The other holds a black powder musket. A businessman in a suit is the only passenger on board.

The lavish Victorian house stands out among the homes in the new neighborhood. The baby blue two-story structure has white trim. Two spiral towers with witch's hat turrets stand guard on both front corners of the structure. The driver directs his four-horse team under the canopy of the carriage entrance on the right side of the mansion.

A well-dressed black man approaches the carriage and stands at attention. He waits for the passenger side door of the stage to open.

The lone man inside holds a top hat in one hand and a cane in the other as he leans forward in his seat. To the butler, "Go let the governor know we are here."

"Who shall I tell him is here?"

"Tell him Cyrus Wyckoff is here."

The servant, Cornelius O'Connor, assures the visitor, "Yes, Sir."

The butler turns and enters the side entrance of the manor.

The top hat-wielding gentleman steps out and dapperly places his top hat over his balding head.

To one of the other four men in his entourage, "See if you can find a freight cart at one of the local stores. Tell them it is government business. Let them know we'll make it worth their while."

"Yes, Sir."

The stout young man and horse dodge other equestrian riders and numerous horse-drawn carriages as he trots down the cobblestone street.

Cyrus to the two stagecoach operators, “Can we get a little help with our cargo?”

The taller of the two drivers says, “Sure thing, just as soon as we take care of the horses.”

“By all means, take care of them.”

Cyrus paces a bit while he takes in the bustling small-town activity. The other riders dismount and mull together on the opposite side of the stagecoach from the man wearing the top hat.

Moments later, the Governor's servant walks out the side door of the nicer than most homes.

Cornelius O'Connor asks Cyrus, “He wants to know the nature of your business?”

Cyrus, “Tell him I am an assistant to Clark Thompson. He is the Superintendent of Indian Affairs in Washington D.C. He'll know who that is.”

“Ok, I’ll tell him.”

The errand guard returns on foot, pulling a noisy but sturdy freight cart with cast iron wheels and a wooden flatbed. His horse tethered to a sturdy handle on the cart.

Cyrus to the other three guards, “Go help him.”

The three men stroll casually to assist. Together, they push and pull the cart up the slight hill.

Cyrus yells at the four men, “Use that rear rail bracket to push. My god, men, use your heads."

The guards glance at each other, infuriated by the disrespect from this pompous ass. They park the cart at the back of the stage.

Cyrus yells, “Are you two about done with the horses?”

The taller driver responds, "Just about, just a second." To the other driver with only one visible tooth, "You go and undo the cargo hold."

“Okay." In a hushed tone, "What an asshole."

“Yes, and we have to take his ass back too.”

Cyrus makes his way around the stagecoach. All four guards step aside and wait as the shorter driver with a long, scraggly beard and a single brown front tooth undoes the tie-downs on the carriage cargo hold.

The older driver, a bit taller with a better-kept beard, arrives and asks, "What do we have here, gents?"

A tap on their shoulders signals the drivers to part and let Cyrus see inside the cargo hold. There sit two chests, each chained and padlocked.

Cyrus, with naked loathing, orders the men, “Ok, let’s get them chests on the cart.”

The four guards separate two to each side, and the closest two men to the stage reach inside and try to budge the chest.

First guard, “It isn’t budging."

Tall Driver, “Here, let me help.”

He splits the two closest men and grabs hold of a leather handle on the short end of the first massive chest. It begins to move slowly, inch by inch.

The single-toothed driver, “What’s in there?”

Wyckoff, “Never you mind. Just get them on the cart.”

A voice from behind the crowd of men says, "What you got there?"

Cyrus turns to see Governor Alexander Ramsey standing with another well-dressed man on the deck of his side porch.

“Two heavy chests for you, sir."

Ramsey cheerfully announces, “Well, well! When you get them unloaded, bring 'em around back. I have a service entrance with a ramp."

Wyckoff, “Sure thing.”

The four guards take positions as if pallbearers. Each side of the chest has two new leather straps, with a man on each. The first chest falls with a loud clang onto the cart. Together, the six men push the clumsy cart around back, then up the ramp and inside the kitchen pantry.

Ramsey instructs the men and points to the open area along the wall, “Over there will do.”

With a giant clunk, the chest hits the floor.

Wyckoff to his helpers, “Ok, go get the other one!”

The six men dutifully turn and follow orders with grumbling heard once they get outside.

Ramsey extends his hand to Cyrus, who takes it and responds with a firm shake. Gesturing to the man next to him, “This is Henry Sibley!”

Cyrus Wyckoff, “We’ve met.”

Sibley shakes the hand but doesn't respond. His puzzled look tells Cyrus he doesn't remember him.

"It was a few years ago, back in Washington, when you were in Congress."

“Sure, I have met a lot of people, sorry.”

“Understandable. I'm Cyrus Wyckoff.”

The two men shake hands vigorously.

Sibley, "Good to see you again. You've had a long trip."

"Yes, a long, bumpy road."

Ramsey, “Once you are done there, would you join us in the parlor?”

“I would love to.”

The two Governors of Minnesota, one former and the other presently, retreat through a pair of tall, lavishly carved French Doors into an adjacent room off the spacious kitchen.

The six men return with the second chest. Cyrus tells them, "After you finish with the second chest, wait for me at the coach while I take care of some business."

Third guard, “Certainly.”

***

CYRUS WYCKOFF ENTERS the parlor where the two governors sit, sipping whiskey.

Ramsey asks, “Would you like a glass?”

“Certainly.”

Ramsey motions to his butler, Cornelius O'Connor, "Pour our guest a glass."

Sibley motions to Cyrus with one hand toward a chair, “Have a seat.”

"I'll stand. Thank you. It has been a long ride."

“Oh, yes, I understand.”

Cornelius asks, "Will that be all, sir?"

Ramsey, “Yes, that will be all. For now.”

Sibley inquires, “How is Cornelius working out?”

“Just fine. He is a great asset.”

Cyrus, “Cornelius? Strange name for a nigger.”

Sibley responds, “Now, now! There is no need for your Southern animosity. His full name is Cornelius O’Connor.”

“He is Irish?”

Sibley laughs.

Ramsey bemoans the humor, "Of course not. His father's southern masters were Irish."

Cyrus squeamishly responds, "No need to get offended. I was just having a bit of fun.”

Sibley, “You are in the north now. We support the Union cause.”

Ramsey, “In public at least. We are sympathetic to the southern plight. So, no offense taken.”

They all lift their shot glasses and take a sip.

Ramsey asks after his sip, “Any troubles along the way?”

“No, nothing to speak of.”

“Good to hear.”

Sibley states, “You say we have met. Where and when was that again?"

“As I mentioned, you were in Congress trying to gin up support from the federal government. You were asking Congress to appropriate money to this territorial legislature to purchase more of the Indian’s land.”

“Yes, they were not very accommodating.”

Cyrus Wyckoff, "You did get them to agree, though, as I remember.”

“Yes, but not to the amount we wanted.”

“We?”

Ramsey laughs.

Sibley explains, "The amount I was sent to garner was nearly $5 an acre. They only appropriated around 30 cents an acre."

Cyrus Wyckoff, “$5 an acre seems a bit rich to pay savages for land they aren’t using.”

Both governors laugh.

Sibley, “You see… “

Ramsey touches Sibley on the shoulder.

Ramsey to Cyrus Wyckoff, “Do I have any paperwork to sign?”

"Yes, sir."

Cyrus pulls out a lightly wrapped and bound ledger.

Undoing the binding, he states, "Those savages sure will be happy to receive this."

Sibley, "Yes, they are always eager to get their hands on their annuities."

Wyckoff slides the ledger and keys to Governor Ramsey. Then he takes another sip of his whiskey.

“That is some good whiskey!”

Ramsey peers over the paperwork and then hurriedly scribbles his name.

Sibley, "Yes, it should be. It costs a fortune."

“What is it?”

“Bowmore, It’s from Scotland.”

Cyrus Wyckoff nods, “Very nice.”

Sibley snobbishly, “It’s a single malt.”

Wyckoff admits, “I’m not a connoisseur.”

Ramsey proudly exclaims, “We are.”

Sibley informs Wyckoff, "It's a mature whiskey, seasoned in specially selected oak barrels.”

“Is that what makes it so special?”

Ramsey arrogantly states, "Yes, it gives it the richness and complexity.”

Sibley haughtily, “It also gives it that full-bodied palate.”

“Palate?”

"Flavors. Flavors from the oak, ginger, and raisins.”

Ramsey proudly holds up his glass, "Just look at the beautiful light mahogany color.”

Wyckoff finishes his glass.

Ramsey smugly, “It’s over sixty years old… Would you like another?”

"No, thank you. We have a long way to go. We need to head back. I want to stay somewhere more civilized. I have to make it back to Washington for an important appointment."

Sibley sarcastically replies, "That's too bad. I hoped to catch up on some news from back in Washington."

“Maybe another time.”

"Maybe next year?"

Cyrus Wyckoff stands, "Maybe. If I’m so lucky to be chosen to make the trip."

He picks up the ledger and turns to leave. Cyrus pauses and turns at the extra tall double doors.

He faces the two men seated in the parlor, "If you are ever back in Washington, look me up."

Sibley, “I will.”

“Safe journey!” Ramsey adds, “Thank you.”

Cyrus Wyckoff raises one hand to wave, turns, exits the parlor, and walks past the heavy chests sitting on the floor in the kitchen.

Ramsey states firmly, "I think I'll have another."

Sibley, "That sounds like a good idea."

After a quick pour, the two men clink their glasses and toast, "To the annuities."

Chapter 10

Near the Wiseman Cabin

Early Summer 1862

HANNAH HAS FINISHED her daily chores and rides Wildfire to the river.

Chaska has set up camp. A circle of river rocks surrounds a fire pit, with burnt and cold coals from last night's fire in the center. He hears Wildfire trapsing through the brush and goes to the edge of the clearing to greet Hannah.

The two lovers embrace and kiss.

Chaska, "Here, lay down here. I have set out our quilt under our tree."

They lay down. Hannah gets comfortable and then to Chaska, "You told me you would tell me the story about the White Buffalo Calf Woman."

"It is a legend, and I said someday!"

"Well, it is someday!" Hannah laughs.

"Ok… Ok, I did tell you this is a long story. So, are you comfortable?"

"Yes, I'm good."

"Like I said, this legend has been passed down to all Lakota people. It explains how we received the Seven Sacred Rites."

"Seven Sacred Rites, ok."

"Yes."

"Oh, I am only trying to make sure I remember." She sheepishly confides.

"I understand… See, a long time ago, this Sacred Woman, who we call The White Buffalo Calf Woman, explained the Seven Sacred Rights to our people. These rituals help us practice our spiritual beliefs and teach us how to stay in harmony with all things.

The first ritual is the rite of "Keeping of the Soul." She explained that it should be a "sacred" day. An example would be when one of our loved ones dies.

Hannah's eyes widened, confirming she understood that would be a sacred day.

"We keep this person's soul through this ritual. By doing so we would gain much understanding. We will increase our thoughtfulness and love for our fellow villagers. So long as the person's soul is kept with our people, through this ritual, we are able to send our 'voice' to Wakan Tanka."

"Wow, how does the ritual work? How do you keep the soul?"

"I will explain the best I can… You are getting ahead of the story… Let me start from the beginning. Many years ago, before our people tamed horses. We could only hunt the buffalo and other game on foot. We used stealth and put camouflage foliage on ourselves to get close to them. This made feeding our people difficult. Our people were hungry and dying. The legend tells us one summer, as is still the tradition, there was a gathering of the 'Seven Sacred Council Fires'… Do you remember the sacred numbers?"

"Yes, seven and four."

"Good, the sacred numbers come from this legend… Well, these seven councils came together. Because our people were hungry, the council tried to decide what to do. Two young braves from the band of Lakota, whose name means 'Without bows', were sent on another hunt. With the blessing of the council, they got an early start. They left camp with high hopes they would finally be able to help feed their village.

As the morning turned to mid-day, it became much warmer. The two hunters were growing discouraged, having spotted no actual game besides the elusive, tiny prairie dogs. Not giving up, the young hunters looked around for the tallest hill. Deciding on one, they made their way to it. They hiked up the long slope, hoping to see where the buffalo herds were. Once they reached the top, they scanned the horizon, again disappointed. They had to shield their eyes from what they thought was the sun's brightness. The intense heat created the familiar haze coming off Mother Earth."

"One of the six grandfathers!" Hannah proudly mentions.

"Yes, good, you remembered… Suddenly, there was movement. But again, the two hunters were disappointed. What they saw was a lone creature walking toward them. At first, they could not tell what it was. Soon, they realized it was walking on just two legs. As the creature got closer, they saw it was a woman wearing a white buffalo skin robe that glowed as bright as the sun."

"Wow, what was she doing out there all alone?"

"Wait, I will explain… The two terrified braves froze in their tracks. Until one was overcome with lust for this woman."

Hannah snickers.

Chaska smiles at her and continues, "He said to his friend, 'What a beautiful woman… How is it she is all alone out here?' "

"I was wondering the same thing!"

Chaska looks dismissively at her.

"Ok, I'll stop."

"It is alright. I don't want you to spoil the story!"

Chaska laughs and puts his arm around Hannah, who is now lying on her back, her head on his lap, looking up admiringly at the storyteller.

"So where was I? Oh yeah, the first brave says, 'I will make her mine!' and approaches the radiant being.

But his companion yells to him, 'Don't… you are a fool. Can't you see this woman is sacred? She is not of this world.' But the foolish one did not listen. He may not have even heard his friend. He was too blinded by his lust."

Chaska hears another little giggle.

It is ignored.

Chaska smiles and continues, "The woman motioned for the first brave to come closer. He did not hesitate. The unwise brave approaches the woman. Sacred Lakota designs cover the white buffalo skin robe. The designs were in all colors of the rainbow. On her back, she carried a bundle and clutched a fan of sage leaves in her hand. Her long and shiny hair, black as coal, floated in the light breeze, except for one strand she had tied with buffalo hide. The foolish brave could see her radiant eyes were full of power. He stands before her spellbound by her beauty. She did not speak. His desire overcame him, and he attempted to touch her… In that instant, a great whirling cloud covered the two of them. Moments later, when the cloud lifted, the woman stood there alone. On the ground, near her feet, were numerous snakes slithering amongst his bones."

"Oh, my! He died?"

"Yes, he died."

"Oh my God."

Let me continue."

"Sorry, it is so sad!"

"I know, but it is just part of the story… Standing a good distance away, the second brave stood shaken and completely silent. The mysterious woman spoke to him, 'Behold!' Upon hearing this in our native language, he assumed she must be from our people. So, he approached her very cautiously. When he saw his friend's remains, he pulled his bow. Trembling, the now lone hunter, tried to load an arrow to defend himself… The woman declared again in our native tongue, 'I am *Wakan*. Put your weapon away. Your arrows cannot hurt me. Do as I tell you. You are safe.' Cautiously, he obeyed. She then explained, 'I come to you with a message for your people from *Tatanka Oyate*.' Which means 'Buffalo Nation'. 'Go to your Chief. Tell him what you have seen here so he will understand. Tell him I will come to your village. Tell him to construct a tepee, one large enough for seven of your elders. Do this to prepare for my coming."

"Oh, my."

Chaska nods that he understands, and continues, "The young hunter returned as fast as he could across the prairie, back to his village. Exhausted and out of breath, he reaches camp. He insistently asks everyone he sees, 'Where is the chief?'

This commotion caused great excitement in the village. A crowd began to follow the messenger until he entered the tepee where the chief was visiting. He tells his chief, Standing Hollow Horn, what he has seen, repeats her instructions, and informs his chief that this Sacred Woman is coming. The chief was initially resistant but relented and instructed the villagers to combine several tepees to make one large gathering place. Everyone got started immediately. The villagers worked tirelessly. Once finished, the entire village waited with great anticipation for the Sacred Woman's arrival.

Scouts were posted to keep watch for a Woman wearing a White Buffalo Robe. Doubt began to set in. The scouts are about to give up. But on the 'fourth day',

"There is that four again."

"Yes, you are paying attention... The scouts saw something strange coming towards them. A glowing, swirling cloud of dust rolled across the prairie unlike anything they had ever seen. Oddly, they did not run for cover. The villagers were not afraid of the strange swirling storm. They understood deep inside it posed no danger to their village. When the cloud reached the village's edge, it disappeared, and all was calm. Immediately, there was a commotion in the newly constructed Great Lodge. The rest of the villagers could see the tepee now glowed from the inside in the middle of the day. The Sacred Woman had suddenly appeared before the few elders assembled inside. The whole village began to gather outside the Great Lodge, and the elders started taking their places inside. The petrified elders who witnessed the arrival sat there in awe. All they could do was watch the Sacred Woman begin walking slowly in a circle inside the immense lodge. She walks in the same direction as the sun moves across the sky, four times."

"There it is..."

"Yes... Then, she stops directly in front of the village chief.

Standing Hollow Horn is as astonished as everyone else. He gathers his thoughts and respectfully tells her, 'Sister, we are glad you are here. We are glad you have come here to instruct us.'

She nods her head in acknowledgment of their appreciation.

She then instructs those gathered on what she wants the villagers to do, 'You will build a Sacred Alter in the center of this now Sacred Lodge… You will make this altar of red earth… On it, you will place a great buffalo skull… Beside the skull, you will place a four-legged rack.'

"A rack? What was that for?"

"The rack is like what we use to stack wood next to our outdoor fire pits. You'll understand in a moment… She continued to instruct my people in all the details as to how to do all these things. The villagers hurriedly complied with her directives. Once the elders complete the altar, the Sacred Woman traces a design with her finger on the red earthen altar.

The Sacred Woman removes the Sacred Bundle strapped to her back and reverently places it on the newly assembled four-legged rack.

Hannah responds, "Oh, now I see!"

Chaska smiles and nods as he continues, "Afterwards, the Sacred Woman began to circle the lodge four more times, again as the Sun circles the earth. Stopping in front of Chief Standing Hollow Hor. She removed the Sacred Bundle from the rack on the red altar and presented it with both hands to the Chief. As is tradition, the Chief was sitting on the Western side of the lodge.

Accepting it and wanting to offer a gift in return, the chief spoke, 'Sister, we are glad you come to us. But we have had no meat for some time. All we have to offer you is water.'

Chief Standing Hollow Horn summoned a young woman to bring a water bladder to him. He dipped sweet grass into a cup of water and gave it to her. We practice this ritual to this very day. Our people dip sweet grass, sometimes an eagle feather, in water and sprinkle it on us to purify our people.

Hannah asks, "Ahh, this is the purification ritual?"

"Yes!"

"That sounds a lot like our baptism and holy water."

Chaska replies, "I know there are a lot of similarities."

"Is there more?"

"Yes, a lot more… Turning to those gathered, the Woman explained the importance of the Sacred Bundle, 'Always care for it with the greatest respect as it is very sacred. Let no one who is impure touch the Sacred Bundle. Because it contains the Sacred Pipe.'

She slowly unrolled the white buffalo skin bundle and removed a long, elegantly carved pipe, then a large round stone, placing them respectfully on the altar beside her. This stone had seven circles perfectly carved on it. She explained to my people that the seven circles represented the seven rites. Our people would learn how to use the sacred pipe through these rituals.

She lifted the pipe above her head so the elders could all see it. She took the long stem with her right hand and placed her left hand beneath the bowl. We have held the pipe in this way ever since.

After presenting the pipe to those assembled, she filled the bowl with a red willow-bark tobacco. She stood up and began walking around the lodge, again circling the Great Lodge four times, always in the direction the Sun passes over us in the sky. We have come to understand this symbolizes the circle without end, our sacred hoop, the road of life.

The Sacred Woman then placed a dried buffalo chip on the fire. Once it took to flame, she lit the pipe with a twig. This transfer of fire from the fire pit to the pipe symbolizes the fire without end. Through this ritual, the flame is passed on from generation to generation.

She explained that the smoke rising from the bowl of the Sacred Pipe was the breath of our Grandfather Sky. Instructing us with these words, 'You will forever gather together, during winters and summers to come, to send your voices, your essence to Wakan Tanka.'

She explained to my people the right way to pray, what words to use, and what gestures to make. She taught them songs to sing when filling the pipe, how to lift the pipe in a specific way to honor Grandfather Sky, and how to hold the Sacred pipe down near Mother Earth and then to the four directions.

She taught my people, 'As you walk the earth, with this pipe, you are walking on Mother Earth. She is sacred, so every step that you take should be taken with respect for her.' She emphasized, 'As you smoke from this pipe, you should be mindful as you sit or stand. It is still upon Mother Earth.' This is why the bowl of the Sacred Pipe is made of red stone. It is of the earth.

She explained that when making a Sacred Pipe, 'I instruct you to carve into the pipe bowl the face of a buffalo calf. This will represent all of the four-legged creatures who live upon Mother Earth. The four legs of the buffalo represent the universe, made up of the four directions and the Four Ages of creation.' "

Hannah lifts her hand with four fingers up.

Chaska nods and continues, "She told my people to remember this when you draw the smoke through the pipe stem made from wood, which symbolizes all growing things. This is why the pipe stem is made of wood.

You will attach eagle feathers and hang them from the stem, representing all winged creatures. Pay attention to the smoke from the bowl as it drifts to the sky. This sacred ritual symbolizes a living bridge between the Sacred Beneath and the Sacred Above. When done with respect and reverence, Wakan Tanka will smile upon us. Because then we will be one with the earth, the sky, and all living things. The two-legged and four-legged creatures. The winged ones, as well as the trees and the grasses. Together with all people and all things, we are all related. We are one family. This pipe holds us all together. The buffalo was put on Mother Earth by Wakan Tanka at the beginning of the Four Ages when water covered the surface."

"That is beautiful!"

Chaska nods, then continues, "She explained symbolically the Four Ages of creation in this way, 'Every year the buffalo sheds their hair and in each one of the Four Ages he loses a leg. The Sacred Hoop of life will come to an end when all the layers of hair and all four legs of the great buffalo are gone. Then the water will come back to cover Mother Earth. All things of the universe are the children of Mother Earth. We are all joined as one family through Wakan Tanka, and we will be reminded of this when we smoke from the pipe. Treat this Sacred Pipe with respect, and our people will increase and prosper.'

The Sacred Woman stood but abruptly turned, speaking directly to Chief Standing Hollow Horn. 'This Sacred Pipe will carry your people to the end of time. Remember, there are Four Ages. I am leaving you only in the physical sense, but I will watch over you and my people in every age of creation, and at the end, I will return.'

Again, the Sacred Woman slowly walked around the Sacred Lodge four times in the direction the sun circles the sky. The elders sat silently, and the people outside did as well, even the hungry young children. Everyone was filled with awe. Looking around at those gathered, satisfied that her message had been delivered, she stepped out of the Sacred Lodge.

The people parted as she walked through those gathered. They followed her to watch as she walked away. After she had gone only a short distance, she turned to face the people and then sat down on the prairie. The people gathered together, staring in amazement from a distance. All were stunned when, right before their eyes, she turned into a young reddish-brown buffalo calf… Then, this calf rolled over, becoming a yellow buffalo calf… Rolling again into a black buffalo calf. Then, this spirit animal began walking further into the prairie and laid down and rolled over one more time. Only this time, she transformed into a White Buffalo Calf… Now complete, the White Buffalo Calf turns and continues to walk away. She kept going, only stopping to bow to the four directions of the earth. My people watched until all they could see was a bright speck of light on the distant horizon of the prairie. Finally, she disappeared."

Hannah reacts, "Oh! Wow…"

Chaska silently held up his hand as if to say, not yet.

"Immediately, when she vanishes from sight, the villagers hear a rumbling in the distance. They saw the dust from a great herd of buffalo on the horizon. Our braves gathered their bows and sheaths of arrows and went out to meet the approaching herd. The buffalo did not run away or try to avoid our hunters. Instead, they allowed themselves to be harvested… From that day forward, the buffalo has furnished our people with everything they need. Meat for our food, hides for our clothing and tepees, and bones for our many tools."

Chaska relaxed at that moment to confirm he was finished.

"Wow, that is quite the legend!"

"I told you it was a long story."

"It is beautiful, so profound!"

"Thank you, it has its lessons… It is a story nonetheless, no different than your Christian story!"

Chapter 11

St Paul, Minnesota

Governor's Mansion

(continued from chapter 9)

On the same day in May 1862, A few hours later, in the parlor.

AFTER DISMISSING THE servants, the two intoxicated governors sit silently in the parlor.

Sibley restarts the conversation, "How do you like being back in the governorship?"

"It's just like old times."

They both chuckle as Ramsey pours another shot.

"Anything happening that you are worried about?"

Ramsey replies, "These annuity payments."

"Why, the chests are right there. What is there to worry about?"

"Remember Chief Buffalo?"

Sibley sips his shot and then responds, "Kechewaishke? The prominent chief of the Ojibway around Lake Superior?"

"Yes, that is the one."

"Isn't he dead?"

Ramsey, "Yes, around six or seven years ago."

"Then what is your concern."

"Remember when Wisconsin became a state back in 1848?"

Sibley spins his empty glass between his fingers on the table, "Yes, that was only fourteen years ago."

"Well, it is time to do the same thing."

"I don't follow you."

Ramsey lifts the bottle to offer another pour, "Remember when President Andrew Jackson authorized the removal of all Indian tribes east of the Mississippi?"

Nods his head at the offer, and he replies, "Yes, that caused a big stir."

"Well, I believe we can accomplish the same thing but just in a different way."

Sibley scoots forward, his arms on the table, "I'm all ears."

"Well, Chief Buffalo was recognized as the leader of most Ojibway bands. But now we are facing these Sioux tribes. They don't have a strong leader we can use."

"What about Little Crow?"

Ramsey squirms in his seat, "Yes, but he has lost his clout with his people. And he has signed a few treaties that his people are not happy with."

Sibley, "But didn't Chief Buffalo also sign multiple treaties?"

"Yes, but his people were in favor of those treaties. That treaty in 1837 assured his people they could hunt and fish on those lands forever."

"But didn't they still move the other tribes out of Wisconsin? The Anishinaabe, the Odawa and Potawatomi."

Ramsey, "Yes, they did, and the Indian agents still get their annual annuity payments and supplies to La Pointe every year."

"Those were some very profitable years."

"We can do it all over again here."

Sibley, "What are you getting at?"

"Remember when Wisconsin achieved statehood in '48, which put Chief Buffalo in the limelight?"

"Yes."

Ramsey, "Just like then, business owners and farmers here are interested in laying claim to land and natural resources of Minnesota."

"Okay, what does that have to do with anything?"

"Just like back then, the La Pointe band of Lake Superior Ojibway controlled the land."

Sibley, "But that was in Wisconsin, but now it is here in Minnesota."

"Yes, But the Sioux tribes control the land here."

"Yes, of course."

Ramsey, “Remember President Zachary Taylor signed an executive order in ‘50 to remove the Ojibway from Wisconsin and Michigan.”

“Yes.”

"Okay, it revoked their rights to hunt, fish, and gather on the land they had secured in those treaties in 1837.”

Sibley, “But that caused a big uproar in the communities, not just the Ojibway but the white settlers and businessmen too.”

“I remember some of the articles praising the move. One journalist called it a new and ingeniously contrived way of effecting the removal of the natives."

Ramsey sips his whiskey, pauses to contemplate his plan, and continues, "Another newspaper wrote something to the effect that this unrequested order would bring disappointment and alarm to the Ojibway all over the Lake Superior area and bring them the most disastrous results.”

“Well, it brought about more reservations, and we have acquired more land. It hasn’t been too disastrous for us.”

“No, it hasn’t.”

Sibley, “Didn’t you have something to do with the Indian agent John Waltrous and the Bureau of Indian Affairs back then.”

Ramsey, "Yes, we worked together."

“You were the territorial governor here back then.”

“Yes, that is right.”

Sibley contemplates and then asks, "Didn't you secure the location here in Minnesota for the Lake Superior Ojibway?”

"Yes, and it was a good financial and political decision."

“How so?”

Ramsey, “By bringing them to our Territory, all of the annuity payments from Washington will come here also.”

“And get spent here.”

"Yes, we had to keep our plan to ourselves. Waltrous, me, and two other men searched for an appropriate site for the Ojibway Indian agency."

Sibley, "That was up there by Sandy Lake. A remote area, not much up there."

"Nope, it was desolate as can be, and precisely why we chose it."

"That is about seventy miles west of Duluth."

Ramsey confidently states, "Yes, that is right. Once we found a spot for the Ojibway bands, we notified them that they must all move to Sandy Lake by October 25, 1850."

"When did you find the spot?"

"Early summer."

Sibley naively mentions, "So they had plenty of time to make arrangements."

"But we had a plan. We needed the Ojibway to move there before winter."

"Good idea. Our Minnesota and Wisconsin winters can be brutal."

Ramsey scoffs at Sibley, "And we would use that to our advantage. So, we told them they wouldn't receive their annuity payments, blankets, or food and supplies if they didn't move by then. Every brave, squaw, and papoose must make the journey."

"So, you were looking out for them?"

Ramsey laughs aloud, then remarks, "You don't get it. It was all part of our plan."

Sibley gullibly asks, "Who's plan?"

"Orlando Brown's and the rest of us."

"The Indian Affairs commissioner? The rest of us?"

Ramsey, "I'm not sure I should continue. I don't know if you are on the same page. I don't know if I can trust you."

"No. Please go on. You can trust me. Please continue."

"Well, a few weeks later, things started to fall apart. Orlando resigns, and President Taylor dies a week after that, only being in office for a little over three months."

Sibley, “That was tragic.”

"That isn't all. The vice president assumes the presidency and screws up our plans even more."

“How is that?”

Ramsey, “He appoints the Secretary of the Interior Thomas Ewing to a vacant Senate seat.”

“Why does that matter?”

“He was one of us.”

Sibley, “He was?”

“I'm worried about you… So, when it is getting close to October 25th, we have thousands of Ojibway on their way to Sandy Lake. They are expecting agent John Watrous to meet them.”

"Of course, he will be there with food, supplies, and cash payments for them."

Ramsey, “I'm taking a huge risk telling you about all of this.”

“No, you are fine. You can trust me. Promise.”

"Well, the way we saw it, they didn't deserve anything from the Government. So, our plan was to provide only the most essential food rations. But not much of it."

“Oh, you wanted to starve them.”

Ramsey, "They are savages. They don't deserve shit."

“I see.”

"To top it off, what the agents supplied was contaminated."

Sibley adds, "Oh, that was a nice touch."

"Okay, good, you finally understand. So, the Ojibway came, and they waited. And they wait. A couple weeks later, over four thousand Ojibway are camped at Sandy Lake."

“Four thousand?”

Ramsey affirms, "All of them think they will receive supplies and payments when they arrive in late October."

“But that wasn’t your plan.”

"No, it wasn't... We also know the Ojibway would be upset with this location and would all want to return to Wisconsin, their ancestral hunting grounds before winter set in."

Sibley, “You stranded them there. Quite the plan.”

"Yes, like I said, they don't deserve anything from us."

“I am glad we are on the same page.”

Ramsey, “The four thousand Ojibway wait for Watrous to bring the life-saving supplies. While they wait, they sleep on contaminated blankets, and the meager food runs out or spoils."

“Your plan is working.”

“It can work again, but bear with me... Watrous does show up at Sandy Lake, but a month late.”

Sibley, “But your plan was working. Why have him show up?”

“Because it would have been obvious, we needed to show we were trying.”

“I see.”

Ramsey, “The scene John described to me was horrific. Death and disease everywhere.”

“Brutal but necessary.”

"Yes, then John tells me he didn't bring anything. John shows up empty-handed."

Sibley, “Remind me not to get on the wrong side of you guys.”

"He said he explained to Chief Buffalo that without congressional authorization, he couldn't pay annuities."

“That was good thinking.”

Ramsey, “So, he contacts the local traders to give the Ojibway modest provisions on credit.”

“And they can charge them an arm and a leg.”

“Yes, but that isn't all of it. A few weeks go by, and he authorizes the distribution of rations in early December, just as winter sets in."

Sibley shakes his head and smiles.

"John tells me he went back to Sandy Lake a week later. In his report, he records a hundred and fifty Ojibway have died from measles, dysentery, starvation, and exposure."

“A good start.”

They both laugh.

Ramsey moves forward in his chair, "John figures up to six of them were dying a day."

"So, your plan was for Watrous to show up late, bring contaminated blankets and spoiled food?"

“Yes, it might seem cruel. But they are just savages. They don’t deserve anything from us.”

Sibley, “That will mean more land for our people, for us.”

"Yes, you do get it. Yes, we planned to delay the annuity payment long enough so the Ojibway would have to travel back home without their canoes. The rivers would be frozen over. They would have to travel on foot or horseback with meager provisions in the dead of winter in Minnesota."

“So many would perish.”

Ramsey, "Yes, by Christmas of that year, reports came out that 167 more Ojibway had died from starvation and disease. With the rivers frozen, those who survived made their way home in the dead of winter. The old cuss Chief Buffalo made it.”

"Damn, he was old then already."

"He was 91 years old then."

Sibley, “And he made that journey! Tough old bird.”

"He made it, but not all of them. The march home on foot with inadequate clothing, shelter, or food took another 230 of them."

“As you say, they don’t deserve anything from us.”

Ramsey, “You got that right. In the end, over 400 Ojibway are dead.”

Like I said before, it is a good start. Genius.”

“I can’t take all the credit.”

“Sounds like you had some unexpected help.”

“What do you mean?”

Sibley explains, "The death of President Taylor had to throw Congress into disarray. That meant they couldn't or wouldn't authorize payment for some time."

“I guess you are right. God works in mysterious ways. We had several months to plan all of this.”

“Did you ever have second thoughts?”

Ramsey, “Not in the least, I think we can do it again.”

"Really? You don't think it would be too risky to try something like that again. So soon."

“No, I don’t think it is too risky. Not at all. There is no oversight, no one to watch over us. We can do it again and even bigger. We aren't getting any younger."

Sibley agrees but adds, "But now we have to deal with reservations and all that comes with that.”

Ramsey, “I had a plan. Hear me out. I covered my ass.”

“How did you do that?”

“I issued a press release explaining it. It read something to the effect, "Far from famine or starvation occurring because of negligence on the part of Government officers, the Ojibway received all that was due them under the treaty obligations. Except for their money, and to all who are familiar with the thriftless habits of these Indians and how they incur debts whenever they get their hands on government money, almost all of the annuities were due to their traders."

Sibley points out, “Ahhh, but I remember Kechewaishke survives the trip back to his home in La Pointe.”

“Yes, he did, and he starts his own campaign asking settlers to support the Ojibway’s claim and desire to stay on their ancestral homeland.”

“The Wisconsinites knew what we know. That if they kept the Ojibway there, they would have the annuity payments spent there too.”

Ramsey asserts, “I guess they weren’t stupid after all.”

“I guess not.”

“No, the people started calling for reservations for the Ojibway instead of moving them out of State.”

Sibley asks, “But I don’t get why Kechewaishke agreed to it?”

"He saw permanent reservations as at least getting something. If he hadn't agreed, his people would have nothing. So, it was the only way for his people to survive."

“Kechewaishke was a smart old bird.”

Ramsey, “That he was. At ninety-two years old in April 1852, he and six other La Pointe Ojibway went to Washington, D.C.”

“Did the Secretary of the Interior ask for them to come?”

“No, they went on their own to protest how they were being treated.”

Sibley, “Understandable.”

Ramsey looks at Sibley with concern.

“You know what I mean.”

"Yes, it seems he was hoping to negotiate a permanent reservation on their homeland."

Sibley, “Ten years ago, roads were nothing but trails.”

“That’s right. The Ojibway traveled in those flimsy birchbark canoes as far as they could. Then hopped on a steamship.”

“That had to take a long time to get there.”

Ramsey, "Yes, it did, and they gathered hundreds of signatures on their petitions all along the way."

“They got people to sympathize with them?”

"Yes, but thankfully, they were stopped by Indian Agents in Sault Ste. Marie and Detroit, who try to convince them to turn back."

Sibley, “But they didn’t.”

“No, they make their way to New York City.”

“But you said they went to D.C.”

Ramsey, "Yes, I did. In New York City, they start creating as much publicity as they can, begin raising money and getting newspapers to support their cause."

"Kechewaishke was a wise man."

Ramsey tilts his head and looks at Sibley over his reading glasses in bewilderment. "They finally set out for Washington, D.C."

“He was quite determined.”

“Yes, he was, but his entourage gets a cool welcome from the Bureau of Indian Affairs.”

Sibley, “One of your men?”

“Yes, but a congressman gets wind of Kechewaishke's arrival and asks him and his followers to meet with him and President Fillmore the next day."

"On such short notice. How did Fillmore make time for that? Getting access to a president is almost impossible in a day's time."

Ramsey, “This was a New York Congressman who had already scheduled a meeting with Fillmore.”

“Oh.”

“After an hour-long presentation by an English-speaking Ojibway, Fillmore is impressed enough to overturn Taylor's removal order."

Sibley, “I guess he was impressed.”

“Not only that, he permanently puts the annuity payment back to La Pointe.”

“All that money could have been coming here.”

Ramsey, "Yes, and that is not all. Fillmore agrees to a new treaty to create permanent reservations in Wisconsin."

"Damn, that old Kechewaishke."

"He isn't done yet. Two-and-a-half years later, at ninety-five years old, he signed a treaty at La Pointe, establishing a permanent reservation."

Sibley, "So, the entire removal process you arranged was for nothing."

"Not entirely. If we do this right this time, we'll be even richer than we could have been back then."

"Didn't that kinda begin the establishment of reservations?"

Ramsey, "Yes, it did. They can be useful for us also. We can slowly dwindle the size of their 'reservations' until they have almost nothing."

"They don't have much now."

"No, they don't, but what they have is bottom ground and riverside land. Prime ground for building farms, homes, towns, and cities."

Sibley, "How do we get our hands on that ground?"

"I have a plan. I have learned how to play the game."

"What game?"

Ramsey, "Land acquisition. These tribes want a separate piece of land to call their own. But we pick it out for them. They want autonomy over their land, but we oversee them. The settlers want some assurance of safety from the savages."

Sibley, "And we sell their land to the settlers."

"Yes, only what we don't want for ourselves... Now, most of the Ojibway bands have agreed to relocate onto these reservations in Wisconsin."

"So, the annuities will go to Wisconsin traders and not here."

Ramsey, "We have the Sioux tribes and a lot more land to the west."

"Did you or anyone get in trouble with the government over the Sandy Lake incident?"

"Nope, like I said, there is nothing to worry about. No one is going to check on any of this. I was able to delay the annuities for the next two years, too. No one blinked."

Sibley, "Eventually, someone will get wise to this."

"You are a worry wart. There is too much going on back East with the war to free the slaves for them to worry about these savages. We, of course, won't do it the same way each time, but there is nothing to worry about. Trust me."

"The natives will complain like Kechewaishke did and go back East to file complaints."

Ramsey, "We can stop that sort of thing from happening too."

"How?"

"Let me worry about that. We were doing well until Franklin Pierce got elected."

Sibley, "How did the new president affect your operation?"

"He put George Manypenny in as Commissioner of Indian Affairs."

"But he has purchased almost all of the Minnesota Territory for the federal government."

Ramsey, "Yes, that was good, but he fired Watrous, and then my first governorship ended."

"Then how are we to move forward?"

"Things changed, but they didn't stop our operation."

Sibley, "So, you took a sort of vacation when you got elected as mayor of Saint Paul?"

"You can say that. It gave me time to associate myself with trustworthy individuals."

"Now that you are governor again, you are back in business?"

Ramsey, "This governorship is just a stepping stone for me. I have much higher ambitions than to be stuck out here in the middle of nowhere, overseeing a desolate State."

An awkward silence follows.

Sibley breaks the tranquil moment, "Let's open the chests."

Ramsey, "That is a great idea."

"Let's go see. It is amazing to see all those coins."

The two middle-aged men stagger into the kitchen and stand over the chests.

Sibley slurs his words, "Well, open them."

Ramsey fumbles in his coat pocket for the key to the padlocks. Pulling it out, he drops it.

Sibley pick it up and laughs, "Here, let me."

"I got this. Never you mind."

Ramsey snatches the key from Sibley's hand and inserts it in the first padlock. With a quick turn, it clicks, spinning the hoop, and the chain clatters to the floor.

"The other padlock."

Ramsey, "I know, just hold your horses."

Unable to hold back his eagerness, Sibley unravels the chains as Ramsey tries to open the second padlock. He tugs at the clasp over the chest latch.

"It won't release... I hope this key works on this, too."

Sibley, "It will."

Ramsey reinserts the key and turns it. He hears another click. He looks up at Sibley with anticipation.

"Well, open it."

The chain rattles to the tile floor. Ramsey flips the clasp and lifts the lid to expose a chest of shiny, newly minted gold coins.

Sibley, "Give me the key. I'll open the other one."

Ramsey buries his hands in the chest of coins, picking them up and dropping them back on the pile of gold. The clinking noise continues as Sibley unfastens the second chest. Soon, both men are shuffling coins.

Sibley, "We should count it."

"That would take all night."

"Yes, what else do we have to do?"

Ramsey, "You have a point."

They both laugh.

Sibley grabs the largest bowl from the cupboards and scoops a pile of yellow gold coins.

Ramsey, "We'll count it in the parlor."

The two men work diligently, removing bowl after bowl of coins to the large table in the center of the parlor. They take turns running back for more after breaks for another glass of whiskey. A large pile of gold coins sits high in the table's center.

Soon, there an organized assembly of dozens of golden towers, each twenty coins high.

Ramsey, "Will this table hold it all?

"We'll find out."

"We are going to need another table."

Sibley, "Isn't there another large table in the grand room?"

"I think you are right."

Late into the night, they drink and count coins.

Ramsey, "One for me and one for the savages."

Sibley, "What?"

"Who all knows this is here?"

"Almost no one. They keep the shipment a secret to avoid drawing the attention of thieves."

Ramsey exclaims, "Precisely."

"But the paperwork."

"What about it."

Sibley shakes his head, "You signed for it."

"Yes, I did, didn't I. The only person with a copy of that is Cyrus Wyckoff."

"I have a few friends in Washington that can visit his office and secure the signed ledger."

Ramsey, "That would help a lot."

"You've given this some thought."

"A little."

Sibley questions, “Can we get away with this?”

“I believe we can.”

“What about the Sioux? They are waiting for this to arrive.”

Ramsey, "It hasn't arrived. We are still waiting."

“If this goes south, it was your idea.”

“It will work.”

Sibley, “I don’t know.”

"Trust me.”

“I'll send a telegram to my friend in Washington in the morning."

Ramsey suggests, "In the meantime, let us finish counting."

"Yes, and then we need to find a place to store it all."

"Somewhere, the help won't find it."

Sibley gets worried, “Yes, the help.”

Ramsey, “Don’t worry about them. I’ll take care of it… Fifty, fifty?”

“Of course.”

Chapter 12

Henson Continues the Journey Home

August 4th 1863

HENSON STOPS TO REST his mount, "Which way should we go, girl?"

Wildfire bobs her head and looks for some grass to munch on.

Henson begins coughing, and he reaches into his pocket for a handkerchief. The coughing continues until he spits out a green chunk of mucus.

"If we follow the river, it will take longer." His coughing continues. "If we go across this bend, we will cut the distance, but the hills are rocky and uneven. We might not save any time going that way."

Wildfire wanders to and fro as she devours small clumps of grass while Henson contemplates which way to go.

"It is going to get warmer. Maybe we should stay close to the river?"

His mount seems to ignore the chatter.

Henson checks his canteen and begins to cough and hack again.

"It is nearly full."

Henson hacks up some phlegm and spits it on the smooth slate rock-covered ground.

"We have water, but will it be enough? The Field Staff took us across this desolate stretch, and we ran out water a couple of days before we got back to this spot."

His headache is getting worse, and he wipes his brow with his shirt sleeve and dismounts.

"By the looks of it, down by the river, the grass is growing back from being trampled by 800 horses and nearly that many cattle. Our making camp here did a number on the grazing too."

Henson stretches his legs and walks off his stiff, aching backside.

"Maybe I should flip a coin? Nah, I'll make the decision. I better practice what I preach."

He takes a drink from his canteen and wipes his mouth with his sleeve.

"I won't put you through that again, girl. So, I guess that means we should stay close to the river. We'll walk down this slope, and then we'll rest again."

His mind goes back to a lesson he taught his son Arthur. About a year earlier.

***

Wiseman Place

Summer of 1862

HENSON ASKS, "ARTHUR, have you picked out the next one?"

Arthur's father stands next to the split rail fence surrounding the hog pen. Henson slides a six-inch butcher knife blade over a sandstone block set on a flat space on the fence. At just the right angle, he systematically slides the steel blade forward, then flips to the other side of the blade, over and over again. A few minutes later, he checks the blade for sharpness by shaving a bit of hair off his forearm. He is satisfied the keen edge is sufficient.

Arthur answers, "No, I figured you wanted to pick it out."

He imitates his father's knife sharpening method as he sits on a barrel next to the hog house with his sharpening stone on another. He has also had plenty of practice bringing the cold steel to a razor-sharp edge.

Henson adds, "No, it is time for you to make the suggestion."

Not lifting their eyes, they speak while concentrating on their knives' steel blades.

"But each time I say which one, you tell me it's wrong."

"No, son, I tell you what to look for. It isn't wrong. It is learning."

Arthur laughs, "What are we looking for today?"

Henson scoffs at the laughter, "We are looking for the best of the lot, the one that is most ready to be harvested."

"Okay, does that mean the largest or what?"

"It means the best."

"Are we excluding any of them for future breeding?"

"Good point, let's go take a look."

They each slide their knives into their leather sheaths and stones in a pouch. Then, each man walks toward the hog gate. A pen of ten nearly mature hogs, each approaching 200 pounds. Some wander unsuspectingly around the pen. Some rut in the mud while other mud-covered swine lay quietly along the stacked corral rails.

Arthur points to a young boar in the corner, "What about that one?"

"What about him makes him the best?"

"He is taller than the rest, a bit skinny, but looks like good meat."

Henson, "Good, but the skinny part concerns me."

"Okay, that one is fatter but a bit shorter."

"We might want to keep him for breeding."

Arthur giggles, "See what I mean?"

"You have to look at all of it to make the right decisions. The same goes for the cattle, the horses."

Arthur, "Okay, what about that one!"

"Which one? The one in the water?"

"Yeah sure. Would you'd consider that one?"

Henson assesses from a distance, "It's covered in mud. It could be a good choice. Maybe we should see what it looks like."

"Then you select."

"Okay, Let's separate that one, wash him off, and see if it is ready."

"Let's go with the first one, then."

Henson laughs, "Oh no, no matter which one you select, we have to clean 'em off first."

"But it is covered in mud!"

"Come on son. Let's go get our dinner for the next few weeks."

When Henson opens the gate, the hogs begin to grunt and squeal. Arthur follows and closes the gate behind them. He tries to step carefully on the rare dry patches of ground between fecal piles, stinking mud, and muck.

Andrew and William have come back from the grove. They climb the hog corral fence, and each lad selects a post to saddle up next to watch.

Up at the house playing with Boots, Loren sees his two brothers scale the fence, and he makes a beeline to their side.

Pheobe and Hannah notice the activity and wonder what is going on. They finish hanging their baskets of clothing on the line and then head towards the pigpen, too.

Henson moves to a dry mound. The two men separate the runts from the more mature hogs. With a branch, Arthur shoos the runts through the doorway to the inside of the hog barn. Henson closes the door each time one runs in. They circle the pen again, trying to stay out of the mud.

Henson, "You can wash your boots!"

"But if I can avoid it, I will."

Henson laughs again.

Arthur, "It ain't funny!" Then he laughs himself.

The target hog is aware he is in trouble. He turns his head back and forth, watching both men coming closer from both sides. It doesn't know which way to go. So, he stays in his pigsty pit of mud.

"He isn't budging Pa."

"Smart pig!"

Arthur laughs, "Does that make him the best then?"

"Maybe!"

Pheobe, "Boys, don't you get that all over you."

Hannah looks at her mother questioningly.

"Or Hannah will have to wash your clothes."

Hannah's face turns to shock, then repeats, "You two better not get that all over you!"

Andrew, William, and Loren all laugh, as well as Pheobe.

Hannah, "Mom, I'm serious. That would be terrible."

After yelling sooie by both Henson and Arthur for quite sometime, Henson suggests, "You might need something to get him to budge. That stick isn't long enough."

Arthur suggests, "A pitchfork would work!"

Pheobe, "Arthur!"

"I'll use the handle side on him, ma."

"Oh, okay."

The standoff continues while Andrew fetches a pitchfork from inside the hog house.

When he returns with the fork, "Here you go, Arthur!"

"Thanks, Andrew."

Arthur holds the prongs of the fork to prods the hog on the rump with the wooden handle. It doesn't move an inch.

Henson suggests, "Try poking him up around the back of his ears, they are sensitive there."

"Okay, but I don't know if I can reach them."

Henson, "Step in the mud just a little."

Pheobe, "Arthur, be careful."

Arthur, "Mom!"

Hannah, "Don't you… "

"Okay, okay, enough already." Arthur pokes the hog behind the ears but still doesn't budge. Henson moves closer along the split rail fence.

Pheobe, "Henson Wiseman!"

"Pheeb, I'll be alright."

The hog turns his attention to Henson. Arthur pokes his ear again. The hog stands abruptly, then darts out of the muck. Arthur is startled and loses his balance. His foot slips. His arms begin to whirl around and around. In one huge splat, he lands back first in the ankle-deep muck of the hog pen.

Andrew and William both laugh.

Pheobe, Henson, and Loren are initially scared for Arthur, then join the two boys.

Hannah sighs in frustration.

Arthur slowly rolls over, placing his hands and knees in the mud, trying to push himself up. He continues to slip and slide, finding it difficult to get footing.

Henson, "Use the pitchfork!"

In as much sarcasm as he could muster, "Why don't you come and help me?"

"Not on your life, son!"

"I'll get the prize hog penned up for you. You might want to take a dip in the horse tank!"

Loren asks his mother, "What will the horses drink?"

Pheobe pats him on the head, “Andrew and William will drain it after he bathes and then refill it!”

In tandem, "What did we do?"

Arthur gets upright and slings the loose, dripping, stinking feces and urine-filled mud from his arms.

Henson coaxes the hog into the holding stall and sighs, "Good job, son!"

Arthur, “Right!”

Henson can’t help but laugh to himself.

Pheobe feels so sorry for her son but still finds it humorous.

Andrew and William wander off, trying to avoid their upcoming detail.

Loren pulls on his mother’s sleeve and points at the two.

Pheobe, "Hey, you two, get back here."

The two boys sigh and turn around slowly.

"Make sure the trough is full, and one of you go to get some lye soap from the cabin."

They both volunteer.

"William, you go."

Andrew, "Ah shucks!"

William turns and says, "Na na na nana!"

Pheobe and Hannah head back to the cabins and urge Loren to come along with them.

Loren, "I wanna watch."

Pheobe takes him by his hand, "No, you don't!"

"Sure, I do."

Hannah agrees, "Trust me. You don't want to watch."

"Why? Because I ain't old enough!"

Hannah emphasizes in a motherly tone, "No. You don't want to watch. And yes."

Pheobe to Hannah, "You gather a clean set of clothes for Arthur and take them down to him for me. I'll start supper."

"Sure thing." Hannah and Pheobe can't hold back their laughter as they walk back to the cabins.

Loren wanders off with Boots to play. But he wants to watch even more now. It is getting dark, and the night air is cooling off. When he sees his chance, he wanders slowly away from the cabins. Then sneaks back down toward the smokehouse. He finds a wooden crate to stand on. Wipes a space to see through the dust-covered window. Inside, two kerosene lanterns light up the room. Loren sees Henson in a garment he has never seen before. A tanned pigskin leather frock covers him from his neck down to his ankles.

Arthur arrives, wet hair and new set of clothes. He grabs another frock and puts it on.

Andrew and William sit on a bench off to the side. Their backs turned to the window.

The sow lies on four-wheel cart.

Henson pulls on a rope attached to one of the hog's hind legs. The other end of the rope runs over a pulley attached to two doubled up ceiling joists. Together, Henson and Arthur slowly raise the unconscious hog off the cart. One leg continues to twitch.

Arthur, "He is going to wake up soon."

Henson asks, "I know. You got her son?"

Arthur wraps the rope around a cast iron tie-off bracket attached to a wall stud, "Yes, I got her."

Henson, "Andrew you get the cart out of here when she's clear."

"Okay pa."

Andrew pulls the cart into the next room.

Henson places a wooden bucket under the hog's snout. With a quick slice, he slits the hog's throat, and a dark red substance drains into the bucket. The hog begins to twitch rapidly.

Loren, "Oh my!" He covers his mouth.

Henson washes the hog with soap and water from a wooden bucket.

Finished cleaning the sow, the two adult Wiseman men steel their knives in preparation.

After a few minutes, Henson announces, "It looks like it's done."

"You want me to go first?"

Henson, "Sure, if you are ready."

Arthur pinches the hog's jowl, inserts his newly sharpened blade, and gets a good grip. He begins to slice downwards, opening the jowl with each slice and removing the hide from the hog's head with expert precision.

"Good job, son."

"Thanks, do you want to…?"

Henson proudly states, "No, you are doing fine."

Arthur cleans his knife with a cloth hanging from his frock's belt. He takes the long steel hanging on a light chain on his other side and sharpens his knife.

One last glance over at his father, he gets the nod to continue. The fifteen-year-old begins a cut upward from the throat of the still-warm carcass up through the center of the hog's chest. He resets his grip every foot or so, only pausing for a moment to steel his knife. He continues up the center of the hog's belly.

Henson, "Be careful!"

"I am."

Arthur makes continuous incisions until he finishes between the hind legs, which are now still.

Henson questions his son, "What comes next?"

"I know."

Arthur clears the hide from the midsection, exposing the hog's belly fat.

Henson jokes, "Bacon!"

Andrew and William both laugh.

William licks his lips, "Yum."

Arthur laughs with his brothers and makes a few more cuts toward both back legs. Then, he returns to the midsection again, carefully splitting the two sides to reveal the entrails. Steam floats off the stomach and intestines.

Andrew and William, "Wow."

Arthur carefully works his way around the guts from top to bottom, now upside down, rear end to front of the chest. The innards begin to sag.

Andrew offers, "I'll get another bucket."

Henson, "A barrel would be better."

"Ok"

"Thanks."

Arthur announces his intentions, “I’ll work on the hide while he fetches that barrel.”

Henson, “Good idea.”

A moment later, Andrew arrives, "Here you go, Pa.”

Taking it from Andrew, "Here you go, Arthur." Henson places the barrel precisely.

Arthur lets the hide dangle, inserts his left hand around the slimy intestines and internal organs, coaxing the bowels out with his left hand, and, with his sharp blade, severs the lining that holds them in place.

***

LOREN’S FACE GOES pale. His stomach starts to churn. He turns away from the window, careful not to make a sound.

***

ARTHUR ANNOUNCES, “It looks clean, no abscesses!”

Henson approvingly states, “Good. Looks like a good one! Here, let me help you."

They coax the entrails into the barrel with a plop.

"Good job, son. We'll have the little boys clean those up later."

Andrew and William look at each other with shock.

Arthur laughs, then to his father, “You want me to finish skinning it?”

***

LOREN STEPS DOWN from the crate, white as a bleached bed sheet in the summer sun. Halfway to the cabins, he releases his afternoon meal on the ground.

***

HENSON INQUIRES, “If you think you are ready?”

“Are we saving the hide?”

“Sure, we can make a few useful things out of it. So sure.”

Arthur asks, "Where is the knife I should use for that?"

Henson turns and pulls a knife from its storage location, "Here, this one works much better.”

Arthur grips the hide at the midsection.

"First, cut the hide from the legs.”

“Right, and work my way down.”

Henson nods his approval. After severing the hide from the hind legs, Arthur slowly and precisely separates the rest of the hide from the carcass. When enough hide has fallen away, Henson assists by holding the excess for Arthur.

Henson, “You two go get a cart for this hide!”

Andrew responds, "Okay, Pa!"

He darts out of the smokehouse door toward the grain bin area.

Henson and Arthur work as a team to remove the hide, all in one piece.

William remains sitting, mesmerized by the process.

Henson turns to William and instructs him, "Take the blood bucket out to the pen."

"Okay, Pa.”

Andrew arrives as William leaves.

Andrew parks the cart in front of the upside-down, nearly hideless and gutted hog.

Arthur lowers the hide into the cart.

Henson takes his knife and begins separating the head from the neck.

Henson to Andrew, “Put that with the innards.”

Arthur looks menacingly at the hog's head that gave him a mud bath just an hour or so earlier, "Gotcha."

Henson laughs and ties the hind legs together, good and tight.

Arthur repositions a cast iron hook over the fire pit.

Together, the two men hoist the much lighter carcass onto the hook.

William returns.

Henson instructs, "Andrew, go get the other cart with the hickory wood in it!"

"Where is it?"

Arthur, "Next to the woodshed, it should be full."

Henson to William, "You go help him then."

William, "Okay."

Henson to Arthur, "You did a fine job, son. No holes in the hide. Your first one without a hole."

Arthur nods with pride, "It is tougher than it looks."

Andrew runs over some squishy stuff in the yard. It smells funny, but he doesn't stop to check what it is. William follows and together they push the hickory cart back to the smokehouse.

William asks his father, "Pa, what are we gonna make out of the hide?"

"I don't know right off. Maybe some bags for shotgun shells? Or tote bags for camping, or anything we need to carry. Pigskin is a very versatile material once it is tanned. Ma and Hannah will know what to do with it."

Henson and Arthur stack the bundles of leaves and twigs first. Then, they position the hickory wood tepee-style over the tinder. Henson strikes a wooden match and ignites the stack of wood. The four men watch and wait as the fire grows. The light from the flames flickers on their faces.

Henson, "Wish I had my pipe."

Andrew, "I'll go get it, Pa."

He rubs his son's head, "Naw, I can wait."

Arthur mentions, "I guess I get to come out and keep the coals going."

Henson, "We'll take turns."

Arthur smiles.

The two men and two boys sit and watch the flames dance as the grease drips into the fire. Satisfied, the logs are glowing red hot, they spread the hickory out below the hog carcass.

Henson announces, "I'll check it after supper. Then you can check again before we turn in."

"Alright, we're going to have a lot of good eating off this one."

"Yes, we will. Okay, let's head up to the cabins."

Andrew and William exit first, followed by Arthur, as Henson shuts the door to the smokehouse. The four men walk side by side up the slight slope to the cabin for supper.

Henson, "Anybody hungry?"

Chapter 13

Second Battle of New Ulm

August 23rd, 1862

WAGONS LAY OVERTURNED across the wide, expansive street separating the scattered buildings. Stuffed between each wagon are empty or dirt-filled wooden barrels of all types. Smaller wooden crates and debris from burned-out buildings fill any smaller gaps. Men with muskets in hand find a suitable location to stare toward the tree line filled with Dakota warriors.

One of those men asks, "What else is there to do?"

A fellow settler answers, "We have done all we can to prepare. Now, all we can do is wait."

A third settler keeps his eyes turned toward the river and states firmly, "They will be coming soon."

The once-small village of New Ulm has become a fortress. Since the start of this uprising, families have arrived from all over the countryside. Farmers and ranchers have abandoned their homesteads for the presumed safety of the town. When they arrive, they are told to prepare for the worst. The women and older children who refuse to leave their men help with preparations. Some prepare meals, while others haul material for the numerous expanding barricades. Still others are employed, melting lead from anything available into musket balls.

Most of the farmers and ranchers have brought their hunting muskets and shotguns. These hunting weapons are now proving to be, more than ever, an even greater requirement for survival.

Flandrau to Boardman, "We need to find out how much ammunition and black powder we have available."

"What good would that do?"

"If one person has a hundred shots and another has none, then that is our weakest link in the chain of defense."

Boardman asks, "So, what do you want us to do?"

"Account for how much lead shot, black powder, and cartridges we have. Then count how many muskets we have."

"There are a lot of different muskets."

Flandrau replies, "I know… just hold on… once you know how much of each type you have, disperse the ammunition evenly."

"But some of these guys won't want to part with their ammunition."

"Bring them to me. I'll explain it to 'em… You better get started."

Half of the men continue to place burnt boards, along with anything they can find from the buildings destroyed in the first attack on the barricades.

Settler with a floppy hat, "What is that?"

One wearing a cap, "I don't know. Thunderclouds, maybe?"

"But there isn't a cloud in the sky."

"Right!"

A man wearing a straw-hat states, "I think it may be smoke.

Another asks, "Is it coming from the fort?"

A third suggests, "It must be under attack."

Numerous gray columns rise over the hilltops.

Man with straw-hat, "The fort is too far away to be seen from here."

Second man asks, "If it isn't the fort, then what is it?"

Man with a cap, "Settlements?"

"Well, we better get this built then. We may be next."

The two settlers finish inserting the charred debris and head out, looking for more.

Another distant crack of cannon fire echoes in the distance.

Another curious onlooker also notices, "Is that a cloud, or is it smoke?"

Columns of dark black and gray smoke clear the treetops, one after the other, closer and closer, leaving an eerie feeling among the defenders of New Ulm.

"That's smoke."

A defender points, “Over there.”

Another man shouts, “There are new columns over there.”

“There is another one.”

Each new column of smoke is closer than the last.

“They are coming.”

A tense Boardman, “Then the Fort must have fallen.”

Flandrau calmly says, "Not necessarily."

“We can’t take our chances. We need to see for ourselves.”

“What do you suggest?”

Boardman, “We should send men to the top of that ridge.” He points to the distant bluffs. “From there, they can see the entire valley.”

"What, and leave us short-handed?"

“Just enough men to make sure they can defend themselves. If they run across a war party, then they come back.”

Flandrau, “How many men are you thinking?

“Say, seventy-five men. That should be sufficient.”

“I don’t know.”

Boardman, "We need to determine what we will be facing."

“It is your call.”

Volunteers are requested, and the men who answer the call gather in the center of the street.

Flandrau to the leader and these volunteers, "This detail is dangerous. You will need to stay together after you cross the river. From there, you need to reach that high ridge overlooking the entire river valley."

Boardman adds, "From there, you should be able to see how many Sioux there are and where they are headed.”

Flandrau, “Precisely!”

Boardman, “If you have your weapons and ammunition, you better get a move on.”

One of the seventy-five volunteers says, "Okay, I think we are ready."

At the ferry landing, the company of men slowly and laboriously cross the river.

***

Earlier that morning.

LITTLE CROW HAS a plan to weaken the town's defenses.

Little Crow offers his plan, "If we set fire to farmhouses, barns, and anything else that will burn, they will see it from New Ulm."

Big Eagle asks, "What good will that do?"

"It will send them a signal."

Wowinape asks, "Are you telling them what we are doing?"

Little Crow responds confidently, "Yes, son. The defenders of New Ulm will see us coming."

"And they will get ready for us."

"They are already prepared."

Big Eagle, "This doesn't make sense."

"We have lost the element of surprise and our overwhelming numbers."

Wowinape inquires, "So, how will this help?"

"First, they will know we are on our way to do battle."

Cheers rise up among the warriors.

"Second, it will send fear through the farmers and ranchers who defend the small village."

Big Eagle adds, "Some may run. Some may retreat from the village."

"Yes, that is possible."

Another robust cheer rises up from the soon-to-be combatants.

Little Crow continues, "Thirdly, we want the defenders of New Ulm to believe that the Fort has fallen."

Wowinape mentions, "But it hasn't."

“But they don’t know that.”

Big Eagle inquires again, "But why let them know we are coming?"

“If I know them as well as I think I do, they will want to determine the size of our force.”

“They will send out scouting parties.”

Little Crow, "Yes, but I'm certain they will send out a larger group. Small scouting parties would be too vulnerable."

Wowinape asks, "What are you thinking?"

“The only place to see how many braves we have is to send a sizable force to the high ridge on the other side of the river.”

Big Eagle, “You might be right.”

“I’m pretty sure I am. We’ll send our own war party ahead to wait for them.”

“We’ll have the element of surprise again.”

Little Crow, “Yes, but that is not all. When they send possibly a company of men across the river…”

Wowinape adds confidently, "We'll be waiting for them."

“Yes, but they will wait and not attack.”

Big Eagle, “What? Why not?”

“When they are on the other side of the river. Our war party will stay hidden and wait. When they go up to the ridge, our braves take the ferry back across, sever the ferry's ropes from the landing, and burn it. That will cut off and strand them on the other side of the river."

"They could still cross on horseback."

Wowinape states, "That's right."

Big Eagle asks, "What will keep them on that side of the river?"

"Those braves that will burn the ferry will be on this side."

“It is a good plan.”

Little Crow explains his plan, “The rest of our braves will surround the town of New Ulm here."

He scratches a rough layout of the town in the dirt.

He continues, "The first group of warriors will line up on the lower bluff that overlooks the village. The second group will take positions that cut off access to the river road, eliminating any chance of a quick escape."

***

FLANDRAU STANDS BEHIND the barricade. He opines, "I hope those men don't panic."

Boardman dismisses the concern, "They'll be fine, sir."

"They are nearly a hundred yards away from these barricades."

"They will be in a better position to see the Sioux coming from there."

Flandrau questions, "I don't know, they are only farmers and ranchers."

"They all know how to shoot."

"But they are not trained in battle. Deer, don't shoot back."

Boardman disregards the comment, "I don't think that will matter."

"But they haven't faced anything like this."

"Well, if they shoot and run, they have a hundred yards or so to reach the second wall of our defenses."

A concerned Flandrau continues, "If they do that, they could be cut down."

"Then their arrows can reach the roofs in the center of town."

"We have enough of our women in that bucket brigade, keeping watch over all these buildings."

Boardman replies, "If they don't hold them off out there, we could be done for… The whole town would be lost."

"I'm not worried."

An emphatic Boardman responds, "We'll know soon enough when we hear those blood-curdling screams."

"That sent chills down my spine."

"Exactly. To these untrained and unseasoned farmers, standing and facing those warriors might be too much."

***

AT MID-MORNING, Little Crow and his closest warriors watch as the plan to isolate the New Ulm observation party is successful. Confident and with the rest of his forces in place, Little Crow orders his men to advance.

***

WHEN THE SCREAMING starts, just as Flandrau had feared, the first set of defenders didn’t even fire a shot before they all broke formation and ran to the shelter of barricades.

***

LITTLE CROW TO his signaler, “That was way too easy. Call them back, get them to hold up.”

Gray Bird sends the signal and responds, "That was surely a trick. An ambush?”

“Yes, very likely. So, instead, have them take control of those outer buildings."

Gray Bird, “Yes, from there, we should be able to begin setting fire to their buildings.”

The runner hesitates.

Little Crow, “Go!”

***

A GROUP OF citizens from a small hamlet of Le Seuer have taken up positions in the local flour mill at the edge of the barricades. The wind-driven mill with sails seventy feet long has become their fortress. The defenders have piled flour sacks high against the doors and lower windows and taken positions on the higher levels of the structure.

The Dakota braves begin to send their flaming arrows toward the buildings they can reach. The smoke from the musket fire and buildings set a flame, curls in the stagnant air throughout the town square.

Little Crow, "This is good. The winds are in our favor."

"What do you mean?"

"Look, the smoke from their muskets and the burning buildings create a cover. There is little to no breeze, the smoke lingers, and our braves can use it to get better access to more buildings."

Gray Bird, "I'll send word to the warriors."

"Have them use caution. Go house to house, building to building. We'll burn them out."

As the battle drew on, the defenders held their ground.

Little Crow watches and sends orders via his most trusted warriors. The outcome is becoming increasingly uncertain.

Gray Bird, "What should we do now?"

"They are weakened. It is time for an all-out assault."

"How many braves?"

Little Crow, "All those to our right, have them assemble at the river's edge."

"But that will be in clear sight of the village."

"Yes, I want them to see this coming."

***

FLANDRAU, "THEY are gathering for an all-out assault."

Boardman, "What should we do? They could overrun us."

“We have drawn back from the barricades. The men are fighting from building to building.”

“Those men not defending a building or wherever we can spare some, have them gather here.”

A volunteer messenger hastily exits.

Flandrau, “What is your plan?”

“I don’t know yet.”

***

LITTLE CROW GATHERS his most trusted warriors and explains his plan, "We are going to rush their defenses. They are weak and scared. It is time."

***

FLANDRAU, “HOW MANY men do we have?”

A questioning Boardman, “Maybe a few dozen?”

“That may be enough.”

“What is your plan?”

Flandrau, “I’m working on it.”

A farmer suggests, "Maybe we should retreat to the woods. There is good cover there. We can pick ‘em off one at a time.”

Boardman, “That won’t work. They are in those woods. Besides, we have too many women and children and too many wounded to make the almost three miles to the security of the thick forest.”

The farmer, “Right.”

Flandrau offers, "We can counterattack."

Boardman states, “What? That’s crazy! You said so yourself. These men are not trained. You saw how they fell back from the first line of defense."

Flandrau suggests, "They are seasoned now! They all know what is at stake here. It is our lives. What we need to do is show them we are not going to go without taking most of them with us."

An anonymous voice asks, "Are you saying attack them, instead of us waiting for them to attack?"

Another counters, “It is always better to defend. We have cover if they are attacking. If we attack, we'll have no cover. We’ll be out in the open.”

Flandrau counters, "But we have seen them turn and run when we send overwhelming fire on a building they have taken. They might retreat if we attack them."

Boardman ponders, “He may have a point. How many men can we spare for an assault?”

One of the farmers answers, "We have nearly forty volunteers, Sir."

Flandrau tries to inspire the defenders, "Men, this may be our last chance to drive the bastards back.”

Both sides prepared for a head-on assault. The New Ulm defenders gather behind the barricade's most mobile section.

Flandrau asks, “Are you ready?”

A nervous farmer replies, “As ready as we are going to get.”

“Open it!”

The nearly forty men rush through the opening. They begin their advance screaming and yelling, much like their adversaries had earlier that morning.

***

A SURPRISED LITTLE Crow, "They are coming to us... Let's show them how this is done."

***

THE NEW ULM chargers get a surprise, too. The Dakota don't turn and run but begin to advance toward the approaching gaggle of farmers. Each brave begins screaming at the top of their lungs, firing as they run toward the group of farmers and ranchers turned militia.

They return fire as they advance toward their adversaries.

Flandrau orders the men behind the barricades, “Lob your fire over our charging men.”

The lead shot drops like black hail on the advancing Dakota. This overwhelming barrage of fire turns the charging Dakota warriors. They scamper for cover.

Flandrau to the bugler, “Sound to halt the advance.”

“But they won't know what it is, Sir.”

“Just blow the damn horn. They'll figure it out!”

Boardman, “Why call them back?”

"Because if they continue, they will go past our cover fire. They could be picked off out there."

The bugler screeches his message.

Flandrau waves his arms to the men to return. The New Ulm charge stops, now out in the open. Many run to the original positions for cover. Others scramble for whatever they could find. Both sides continue to exchange fire.

Flandrau assesses the new situation, "The counterattack has advanced past those structures." As he points in the general direction.

“What are you thinking?”

"Well, those buildings over there can be used against those men if the Sioux are able to take control of them.”

Boardman, “They would be sitting ducks out there.”

“Precisely, we need to burn those structures and anything that could be used as shelter.”

"I'll get right on it!"

"Hold on, when that is complete, have all the men use the smoke screen to fall back again to the town's center."

"But, Sir?

"Do it. You will see that when the shelters are all gone, the only thing out in front of our barricades will be open ground."

***

LITTLE CROW, "They are burning their own buildings."

Gray Bird, "They are doing our work for us."

"No, they are preventing us from using them. When those structures are gone, we will have nowhere to find protection. We won't be able to advance our warriors."

"What shall we do?"

He assesses the time of day. After a long pause, he answers, "Nothing, it is over. It is done."

Chapter 14

Chaska's village

Yankton Dakota Reservation

Late summer 1862

THE ELDERS HAVE gathered in the Council Lodge of the Yankton Dakota Village across the river from Fort Randall. All of the local Chiefs are present.

Smutty Bear, the leader of this village, inquires, "Why are we called together?"

Black Elk, "My son wishes to nullify his marriage arrangement."

Crazy Bull asks, "For what reason does he make this request?"

Black Elk, "He says he cannot get along with her."

Most of the chiefs laugh.

Standing Elk, "That is life."

White Medicine Cow questions the father, "Is this your son?"

Black Elk, "Yes."

To Chaska, "What have you to say to the elders?"

Chaska begins to stand.

Crazy Bull, "Tell us your name for the other chiefs."

"Chaska."

Standing Elk inquires, "You have not chosen your brave name?"

Chaska answers, "No, I have not."

"How old are you?"

"I am nineteen years old."

Crazy Bull to the other chiefs from distant villages, "He has done well for himself." To Chaska, "You have many horses and are a good hunter."

"Thank you."

"Why do you wish to end this arrangement?"

Chaska humbly answers, knowing the response, “No offense to her father, but she is unbearable.”

Laughter among the elders ensues.

Smutty Bear, “Your parents have already given the price for her.”

Chaska, “I realize this.”

Not wanting to be disrespectful, Chaska doesn't explain that he supplied the price for Little Thunder by himself.

Smutty Bear, "Are you asking her parents to return the price?"

"No, I am not. I will respectfully pay them to end this arrangement."

An astonished gasp is heard from the elders.

“You will pay them and let them keep the price.”

Chaska assures the elders, “Yes.”

Chief Smutty Bear is adamant, “You realize that is a great insult to both the parents and the young woman.”

"I don't mean it to be. I respectfully wish to be free of this arrangement. That is all."

Roaring Cloud asks, “You do not believe you can reconcile with my daughter?”

“I am sorry, but I see no way that will happen.”

“We could have a talk with her.”

Chaska explains, "I have already tried everything I can. She doesn't listen. She talks endlessly."

Laughter begins and is squelched quickly by Smutty Bear.

Roaring Cloud reminds Chaska, “You were friends growing up.”

“Yes, we were, but she has changed.”

“Could it be you have changed?”

Chaska, “That is possible, but she is insistent and doesn’t listen. She does not obey me.”

A low rumble of disbelief rolls through the council lodge. This statement has the attention of the elders.

Roaring Cloud offers, “Sometimes these things take time to work themselves out.”

“I have heard this. But I don’t wish to wait to find out if it works itself out or not.”

Roaring Cloud proposes another option, “You are permitted to have more than one wife.”

"No. No, thank you. I don't want more than one wife."

“Have you taken up the ways of the white man? The practice of only having one wife?”

Chaska hesitates and then answers, "No, I have not taken up the way of the white man."

“Have you found another woman?”

Chaska hesitates again.

Roaring Cloud restates his question, “I’ll ask you again. Have you found another Dakota woman you desire more than my daughter?”

“No, I haven’t.”

Crazy Bull interjects, “No matter if he had. This is his decision.”

Roaring Cloud offers an explanation for his question, "I understand this. I only wish to understand his reasoning."

Black Elk to Chaska, “Son, is your mind made up?”

"Yes, father, it is."

Black Elk to Roaring Cloud, “What will you ask of my son to relieve him of this arrangement?”

Roaring Cloud, “My wife will be very angry… Not to mention Little Thunder.”

Chaska, "I mean no disrespect to you, your wife, nor your daughter."

"This sort of thing may mean other braves of our tribe will shun her."

Smutty Bear to Roaring Cloud, "She is a good woman. There will be others."

“I hope so.”

Black Elk to Roaring Cloud, "Do you have a price at which you desire to end this arrangement?"

"I will think about it."

Smutty Bear, "Your families have one week to decide and come to an agreement."

Chapter 15
New Ulm

August 24th, 1862

LESS THAN A couple dozen buildings remain intact, but all have battle scars from the struggle to save the besieged village of New Ulm. Nearly a thousand people remain. Low on food and provisions, they face a new dilemma.

Reinforcements arrived the day after the Dakota attackers left. Their arrival is both a blessing and a curse. They now have another 150 men and horses to feed.

Flandreau to Boardman, "Call all the officers and leading townspeople together. We need to make a decision."

Within the hour, a small group of officers and local leaders assemble outside one of the remaining buildings.

Captain Cox announces, "They are all here, sir."

Flandrau begins, "With all of these additional mouths to feed. We need to make a decision, and soon."

Boardman, “We can send out hunting parties.”

Cox argues, “For the Sioux to ambush?”

“What then?”

Flandrau adds, "With our ammunition so low, our powder almost gone. If they come back, I don't believe we could hold them off again."

Boardman, “But we have all of these troops.”

Flandrau explains, "They are volunteers, no different than you and I. They carry a limited number of provisions and ammunition."

Cox interjects, "If we stay here, we'll soon starve, or worse, die of disease or at the hands of the Sioux when they come back."

Flandrau states, “Or we gather everyone together and head east.”

“But what about the Sioux?”

"That is a grave concern, no doubt. But the Sioux villages are West of here. They didn't take our fair city, so the likelihood of their taking the fort is also questionable."

Boardman asks, "You mean you think Fort Ridgely could still be there?"

"It is possible. The fort is better equipped with better-trained men. So, it is possible."

"We should send someone to find out."

Flandreau shakes his head, "No more details like that. Not after the ferry disaster. Sorry, we can't afford to lose any more fighting men."

Captain Cox interjects, "We need to do what is best for those we have here."

***

FLANDRAU CALLS THE townspeople together to tell them their plan, "We need everyone to prepare to leave."

One well-dressed man, "For where?"

"To the nearest town downriver."

The dapper man responds, "With what? We supposed to walk?"

"Some of us. Yes!"

Captain Cox yells to the crowd, "I will have my men gather all the horses and prepare them to pull the wagons. We will assign another detail to turn the wagons upright. Then, we will see how many we can repair. Those that are salvageable, we get them ready for transporting the wounded and children."

Flandreau states firmly, "If we don't have enough wagons for all. Those men and those women capable will walk."

Cox adds, "We won't have enough room for any excess provisions. So, clothes you have on, bags and boxes of food you can carry, nothing else."

The businessman objects, "But what about our things, our possessions?"

Captain Cox answers, “They will have to wait until you can return.”

“We’ll see about that.”

Captain Cox looks threatening at the well-dressed gentleman, who obviously has never missed a meal.

Flandreau to Cox, “Leave him be.”

Flandreau to the crowd of townspeople, “We will still need your cooperation. We need men to continue to guard our village. They also need to know about this plan. The Sioux may attack at any time. Therefore, women and children must be kept off the streets while the men make preparations.”

Cox adds, "All men not working on the wagons or preparing the harnesses will be asked to stay at their posts. That will be both behind these barricades or out on picket duty. Just in case the Sioux return."

Flandreau insists, "We will work all night, if we have to, to prepare the wagons, so hopefully, we will be ready to move out at sunrise."

Cox to the defiant, heavyset man, "You may want to bring another pair of shoes."

Flandrau chuckles, then continues, "We will need all of you to pitch in and help, so let's get started."

***

IN THE MORNING, the well-to-do businessman arrives carrying much more than he was supposed to bring.

Cox to the overweight, obstinate man, "You will have to leave those things here."

Oblivious businessman, "You don't know who you are talking to, do you?"

“No, and I rather don’t care.”

“Well, I am … “

Flandrau pulls Cox away from the conversation, "I know you are a worthless piece of shit. After the fighting was over, I saw you come out of the building with the women and children. You didn't lend a hand to build the barricades. You didn't help with preparing ammunition. I know what you are."

“Well, I’ll be!”

An insistent Captain Cox reenters the fray, “You’ll be leaving your luggage and your boxes of papers. That’s what you’ll be doing.”

"Now, you just hold on a second, young man. Maybe I can make it worth your while!"

“You know what would be worth it for me?”

“Name your price.”

“I wanna see you walk from here to Mankato.”

The shocked look on his face is all anyone needs. He turns and leaves disgusted and doesn't feel a bit of shame as he huffs past the giggling crowd.

Other arrogant traders and store owners also argue adamantly for their possessions and a place to sit on the wagons rather than walk. They are granted neither. Food and water are allowed. Luggage and knickknacks are refused. Children under twelve and the severely wounded are loaded first. Then, only the most elderly women are given a place to ride.

The chaos slowly turns more harmonious after the incident with the proud heavyset trader. The able young people make way for the elderly, the middle-aged for the youngest.

The farmers and craftsmen repair the wagons that can be fitted and used for travel. Captain Cox's men have converted their horses to teams to pull the wagons. Those men, still on horseback, spread out the length of the long ragtag caravan of over sixty disheveled wagons. The soldiers who have given up their horses to pull the numerous wagons walk like the rest, with muskets at the ready. Many of the prominent women scowl as they walk along with their well-dressed men.

***

Little Crow sits staring into his campfire. He tells his son Wowinape, who sits opposite him, "It is over. We have lost this fight."

His son is startled by the comment, "Father, we can still win."

"No, son, it is lost. There are too many of our people leaving for the West. Too many warriors are leaving with them."

Little Crow picks up a partially burnt stick and nudges a burning log. Sparks fly into the air with the heat of the flames.

“You are going to give up?”

"No. But we will have to move away from here."

Wowinape, “Where will we go?”

“I am not certain. West? … Maybe north.”

He stirs the burning logs, turning them over one by one. The red embers glow, and the heat of the flames grows.

"What if we go to the upper agency, the Yellow Medicine Agency? Maybe they will join us."

Little Crow sets his stick down and stands up, “Son, we have been fighting for seven days. If they were going to join us, they would have by now.”

“We must continue.”

"There have been too many defeats. Without victories, we have nothing."

Wowinape stands up also. Brushing off his backside, he insists, "Father. We can't give up."

Little Crow gathers his things, “So many are choosing to leave for the western lands.”

“We still have warriors that are willing to fight. Red Middle Voice and Shakopee still have their warriors.”

“Son, they haven’t joined us in any of our battles.”

Wowinape walks closer to his father, “They have sent the settlers back to the East.”

“They have butchered women and children. That is not what Dakota warriors do.”

Wowinape counters with, “They have brought back food and supplies.”

"They have brought back shame on our people, and it will bring back a furious vengeance when the white man's army returns."

“They have brought back captives.”

Little Crow stands face to face with his son, "Yes, they have, and we may have to use them to negotiate an end to this."

Chapter 16

Henson On His Way Home.

August 4th, 1863

HENSON SPOTS A grove of trees. He stops to relieve himself and to stretch his legs. He coughs and holds his hand to his head trying to relieve the ache that is getting worse.

Wildfire begins grazing immediately.

After taking care of business, walking to get rid of his aching backside. Henson takes care of Wildfire, grabs his pipe, and locates a shady spot to lie down under a tree. He pats his shirt pocket. Then, he removes his tobacco pouch and begins packing the bowl of his pipe. His thoughts go back to home and an incident that happened not that long ago.

***

Wiseman Cabin

Summer of 1862

ANDREW THINKS TO himself, *'There never seems to be anything to do.'*

Pheobe and Hannah are nowhere to be found. Left alone in the cabin, he wanders aimlessly from here to there.

'Pa's chair. No one is here. What if he finds out? How will he find out? He'll never know.'

Henson is the only person who sits in this familiar chair. Andrew goes over to the oversized wooden rocking chair with an old, worn pillow for the seat cushion. Andrew turns and sits down. The tip of his worn shoes barely touch the rough-honed wooden floor of the cabin. He scoots back, his legs straighten out as his back meets the three spoked back-rest. He smiles and tries to get it to rock. It barely moves.

'Why won't it rock?'

Frustrated, he scoots forward, pulling on the chair's armrests. Something falls off the small wooden table next to the chair.

"Uh oh, what was that?"

Concerned, he looks at the floor beside the rocking chair.

"Pa's tobacco pouch."

Tobacco has spilled out and is scattered all over the wood plank floor. Frantic, Andrew begins to scrap up the tobacco leaves into a pile.

Andrew to no one, "I'll put it all back in the pouch."

But the smell of the tobacco is strong. He continues picking it up and stuffing it back in the leather container.

"He'll never know."

Instead, he puts a few pinches of the scrapings in his shirt pocket.

"That doesn't look like much."

So, he pinches a little bit more from the open pouch.

"I'll need something to light it."

He begins looking around.

"Where does he keep them?"

On the lantern table, he spies stick matches neatly arranged in a small upright cup. He grabs a handful. Out the door he goes with his bounty, walking at first, then running. He makes his way to the barn and his secret hiding place.

After retrieving an item, he sees Arthur grooming his horse.

His older brother asks, "What you up to?"

"Nothing."

"Well, if you ain't doing anything, you can help me."

"No, I'm busy."

Arthur laughs and continues brushing his black stallion.

Andrew wanders outside the barn and into the corral, climbs between the split rail fence, and heads toward the hog barn and smokehouse. There, he sees his father scooping the hog pen. He turns and heads toward the grove.

William and Loren are playing fetch with Boots when they see their brother coming.

William asks, “Wanna play?”

“Naw.”

He continues into the grove, leaving the two siblings behind. He finds a familiar stump and pulls out his treasure.

A few minutes later, William asks, “What you got there?”

Andrew tries to hide it the best he can, “Nothing.”

Loren looks on with his querying eyes. Boots just pants as he recovers from playing fetch.

William continues, "You got something there. What is it?"

"It's nothing. Just leave me be."

William spies the matches sticking out of Andrew's pocket, "Matches?"

“Shhh, be quiet.”

“You know you aren’t supposed to play with matches.”

Andrew, "Shhh, be quiet, I tell you. Especially with him here."

Loren understands what Andrew means.

Andrew to Loren, “You should go back home.”

"I don't want to, and you can't make me."

Andrew stands up, and Loren steps behind William.

William, “Let him be. What are you going to do with the matches?”

Andrew pulls some tobacco out of his pocket, trying not to let Loren see.

William, “Dad’s tobacco!”

“Shhh, now he knows.”

"Oh, right."

William to Loren, “You should go back home.”

“I’m not going.”

William, “If we make him. He’ll tell on you.”

“Me? Us.”

“What, I haven’t done anything.”

Andrew, "That isn't what I'll tell them."

"So, how are you planning to smoke it?"

Andrew pulls a crude corncob pipe out of his back pocket.

"I hid this in the barn."

"We'll, fill it up. Let's try it."

Andrew, "Not with him around."

"I can hear you."

William to Loren, "We know you can. So why don't you just run off and play."

"I don't want to. I want to try it, too."

Andrew to Loren, "You are too little."

"No, I ain't."

"Yes, you are so scram."

Loren turns to leave.

"And don't you say anything if you know what is good for you."

"Or what?"

"You know what!"

Loren leaves, upset, "Here, boy. You come with me."

Boots pounces at the call, joining his best friend.

William to Andrew, "Okay, let's try it."

"Let's find a hiding place first."

"Okay, where?"

"Let's go to our fort in the back of the grove."

"Okay."

Moments later, the two boys crawl into the fort, initially carved out of the hillside by erosion from heavy rainfall. Benjamin, John, and Arthur piled branches across the top the first year they arrived in Nebraska. Then John, Arthur, and Hannah improved on the fortress. Now Andrew and William have added even more to it. This washout gully is big enough for the entire Wiseman family to fit inside. Over time, the boys have dragged stumps inside the fort for places to sit.

William, "Okay, let's try it."

“Hold your horses.”

In the relative darkness, the only light is the afternoon sunlight coming through the fort opening, Andrew pulls out the pipe and stuffs the tobacco in the hollowed-out center.

And anxious William, “Light the match!”

"I am. Just wait. Damn!"

Andrew pulls out a match and looks around for something to strike it on. Nothing rough enough. They both look at each other in bewilderment.

Andrew, “What would Pa do?”

“I have seen him use a button on his jacket.”

“Me too, but I don’t have a jacket.”

William, “The buttons on our jeans. Maybe we can use those.”

“Good idea.”

Andrew hands the pipe to William while he tries to light the match. After five or six tries, the match breaks.

“This isn’t working.”

"Keep trying. You have more matches."

He tries again, and after another few attempts, the match fizzles and goes out.

William, “You almost had it, try again.”

Andrew pulls out another, and on the second try, it lights. William holds the pipe to Andrew's lips.

“I got it!”

Andrew takes the pipe by the cob bowl and holds it in his left hand, with the flame over the bowl. He puffs a couple of times, drawing the flame into the bowl. When he stops, the smoke curls upward to the ceiling of the fort. Andrew coughs harshly.

William, “My turn.”

William puffs quickly. The bowl glows red, and between puffs, smoke rises. William begins to cough, too.

Andrew, "Not bad."

Still coughing, "Right, not bad."

Andrew takes the still-smoldering pipe and takes another puff. He passes it to his brother for another draw.

"After the first one, it isn't bad at all."

They begin to giggle and laugh.

***

At the Main Cabin

PHEOBE ASKS LOREN, "What have you been up to?"

"Nothing."

"Where are your brothers?"

"In the grove."

"Raking leaves?"

"No."

"Playing then?"

"No."

Pheobe gets a little suspicious at Loren's solemn demeanor.

"What, they didn't want to play with you again?"

"Kinda."

"Son, you are a little younger than they are. Someday, that won't be an issue."

"I'll always be younger."

"Yes, you will. But as you get older, it will become less of an issue."

"How long will that take?"

"A while."

Loren saunters over to his chair at the dining table.

"Were they playing Cowboys and Indians again?"

"No."

"What then?"

"They are smoking."

"What?" Pheobe turns wildly toward her almost-four-year-old son.

Loren just blurted it out without any thought of the threat by his two brothers.

"No, I mean they are playing."

"Don't you lie to me, young man!"

She now hovers directly over him.

"They told me not to tell. They said they'd hurt me."

Loren begins to cry. Pheobe pulls her son's chair back, picks him up, and puts him over her shoulder to soothe him.

"Don't you worry about them?"

Loren hugs his mother's neck and lays his head on her shoulder.

***

A COUPLE OF hours later, the two boys walk casually down the ridge from the grove. Pheobe watches from the cabin window, dries her hands, throws the towel down over the not-yet-dried dishes, and then goes to meet them at the door.

Pheobe snidely asks, "Did you two have fun in the grove?

Andrew answers, "Sure, we had fun."

She bends down to give them a casual kiss on the foreheads.

She can smell the smoke and tells them, "Good. Get washed up. You two are going to have to wait until your father gets home."

The two look around the main cabin. There is no sign of their little brother. They look at each other in despair.

***

ARTHUR AND HIS father ride up to the wood pile in the empty work wagon. They have been loading and unloading split firewood all day. They unhook the horses, leave the wagon, and escort them to their pen. They check the feed and water troughs and head up to the cabins.

Pheobe waits by the door for Henson as he comes up the hill, "You know what your sons have been up to today?"

"My sons? Uh oh."

A bit taken aback by the announcement he looks around the cabin. Andrew and William are sitting at the table, hands on top, both perfectly still.

Henson asks, "What now?"

"I'll let them tell you."

He turns to the two silent lads. Neither one looks up from the table.

"Well?"

Silence.

Andrew, "We've been smoking."

"Really? Where did you get that?"

Pheobe interrupts, "Out of your pouch on the table next to your chair. I have told you a thousand times to put it away."

"Pheeb, not now."

Pheobe fumes at the reprimand and returns to her cooking.

Henson turns to the two boys, "Which one of you took the tobacco?"

Silence.

Henson raises his voice, "One of you is going to tell me."

"I told them you'd tan their hides when you got home. I was about to send both of them out to fetch a switch for you."

"No need for that. I have a better idea."

Henson walks over to Pheobe and whispers, "You know you hate my smoking. You don't want them to pick up this habit."

"No, I don't."

"Well, it's too late for me, but it isn't too late for them."

Henson turns to the boys, "So, you want to smoke?"

Pheobe, "What are you thinking."

"Pheeb."

"Don't you, Pheeb, me."

"Pheeb, let me handle this."

Henson goes to his rocking chair, pulls out a box from under the table next to it, flips the lid, and grabs two cigars.

Henson to his two sons, "These cigars are usually for a special occasion or a change of pace."

"Henson Wiseman!"

She picks up her youngest.

"Pheeb, hold on. I know what I'm doing."

"Oh, Lord."

She squeezes Loren tight. He squirms in her arms from the pressure.

Arthur suggests, "I'll go do chores."

Henson, "Not a bad idea."

"Or I could stay and watch."

Pheobe adds, "No, you take Loren with you."

"Okay, let's go, little guy."

Loren is set down from his mother's arms. He quietly walks to Arthur's side, not looking at either of the two boys glaring at him from the dining table.

As Arthur and Loren exit the cabins, they see Hannah and Wildfire coming down the trail that leads to the river.

Arthur laughs and yells to his sister, "You might want to help us with the chores."

Hannah scoffs at the invitation and asks, "Why would I wanna do that?"

"Because Andrew and William are in trouble, and Pa is setting to punish them."

"I'll go watch."

"Not a good idea, Ma is not happy."

"Okay, I'll do the horses."

Arthur, "We already did them. I'll get the cattle."

"I'll do the hogs." Hannah laughs, "Okay, Loren, why don't you come with me? We'll take care of the chickens, too."

***

BACK IN THE main cabin, Henson hands each of the boys a cigar, "Here, you both get one of these."

Pheobe is beside herself, "Henson Wiseman, are you out of your mind?"

"Trust me, Pheeb."

"I can't believe you."

Pheobe keeps herself busy making the evening meal, cutting up potatoes and carrots for the evening pork stew.

Henson begins, "Okay, boys, you wanted to smoke, here you go. Put it in your mouth."

Each of the boys looks at the other in bewilderment.

Andrew says, "No, Pa, we shouldn't."

"You are correct. You shouldn't have. But you are going to now."

William sheepishly asks, "Do we have to?"

"Yes, you have to."

Pheobe glances over while stirring the stew, "Henson, this is crazy."

"Trust me."

Each of the boys places the cigar in their mouths.

Henson offers, "Here, let me light 'em."

He takes a match from his shirt pocket and flicks the tip using only his thumbnail. There is a snap and then a fizzle. The flame leaps to life.

Each of the boys' eyes light up at the feat.

Henson places the flame under each dangling cigar, "Puff, puff hard. Don't let those cigars go out."

Pheobe continues to protest, "I can't believe you."

"You'll see."

Andrew and William puff and puff and then blow out the smoke.

"Keep 'em going, don't stop."

Andrew tastes the flavor. He likes it. 'This is different from the tobacco this afternoon. It has a pleasant taste and aroma.'

William is indifferent.

Henson pulls up a chair at the end of the long table, his usual spot. The boys to his left continue to puff and blow out the smoke.

Henson, "Now. I want you to inhale."

Andrew asks meekly, "Inhale?"

"Yes, draw it in and hold it a second."

Pheobe is getting worried, "Henson Wiseman!"

"They'll be alright, Pheeb."

Both boys look at each other.

"Now, take another puff, hold it, and then let it go."

Andrew, "Like that?"

"Yes, like that."

William, "Am I doing it right, Pa?"

"Yes, son, you are doing it right."

Andrew sits back in his chair, feeling pretty big about himself. Then he puffs and blows out a smoke ring.

"Look, Ma, I blew a smoke ring just like Pa."

"Oh, my God."

Henson laughs a bit and then offers his instructions, "Don't stop. Don't let them go out."

Each of the boys continues puffing and practicing their smoke rings.

Pheobe is furious and states, with frustration, "I'm going to open the door. It is getting too smokey in here."

Henson agrees, “Good idea.”

“I hope you know what you are doing.”

“I do.”

Henson to himself, *‘My old man did the same thing to me when I was their age. But he didn’t…’*

Each cigar is burning down quite nicely. The boys are getting comfortable puffing away.

Arthur, Hannah, and Loren walk up the path from the barn to the open door.

Hannah reports, “Ma, you can see the smoke rolling out of the cabin from the barn."

Andrew asks impressively, “Really?”

Pheobe responds, “I’m not liking this at all.”

Henson assures his wife, “They are almost done.”

“I hope so. Supper is almost ready. Hannah, you watch the stew?”

"Sure, Ma.”

Henson to the young smokers, "Okay, you can put them out now."

Andrew, "But Pa, they are only half done."

William stares at his brother.

Arthur giggles.

Pheobe and Hannah look at each other and shrug.

Each of the smokers snuffs out their cigar in Henson’s ashtray.

Andrew proclaims proudly, “That wasn’t so bad.”

Henson adds sternly, "You are not done."

William exclaims, "But we just put them out, Pa."

“Now you are going to bite off the end.”

Andrew, “Which end?”

Henson laughs under his breath, “The wet end.”

Pheobe asks, “What in god’s name?”

"Pheeb, trust me."

Andrew and William both look at their cigars and grimace.

Henson insists, "A big bite."

Andrew, "Huh?"

"A big bite."

Each child nibbles at the soggy end of the cigar in their little hands.

"Bigger bite."

Arthur's eyes get really big. Hannah stirs the stew faster and faster. Pheobe cuts fresh vegetables. Loren stands beside his mother, staring at the dining table with his two brothers and father.

Each of the youngsters takes a good-sized bite of the cigar, and then both start to spit it out.

"Oh no. Don't spit it out. Chew it."

"Hmm?" from both

with a mouth full of tobacco. They both begin to chew.

"Keep chewing it. That's right, just like that."

Hannah scowls with pity for her little brothers.

"When I tell you, swallow it."

"Hmm?" from both of the youngsters.

Pheobe utters, "Oh my god."

Henson to the two smokers, "Do as I say."

Each child continues to chew, and the color on their faces begins to change.

"Okay, now swallow it. All of it."

Andrew is first, a big gulp, and down it went. William takes a bit longer, gagging first, then swallowing it.

"Okay, show me your tongue, each of you."

Arthur looks on, astonished. Hannah can't bear to watch. Pheobe is furious. Loren is scared.

Henson states confidently, "See, Pheeb, they'll be just fine."

"Why in blazes did you do this?"

"You'll see."

Pheobe mentions, "Well, we need some water. We are almost out."

Arthur, “I’ll get it.”

Pheobe, “No. Have one of the young smokers fetch it.”

“Which one?”

Henson, “Andrew, you go get the water.”

William's face is turning yellow. His eyes are going a bit blurry.

Andrew’s skin tone is a bit greener. His stomach is making funny noises. He grabs the two tin buckets and heads outside.

Pheobe declares and instructs, “Supper is ready. William, you get to set the table.

"Okay, Ma."

His voice is a bit soft. He slides out from behind the table and heads slowly to the shelves with the plates and cups. His stomach lurches, and his body heaves.

Henson yells, “Outside.”

Arthur opens the door. William dashes outside, turns to the left, and sprays the contents of his stomach on the ground. Uncontrollable heaves continue, even when there is nothing left to vomit.

Minutes later, Pheobe brings him some water, "Here, drink this."

He throws that up immediately.

She implores, "Keep drinking the water, William."

***

DOWN AT THE water pump, Andrew has a similar reaction. The fresh air has lessened the effects, but he, too, leaves his lunch on the ground by the long-handled water pump platform. He is careful not to get any in the two water buckets. Once his convulsions are over, Andrew begins pumping the handle to fill the buckets. After five or six pumps, the water spurts out of the mouth of the pump in much the same way the two smokers had expelled their contents.

Chapter 17

Little Crow's Village

August 24th 1863

LITTLE CROW TO Gray Bird, "Gather all of our people. We need to leave here."

"What will I tell them?"

"That we must leave here. Our village is too close to the fort. The soldiers will regroup and attack us here if we don't."

Gray Bird, "We are not giving up the fight?"

"No, we are going to the Yellow Medicine Agency to convince those Chiefs to join us. We will see if they want to rid the valley of the whites."

"What about the Redwood Agency Chiefs?"

Little Crow, "I will send runners to them also. They can stay if they want, but we are going to the Upper Agency today."

"But Red Middle Voice and Shakopee are in the Big Woods. What about their villages?"

"That is up to them. They have not joined us. They have sought easier targets. When we needed them, they did not show."

Gray Bird asks, "But their people?"

"Let their people decide for themselves. Tell them they are welcome to come with us… Now Go!"

Little Crow tells his son, "Let the chiefs and members of the Soldier's lodge know I am calling for a tribal council once the camp is set up near Yellow Medicine Agency."

"Yes, Father, I will let them all know."

"You are a good son."

"You are a good father."

***

THE SISSETON SCOUTS report back to their Chiefs as they approach the Upper Agency, “Little Crow’s caravan stretches for miles.”

The majority of the Upper Agency villagers are Farmer Indians who live near the Yellow Medicine Agency. Their lives were in a much better situation than the 'Blanket Indians'. The white Indian Agents bestowed more food, clothing, medicine, and supplies to those Dakota who agreed to till the land. There was a motive for this arrangement. It divided the villages and pitted Dakota against Dakota.

***

AS LITTLE CROW arrives, he finds many villagers surrounding the agency. They are mulling around the vacated structures left standing.

Little Crow to Chief Iron Walker, "The white soldiers that will follow us will want these structures for themselves. We cannot leave them standing.”

“But they are useful. We can use them.”

“You are still fools. The whites will come and put you out. They care nothing for you.”

Iron Walker insists, "We have not participated in this war of yours. The whites will understand."

“You don’t understand. Their soldier will come, and you will have nothing. Unless you join us in ridding the valley of all whites.”

“We will not join a fight we cannot win.”

Little Crow grows more irritated, "Then you must leave these buildings. If you don't, I'll have my warriors burn them down with you in them."

Iron Walker stares back at Little Crow.

Little Crow, "We attacked their fort twice, and you still did not join us."

Iron Walker, “It was a fool’s errand to take on the whites.”

“If you would have joined us, we would have taken the fort.

"You speculate. You do not know."

Little Crow to the other Sisseton Chiefs, "We also fought at New Ulm twice, and you did not join us either time."

"You have started something you cannot finish. You want us to join in your defeat. We will not."

"If you would have joined us, we would have their big guns and their buildings. If you had joined us, we could have made sure no reinforcements could have reached the fort."

Iron Walker, "You are a fool."

"No, you are the fools who believe the word of the white man."

The farmer chiefs leave the council furious. Little Crows' braves torch every building and everything else that will burn. Anything that would be useful to Sibley.

***

LITTLE CROW HOLDS another council of his best warriors.

The next day, nearly two hundred warriors ride into the Sisseton and Wahpeton villages.

Chief Iron Walker shows himself.

Gray Bird of the Little Crow's band of warriors demands, "Your warriors must join us. Our soldier's lodge has decided you must join us. It is the way of our people to follow what the Soldier's Lodge has decided."

"Your Soldier's Lodge." Iron Walker scoffs, "You act like children. You ride in here making demands you have no authority to make. This is our village, not yours. You were not invited, nor are you welcome. Your chief is a crazy man. You follow a crazy fool."

"You have until tomorrow. If you do not join us, we will burn your lodges."

Iron Walker responds, “We will gladly make war with you and your crazy chief. We are not afraid of you who cannot win battles.”

“We could have won had you joined us, but you cowards refuse.”

“You have created this war. It is up to you to fight it. It is not up to us to fight your war."

Gray Bird turns his mount and says, "You will have to fight, also. The white man's army is forming, and they will not distinguish between Sisseton, Wahpeton or Mdewakanton Dakota. They will make war with us all.”

"That we will have to find out for ourselves. If you give up the hostages, you may have a chance at peace. If you don't, you will all die."

“Then we'll die as Dakota Warriors.”

Iron Walker, “You are all fools… Enough talk, you are not welcome here.”

***

THE NEXT DAY, Little Crow's warriors ride to the Yellow Medicine village again. This time, they anticipate that the upper agency village will be ready to battle if necessary. Instead, to the surprise of Little Crow's men. They are met by Iron Walker's most trusted warrior.
Who announces, “We invite you and your men to feast with us.”

The smell of roasted beef wafts in the air.

“Little Crow told us you and your warriors have been on the move and at war for over a week."

Gray Bird shakes his head, “This is true.”

The braves surrounding Gray Bird smell the sweet fixings of a feast.

"We have come here to do battle, not to eat with cowards."

Iron Walker's representative, “We have come here to make peace and offer you a meal. We can council while we eat.”

Gray Bird can see his warriors struggle to resist this temptation.

One brave to the Gray Bird, “What harm could it do?”

Gray Bird states, “We are here to make them join us or else.”

“Or else we eat and discuss it. What is the harm?”

“Okay, what is the harm.”

All of the warriors dismount and join their Sisseton brothers in the feast.

***

IRON WALKER WAITS until the visitors have eaten their fill.

He announces, “Dakota warriors only fight the white man. Not his women or his children. We believe you should let the women and children go.”

Gray Bird finishes his roast beef and says, “It won’t matter if we let them go or keep them. Our scouts tell us the white soldier’s number in the thousands.”

“What have you fools done? … If you let the captives go, maybe you can talk peace?”

"We will keep them as bargaining chips. So, the white man soldiers do not attempt to overrun our village."

Iron Walker scolds, “Yes, so you use them as protection. That is not the way of a Dakota Warrior. It is the way of a coward.”

Infuriated by the insult, "If you join us, we can defeat their army. Like we did at the ferry landing. We can drive the whites from the valley forever. Their farmers have already fled.”

"You are dreamers, just foolish dreamers. More whites will come after those you kill. They are endless in their numbers. Give us your captives. You go fight the white man. Leave us the women and children so we can return them to their people.”

Gray Bird insists, “No. The captives will stay with us. If need be, they will die with us.”

The council ends as abruptly as it had started. Little Crow's soldier lodge leaves the Yellow Medicine village and return to their new camp, just over a mile away.

The next day, they return, hoping the Upper Agency village would join them in the fight.

Gray Bird announces, "They have put up a Soldier's lodge in the center of their village!"

A warrior states, "This means they will not be joining us?"

"No, they are preparing to take up arms against us."

"What will we do?"

Gray Bird, "We go back to Little Crow and see what he decides."

When the Sisseton village braves saw Little Crow's band of warriors turn around. They mount up and follow them back to Little Crow's village.

There, they put on the same display of insistence they had received from the Little Crow's band two days earlier.

Iron Walker, leader of the Sisseton band, dismounts and demands, "We ask that you release all white captives."

Little Crow stands face to face, "We will not!"

"You have taken much property that belongs to mixed-bloods. We demand that property back."

Little Crow, "We will grant you that request, but that only."

The Sisseton and Wahpeton warriors search the village, collecting property of the mixed-bloods and counting the number of captives.

When they finish, Iron Walker rides up to and stops a short distance in front of Little Crow, who is standing with his warriors.

Iron Walker shouts to Little Crow's band, "We welcomed all warriors tired of fighting a losing battle against the whites. Come with us and live in peace."

Slowly, a few braves cross over to the Sisseton and Wahpeton band's side.

When the few warriors who abandoned have changed sides, Little Crow says proudly, "We will not stop our fight to reclaim our lands. It is Dakota land for all of eternity. It is ours… Now go, you who feel the need to become slaves of the white man."

The band of Sisseton and Wahpeton warriors mount up. They take with them a few stolen possessions and a few of Little Crow's soldiers.

Chapter 18

Chaska's tribal village

Mid-September 1862

FOUR RIDERS APPROACH a solemn Yankton Lakota village on a cool, heavy, overcast fall day. Sun-scorched, whitened buffalo hide tepees are arranged in the traditional circles around the center of the village's ceremonial unlit fire pit. Most of the smaller fire pits also sit unused throughout the village.

Usually, each fire pit would be surrounded by diligent workers. Chaska's home village should be preparing for the coming winter.

Only a few years ago, the roaring fires would be encircled by men, women, and older children. The entire village would be involved in the numerous processes it takes to make jerky, pemican, and numerous tools out of buffalo sinew and bones. But now there is no buffalo to process.

Groups of braves should be building pole structures to hoist the buffalo carcasses, to remove the thick hide and dissect the meat. The meat passed off to groups to carve it up into smaller cuts.

The hides passed off to the women who should be tanning and preparing the hide to be made into tepee coverings, blankets, and carrying bags.

The meat would become jerky or packed in salt and stored for future consumption. The best cuts would be reserved for the evening celebration of the successful hunt. But there is no hunt. There is no buffalo.

Now the Yankton Lakota people are restricted to this reservation.

***

KILLING GHOST BREAKS the silence, "This is a lot like our village."

Brave to his right, "They might be ready to listen."

Brave to his left, "We might be able to convince some to stand up and fight."

***

THE ONLY SIGN of happiness is the younger children playing kickball and other groups playing a form of tag. An older boy stops suddenly and stares at the four visitors. He doesn't recognize them. He turns and runs back to tell the village elders.

Killing Ghost and his three companions continue to the center of the village. Heads turn as they pass by. Old and young glance up, then return to their tedious tasks. The riders solemnly proceed, watching the gossip they are inspiring spread throughout the village. Women scurry to gather their small and infant children.

***

A YOUNG BOY messenger reaches a small group of elders gathered under a large Weeping Willow tree.

"We have visitors!"

Smutty Bear, "How many?"

"Four."

Brings Back Buffalo asks, "What tribe?"

"I don't recognize anything familiar."

Smutty Bear, "You have done well. Go, tell the other elders They'll want to know too."

***

MOST OF THE young men should be assisting in carving up the buffalo carcasses. A few would still be on a hunt out on the western plains. Today, these braves can only fish up and down the Niobrara and Missouri Rivers.

Killing Ghost and his friends have seen many villages just like this along their journey. The four travelers come to a stop near a group of women near the center of the village.

Killing Ghosts asks, “Where can we find your chief?”

A young woman, carrying an infant child, points toward the grove of trees, “There.”

She watches with concern as the strangers turn to leave.

***

THE ELDERS SEE the visitors riding up to the willow tree grove. Each nod to the other, bewildered by the visitor's appearance.

“Not from around here.” One of the oldest remarks.

Smutty Bear adds, “Not Ogallala.”

Brings Back Buffalo, “Not Teton either.”

The four Santee Dakota stay seated on their horses.

Killing Ghost speaks first.

He asks, “I am looking for your chief. Which one of you shall I talk to?”

Smutty Bear answers, “I am the one you are seeking!”

“Good. I am Killing Ghost. We have come a long way.”

"Where is it you come from, this long way, you say?"

Smutty Bear is pretty sure he knows the answer. He checks to see if they’ll tell him the truth.

Killing Ghost proudly proclaims, “The Big Woods of Minnesota.”

Brings Back Buffalo, “Minnesota. That is a long way.”

“Yes, it is a four-day ride to the east.”

Satisfied they are who they say they are, Smutty Bear says, “Come join us. You are welcome here. Eat and rest here.”

“Thank you.”

The riders dismount, dust themselves off, and stretch their legs.

The elders present a place to sit for each.

Brings Back Buffalo, “Here, over here, help yourself.”

They step aside for the newcomers to sit.

Smutty Bear begins, "What brings you to our village? Four days ride, you say?"

"We have been traveling for nearly a month."

Brings Back Buffalo, "But you say it is only a four-day ride."

"Yes, that's if we had ridden straight here."

"I see."

One of the oldest elders to Killing Ghost, "Here you take a seat here."

Killing Ghost to the elder, "Thank you!"

He settles in on a buffalo robe, then continues, "We are on a mission."

He recalls the day Little Crow's assigned the four hunters to their separate missions.

Brings Back Buffalo, "A mission you say."

"Yes, we have stopped by as many villages of our people as we could find along the way."

The oldest elder asks, "A Mission. So, what is this mission of yours?"

Killing Ghost asks, "Has the news reached you of the uprising in our lands?"

Smutty Bear acknowledges, "Yes, we have heard. Others have told us of your journey, your mission."

"Then you have had time to consider what we have come to request."

"Yes, we will call a counsel. We will let you speak to our elders."

Killing Ghost, "Thank you!"

Smutty Bear to the four braves, "Eat, drink."

Each respond with a thank you.

***

Earlier When The
Four Messengers Arrive

LITTLE THUNDER WORKS with a small group of women doing laundry. When she sees the four riders enter the village, she slowly makes her way to the girl who pointed the visitors towards the elders.

"Who are they?" she asks eagerly.

"I don't know, but it is probably the runners we have heard about."

Little Thunder exclaims, "The tall one is cute!"

"But you are taken!"

"Not anymore. I was, but a new plan just rode in."

She grabs the girl by the shoulder and turns her back to the grove of trees. Little Thunder can now see over the girl's shoulder.

The young girl asks, "What happened… Chaska and you?"

She squirms, trying to turn to see the visitors.

"Be still. Chaska has asked the elders to allow him out of the arrangement. He is…"

Little Thunder hesitates and then decides to keep the rest to herself.

***

CHIEF SMUTTY BEAR announces to the four braves, "We will listen to your message at the council, and then we will decide. If our council determines your message should be heard by the entire village, you may make a presentation in our village center."

Killing Ghost nods in respect, "Thank you very much. It is for all of our people that we come to you. You will see."

Smutty Bear, "Let's go."

The group of elders begin to stand, so the visitors stand also.

Smutty Bear continues, "Have some young braves take care of their horses."

Brings Back Buffalo, "I'll take care of that."

The entourage of elders and messengers make their way through the village. Young boys and girls spread the news by running in all directions.

The elders invite the visitors to gather in the large council tepee at the center of the village.

Chaska and the other warriors wait outside. The discussion goes on for over an hour. Killing Ghost explains what has happened. The elders question the reasons why.

Chaska and many of his fellow braves listen intently outside the council tepee.

A brave whispers, "They are done."

A few moments later, the council members exited the council lodge.

Smutty Bear announces to the crowd, “They will make a presentation in two days. All of your questions will be answered then.”

The elders and men of the tribe scatter into small groups.

***

LITTLE THUNDER CONFRONTS Little Eagle, “Where is he? Have you seen Chaska?”

“I don’t know. He was here a minute ago!”

In a distraught, sullen voice, “Is he avoiding me?”

Little Eagle shrugs his shoulders.

She becomes insistent, “He has changed. Ever since you two came back from downriver. He has changed.”

Not wanting to say a thing, Little Eagle looks away.

Little Thunder insists, “What happened to him?”

“I don’t know what you are talking about!”

“Chaska doesn’t talk to me anymore.”

Little Eagle stumbles over his words, “I heard you two are no longer a couple.”

“This is true. But he changed his mind once, he can change it back. He should still talk to me.”

“He has a lot on his mind!”

Little Thunder's frustration peeks, “What? What does he have on his mind!”

“I don’t know.”

“You do know. You just won’t tell me. What did he say about me?”

Little Eagle sheepishly announces, “I got to go.”

***

KILLING GHOST AND his three fellow messengers pass by, walking with a few of the elders of the Yankton Lakota tribe. He spies a beautiful young girl standing along the path.

Little Thunder smiles deviously at Killing Ghost. He returns the smile. She and her friends follow them at a distance.

***

Later that evening

LITTLE THUNDER TO her mother, who is cooking over a fire pit. “Where will the visitors stay while they are here?”

"It is none of our concern. You can help me with this."

She steps in and begins to assist.

Red Dove continues, “The elders will take care of it. Why do you ask?”

"No reason. Isn't Papa an elder?"

Red Dove turns to her daughter, annoyed, "Yes, you know he is."

“Of course.”

“What are you up to?”

Little Thunder denies, “Nothing.”

"Your father and the elders will care for those young braves."

"We have extra tepees we could share. I mean, make room for them."

Red Dove asks, “Who would move all of our things?”

"I would. My friends and I can move our things into one tepee."

“You have trouble getting your chores done as it is.”

Little Thunder suggests, “I can do it. Me and my friends.”

“I don’t know.”

“It would be only for a little while. They are on a mission.”

Red Dove queries, “Where did you hear that?”

“Around. Everyone is talking about it.”

“Well, they seem like nice boys. But what they are asking is only going to bring trouble.”

Little Thunder asks, “What have you heard?”

"They want our young men to join in their rebellion. Their people started back there in Minnesota."

“They didn’t start it.”

Red Dove dismisses the response, “How do you know?”

“I listen to what people are saying.”

"No matter who started it. We need our young men here. They will try to convince our men, like Chaska, to join them."

Little Thunder is concerned briefly. But it is short-lived.

***

ROARING THUNDER, Little Thunder’s father, to Black Elk, “They are fools on a fool’s mission.”

Black Elk, Chaska's father, says, "I know, but we must consider what they are asking."

“You heard what they claim. We don’t have any problem like that here.”

“Not now, but you remember what Burleigh did?

Roaring Thunder, “That was a few years ago.”

“What if things get worse?”

"We received our annuities."

Black Elk reminds him, “Not all of it.”

“Burleigh isn’t fair, but we still received the annuities.”

“They say theirs didn’t arrive.”

Roaring Thunder, “That is what they say.”

“You don’t believe them?”

"I didn't say that. They are strangers from a different band."

Black Elk, “They are still Lakota.”

“They are Dakota.”

“We are all the same people.”

Roaring Thunder, “They say they signed a treaty. We are not bound by their treaty.”

“What if our annuities didn’t arrive?”

“But it did.”

Black Elk, “Burleigh stole some of it.”

“But it arrived.”

“Things could get that bad here.”

Roaring Thunder, "But they aren't that bad here. Suppose our braves join this uprising. Things will get that bad here."

“Our braves are not allowed to hunt. We were forced to move our village. The whites have built their town on that former site.”

Roaring Thunder adds, “Our elders signed that treaty.”

“Just like they say theirs did.”

“There is nothing we can do.”

Black Elk adds, “The white settlers continue to arrive. Just like what they say happened back there.”

“Yes, but we are fine here.”

“For how long?”

Roaring Thunder continues, “I don’t understand how you could support sending Chaska out to fight the whites.”

“I don’t want him to go. Any more than any other father would want to send their sons.”

“You heard their leader speak. You saw he is full of anger. He is filled with hate.”

Black Elk agrees and then asks, "Yes, I did. But there has to be a reason why?"

***

BLACK ELK AND Roaring Thunder arrive at the Chief Smutty Bear's tepee. Killing Ghost and his friends are about to leave.

Smutty Bear to Killing Ghost, "How long will you stay with us?"

"Not long. We must continue on. With your help, we hope. How many tribes are in your band?"

"Many."

Killing Ghost requests, "Can you tell us which ones are the closest and where to find their villages?"

"Yes, we can, and I will let you know."

"Thank you."

Smutty Bear, "You haven't brought anything with you. No tepee, no provisions. How do you cook and eat?"

"We rely on the hospitality of our people. We repay with work if required."

"No work is required. You can stay as long as you like."

Roaring Thunder, "You may stay with my family."

Smutty Bear and the other elders turn toward Roaring Thunder.

Black Elk is shocked, "Really?"

Roaring Thunder to the elders, Killing Ghost and his friends, "My children will sleep in one tepee while you are here."

Roaring Thunder informs his friend, "Red Dove has made arrangements."

***

TWO DAYS LATER, the ceremonial fire in the center of the village is ablaze. The entire tribe surrounds the presentation area. Torches are lit, and families gather to hear the stories by the four visitors.

Children wander off from lack of interest. Mothers chase them down and bring them back.

Chaska and Little Eagle find a seat with their fellow hunters and braves.

Little Thunder watches them from a distance with her female friends.

The four messengers put on an emotional demonstration. When it is over, most of the tribe's men respectfully thank the visitors for their story.

Little Thunder makes her way to Killing Ghost, with whom she has become more acquainted.

***

LITTLE EAGLE NUDGES Chaska, “Look.”

***

KILLING GHOST CHATS with the younger male villagers when Little Thunder approaches. He turns to her and hugs her.

She turns to check if Chaska is watching.

***

LITTLE EAGLE, “See that?”

Chaska proclaims, "I don't care. Good, she can be his problem."

***

LITTLE THUNDER WRAPS her arms around Killing Ghost's waist. She frequently turns toward Chaska's group. She touches Killing Ghost on his chest and laughs aloud, then glances in Chaska's direction.

She is furious by Chaska’s lack of concern.

Killing Ghost notices the distraction.

***

CHASKA SNIDELY ADDS, “Good luck to him. He is going to need it.”

Little Eagle laughs.

Chaska gets up to leave, and his group follows.

***

SHE STEPS TO the side of Killing Ghost to see if Chaska is watching. He isn't. She sees him turn and walks away with his friends.

Little Thunder gets upset that they are leaving.

She asks Killing Ghost, "When did this happen?"

“Less than a year ago.”

“It is so sad you lost your family.”

Killing Ghost replies solemnly, “Thank you for your concern.”

Little Thunder continues to glance in Chaska's direction.

Killing Ghost is becoming aware of the young girl’s ploy.

The village elders bid the visitors good night and leave her alone with Killing Ghost. He smiles at Little Thunder.

Killing Ghost, *'I will take advantage of this situation.'*

***

LITTLE EAGLE NOTICES Killing Ghost put his arm around her as they walk away together. Little Eagle wanders off with some of his friends and says nothing to Chaska.

Chapter 19

Sibley's March to Fort Ridgely

August 25th, 1862

THE EVACUEES OF New Ulm make it to Mankato in two days.

Flandrau to a group of men he has led to safety, "Men, now that your loved ones are safe, let all able-bodied men join me in returning to New Ulm."

Many of those gathered shake their heads no.

One of them asks, "Why would we want to go back?"

"To protect what remains and not let the Sioux take over the town."

A settler, "With what? I am almost out of ammunition."

A bystander says, "Me too."

Flandrau, "We'll get you some more powder and lead."

"What about provisions? What would we eat? What would we use to cook?"

A businessman, "You go back if you want, but I'm staying here."

Not all refuse.

***

FLANDRAU AND COX report to Colonel Sibley, who is still in camp at St Peter.

Flandrau states, "Sir, we are here to report that the town of New Ulm has been vacated. The people from that fair town and the surrounding area are now in Mankato."

Sibley asks, "You've seen the Sioux fight. What can you tell me of their strength?"

Flandrau, "We fought them off twice, but we had very little ammunition and or provisions left. We didn't believe we could hold them off again."

“We don’t have much here either, but if you continue downriver, there may at least be food available.”

"We have many men willing to join and return whenever you are ready to move out."

Sibley answers solemnly, “That may be a while.”

“What about the Fort?”

“What can you tell me of that situation?”

Flandrau, “Not much, Sir. We can only guess they are still holding out. We were only civilians. We held ‘em off.”

“That does give us hope, but they would be running out of ammunition and food also. Just like you were.”

“What do you want me to tell my men?”

Sibley responds, "We'll take anyone willing to fight." Then turns to a sergeant, "Get me, Colonel McPhail."

"Yes, sir."

Sibley sits at a folding table, writing another of the many letters to his successor, Governor Ramsey.

“Where are the provisions I've asked for? We need food, cooking equipment and tins. Most of all, we need powder and lead. We can't proceed without these provisions.”

Colonel McPhail enters Sibley's tent, comes to attention, and salutes, "Sir, you called for me?"

Sibley returns the salute nonchalantly, “I am sending you and three companies of fifty men each ahead to Fort Ridgely.”

"All calvary, I presume?"

“Yes, and with provisions and ammunitions as much as we can spare.”

Colonel McPhail, “When are we to depart?”

“First thing in the morning.”

"Yes, Sir."

***

Fort Ridgely

August 27th, 1862

A PICKET ASKS, “What is that in the distance?”

A dust cloud wafts above the trees.

Fellow picket with a telescope, "They have gone downriver. They are surrounding us."

"Send word to Lt. Sheehan."

Lt. Sheehan arrives and makes his decision, "I am not waiting to be sure. Sound the alert."

The fort's defenders rush to their positions to prepare to fight once again. Tension builds as the sun beats down on their heads, and beads of sweat flow freely down their noses.

Horses and riders emerge from the gorge surrounding the fort. A chorus of sighs emerges from behind the barricades. Their relief is in sight as Colonel McPhail and his troops ride up from the vale. Two by two, the horses and riders pop out of the ravine with their flag flying. McPhail arrives at Fort Ridgely with 150 men the day after the second attack on the fort.

Sibley arrives two days later. All officers gather to receive their commander. The townspeople and refugees surround the military entourage. Salutes and greetings are exchanged.

Sibley dismisses the officers and asks, “Where is the officer’s quarters?”

Captain Grant answers, “This way sir.”

Joe Carsoulle steps forward out of the crowd of refugees and asks, “Mr. Sibley?”

“Yes, oh my word. Son what are you doing here?”

Captain Grant, "Son?"

"Yes, I adopted Joe when he was just knee high to a grasshopper."

They all laugh.

Sibley continues, "His parents passed away when he was very young. My wife and I adopted him, we took him in as our own."

Sibley to Joe, "How are you doing?"

"Surviving Sir. We made our way to this fort after our cabin was destroyed."

Sibley, "Destroyed?"

"Yes, the first day of the attack we were warned to leave."

"We?"

Joe Carsoulle, "Yes, my wife and children." He turns to his wife, "This is Jane, and my son Little Joe."

"He is a good-looking young man."

"We have two daughters also."

Sibley, "Where are they?"

"We don't know, we hope you can help us find them. We fear they have been taken captive."

"We will do everything in our power to find them and get them back to you."

Joe Carsoulle, "I'm willing to help."

"Good, we'll need all the help we can get... It has been a long time. Join us we'll catch up."

Joe turns to his wife, "I'll only be a minute."

She nods and returns to the crowd of refugees.

***

Little Crow's village
North of Yellow Medicine Agency

NONE OF THE five Dakota villages are celebrating. Quite the opposite. In each village, groups of warriors and their families gather to discuss their options.

Red Feather, “We cannot win this.”

Little Horn, “We must. There is no other option.”

“But there is. We can leave. We can move west. Where the whites are not.”

“They are everywhere.”

Red Feather, “Not in these numbers.”

“You cannot escape. We must stand and fight.”

"We have fought right alongside you. My brother and many others have died. But we have not won.”

Little Horn, "We defeated them at the Redwood Agency, and the settlers fled. The valley is ours."

"Not for long. We couldn't defeat a fort held by a hundred men or a village of even fewer farmers. We will most certainly be defeated when their army comes.”

“I will stay.”

Red Feather, “I have made my decision for my family. After we lay my brother to rest, we will head west.”

“There is no time to have a ceremony. Those ceremonies are for the old and sick.”

“He deserves a respectful burial, and I and my family will give him one."

Little Horn, “We need to get ready for battle. We are not cowards.”

“Neither are we. We fought alongside you, but we will survive.” He turns to those gathered nearby. “Anyone else wanting to join us are welcome.”

A large group of Dakota families with many braves disperse. They gather their belongings, break down their tepees, roll up the buffalo hides, bundle their infants, and prepare to leave the homeland of their ancestors.

Chapter 20

Wiseman place

Summer of 1863

HENSON CONTINUES HIS journey south along the Missouri River, cutting across bends and going around steep hills. He keeps up a steady pace, riding up the slopes and walking down the other side to rest Wildfire. The glaring sun is high overhead, and his headache increases its torment. His cough is getting worse and becoming more frequent. It is time for another break from this hard leather saddle. With no trees in sight, he dismounts and stretches his weary legs and sore behind.

Wildfire begins grazing as Henson checks his saddlebags for anything to dig a hole. He finds nothing useful and turns his attention to searching for a washcloth. His mind returns to home and a much bigger task for the little boys.

***

Early Summer of 1862

EARLY MORNING BODILY functions have called each family member one at a time.

Andrew returns to the cabin, “It's getting pretty full.”

Pheobe “What is dear?”

“The outhouse.”

"Oh dear, I'll remind your father."

Pheobe takes another long-stemmed ladle of water from the crock and pours it into a cast iron pot.

She continues, "Can you set that over on the stove?"

Andrew responds, "Okay. Sure."

The youngster grabs the pot with both hands. He gingerly walks it across the cabin to the warming stove, and with a clang, he places it on the warming hot plate.

He asks, "What's for breakfast, Ma?"

"I haven't decided yet. Go wake up William and Loren."

"What for?"

Pheobe, "For breakfast. Silly."

"Oh."

Andrew rushes into the kid's cabin. The boy's ruckus can be heard in the main cabin. Soon, three sleepy little boys are sitting by the table.

"How does eggs and bacon sound?"

Andrew, "Do we have enough of both?"

"Nope."

William suggests, "What about grits?"

How about you three go gather eggs?"

All three in harmony, "Ahh Ma."

"Pa, Arthur, and Hannah are already out doing chores. They'll be hungry when they get done, too."

Andrew, "But we can't get the bacon Ma."

"You find Arthur or your father. Let them know I'll need a few pounds of bacon."

Andrew finds Henson and Arthur coming out of the barn.

"Ma says she needs some more bacon."

Henson turns to Arthur, "I guess our chores aren't done yet."

The three men head toward the smokehouse.

Hannah sees where they are going and yells, "I have the eggs."

A short while later, the three men enter the main cabin.

Henson announces, "Here you go, Pheeb, fresh bacon."

Arthur and Andrew head to the wash basin to clean up.

Pheobe smells the stack of bacon, "It is beginning to get ripe."

"That is about the last of it. We'll need to finish the rest with baking or frying it."

Pheobe agrees and says, "Speaking of smelly, Andrew says that the outhouse is almost full."

Henson proclaims, "Damn, I was meaning to get to that."

Arthur stares straight ahead because he knows what it takes to dig a new pit. He and John got to do the last one.

Hannah continues scrubbing clothes in the corner of the cabin.

Pheobe, "Well, it has to be done. We can't wait much longer."

"I know, I know. Well, it might be time for Andrew and William to have a go at it.

Pheobe asks, "Aren't they a little young to be doing that type of digging?"

"Not really. They help dig in the garden."

"They pick up the potatoes and carrots."

Henson, "Either way. It will be good for them."

Arthur smiles at the thought, then instantly wipes the grin off his face so as not to draw attention to his delight.

"Arthur, do we have a couple of good shovels sharpened and ready?"

"I think so. They should be in the wagon shed."

"After breakfast, go fetch those and check if they are good and sharp. Today, before we set out to the grove. We'll get those two started on a new pit."

"Okay, Pa."

Later that morning, four Wiseman men stand staring at the ground, a good twenty feet away from the present latrine. A wooden structure about eight feet wide along the front with a door in the center and four feet from front to back wall. Inside is a bench seat with two oval holes cut in the top.

"Why did you make it with two seats, Pa?" William asks.

Andrew chimes in, "Yeah, only one person uses it at a time."

"It was your mother's idea. Just in case someone was in a hurry, I guess."

Henson and Arthur laugh.

Henson adds, “It leaves more room to store newspapers to read.”

More laughter.

William innocently asks, "What are we going to do, Pa?"

"You and Andrew are going to dig a nice rectangular hole. Right over here."

“A what?”

“Arthur and I will stretch some string lines for you two to make sure the hole is the correct size.”

Andrew, "We gonna do this all by ourselves?"

“Yes. Arthur and I will be busy cutting and splitting wood. We don’t have time for this.”

William ponders, “How deep do we have to go?”

Arthur offers his advice: "The deeper, the better. Then the next time we have to dig another hole, it will be a lot further off."

Henson agrees, “That’s right, so the deeper the better.”

Arthur informs his two younger brothers, "Me and John had to dig the last one."

Andrew asks, "How long ago was that?"

Henson responds, "Quite a few years ago…That was the first one here."

Arthur, “Yep.”

Henson, "Here you two watch, and Arthur and I will get you started."

Henson and Arthur quickly dig an outline inside the string boundaries.

Henson hands his shovel to Andrew, and Arthur his to William.

"Okay, now you two have at it."

The two youngsters each step inside the perimeter and look at each other in bewilderment.

Henson instructs them, "Just like digging potatoes, carrots, or beets."

Each boy places the shovel in the dirt and jump on the shovel to drive it down into the soil.

Henson encourages the two youths, "Yes, just like that, but you might have to put a little more effort into it."

Arthur adds, "The surface crust will be the most difficult, but after that, it will get much easier."

After more encouragement and a few shakes of the head by the older men, the two diggers get into a rhythm. They stand on one side of the string boundary, tossing their half-full shovels of dirt on opposite sides.

Henson sees a problem, "Okay boys. If you both throw the dirt to one side, it will save a lot of work."

Arthur nods in agreement.

After watching them work for a moment, Henson continues, "It looks like you two have this. Ma will come out to check on you, so don't be messing around."

Arthur smiles, "That's right. We expect this to be done when we get home tonight."

Andrew exclaims, "Pa, there is no way."

Arthur giggles, and Henson holds back his chuckle.

Henson assures them, "Don't listen to him. This hole will take a week or so."

William in a defeated tone, "A week?"

Arthur affirms, “At least. It took me and John at least that long.”

Andrew pleads, "Pa, really?"

"It'll get done much faster if you get started digging."

Henson and Arthur pat each young man on the top of their heads and turn to leave.

Henson to Arthur, “How long before those two are fighting?”

"I'll give 'em five minutes."

The two boys begin to dig at a slow but steady pace. Each young man starts shoveling along the short side of the rectangle with their backs to each other. Andrew begins going from the left long side to the other long side along the string line. At the corner, he stops, walks to the original side, and begins again. Andrew widens his new trench with each half-full slice of the shovel.

William works on the other end of the string-bordered hole. He works along the long side until he figures he is halfway. Each time he tries to dig, he has to jump on his shovel to get it to penetrate the hard crust.

In frustration, he says, "This sucks."

Andrew, "Yes, it does." Andrew stops to watch his brother's process. "Here, let me show you."

William responds, "I don't need your help. I can do it just fine."

"It's easier if you only take a thin slice instead of so much at once."

"I know that."

Andrew, "Then why are you taking such large chunks?"

"To get done quicker."

"But it takes longer to do it your way, and it's harder."

William insists, "I'm doing just fine."

"Well, look how much I have done, and see how much you have done."

"I don't care."

Andrew, "Well, I do. I'm not going to do it all by myself."

"You're not. I'm doing it too."

"Then I'll just take a break while you catch up."

William, "You can't do that."

"Watch me."

The two boys come face to face with shovels in hand.

Pheobe interrupts, "You two better put those shovels to work."

William complains, "He was going to take a break."

Andrew whines, "He isn't doing as much as I am."

Pheobe intrudes, "I see the problem. You are both doing it all wrong."

Both, “Huh?”

"Here, let me show you. First, you dig a trench down the middle, and then both of you face each other and work back to the outer edge."

Both boys stare at their mother in astonishment.

“I’ve dug my share of shit holes.”

Pheobe turns, hiding her smile, and heads back to the two cabins.

Both boys’ eyes widen in shock, then turn to stare at each other.

A few hours later, Pheobe, Loren, and Hannah come out to check on their progress. They have dug down a couple of layers, but the edges are beginning to taper in from the top down.

Pheobe announces, "It's time for lunch."

Andrew, “I’m hungry.”

William, “I’m thirsty.”

Pheobe, “Before we go eat, we need to tell you something.”

Both boys ask, "What?"

“The sides need to be straight up and down.”

Hannah holds out her hand, “Here, hand me your shovel. All you have to do is scrap the sides like this.”

She runs the shovel along the sides, curling the soil until about a six-inch ledge of soil remains, "See here, that's how it should look."

Andrew pipes up, “You dug shitholes too?”

Hannah asks in astonishment, “What did you say?”

William adds, “Mom said it.”

Pheobe begins to laugh, “I have.”

Chapter 21

Fort Ridgely

August 31st, 1862

SIBLEY SITS BEHIND a desk with his back to the wall, surrounded by a half circle of Captains and Lieutenants. He discusses the situation when the door opens and Sergeant Bishop enters.

Captain Grant, "What is it, Sergeant?"

Bishop to Sibley, "Sir. We have a delegation here to speak with you."

"How many?"

"Seven, Sir."

Sibley sighs and relents, "Let them in."

The men enter and spread out around the now crowded room.

One of the captains asks, "Would you like us to leave, Sir?"

"No, unless they prefer."

Indian Agent Joe Brown, leader of the delegation, answers, "No, that won't be necessary. This won't take long."

Sibley asks impatiently, "How can I help you?"

"Sir, as you know, some of our families' bodies have been lying out there for over two weeks."

Whispering among two officers begins. Sibley stares at the thoughtless two officers. They stop their conversation.

Sibley, "I know. I am sorry for your loss."

Another man from the group speaks, "Thank you, but we have come to ask you to send out a detachment at least."

"A detachment, to do what exactly?"

A bit annoyed by the question, the settler suggests, "To gather our loved ones remains and provide a decent burial for them."

"Yes. Of course." A bit humbled, he continues. "You do realize there are hostile Sioux out there."

"Yes, I… we do, but we were thinking… "

Sibley interrupts, “I think we can do that… Captain Grant, can you assemble a company of men to take care of this matter?”

Hiram Grant, a thirty-four-year-old Captain, “Yes Sir.”

Sibley turns to Grant, "Don't take any undue risks. Stay together, and when you can, search for any survivors that may still be hiding out there."

“Yes, Sir.”

“Take at least two days rations and report back to me as soon as you return."

"Yes, Sir."

Sibley reminds him, "There is still a good prospect that roaming bands of these renegades are still in the area.”

“Yes, Sir.”

"We have all heard the reports from the survivors who have been straggling in here every few days."

A settler adds, "But, we have heard Little Crow's village is deserted.”

"I have heard the same rumors. If you believe this rumor. It still doesn't reassure me."

Grant asks, “Why wouldn’t that be good news… Sir?”

"It isn't good news because now we have no idea where those renegades may be."

Bishop speaks up, “With your permission, Sir?”

Grant, “By all means.”

“I’ll have the bugler call the men to assembly.”

Sibley adds, "Don't forget the volunteers. They need to assemble also."

***

A few minutes later

CAPTAIN GRANT TO the men gathered in the fort's square, "I will need volunteers for a gruesome detail."

One soldier asks, "What is the detail? Sir?"

"You will be finding and burying bodies. Some dead over two weeks."

A settler, "Oh, god!"

"You will be digging temporary graves."

"Temporary, why temporary? Sir."

Grant, "Because we don't have the time to transport all of them to a cemetery. There are hostiles still out there. This detail will be a very dangerous mission."

Sibley directs Grant, "Take two of our Indian Agents with you."

"Thank you, Sir."

"Yes. Have the Indian Agents accompany the detail. Just in case your detail encounters any Sioux noncombatants and to act as interpreters if needed."

***

GRANT RETURNS, "We have seventy corporals, privates, and fifty civilian volunteers."

Sibley, "Have a detail of privates gather a dozen wagons."

"Yes, Sir."

"Have them fill a couple of the wagons with picks and shovels. The rest are to transport the remains to suitable locations."

Grant asks, "How should I delicate duties?"

"Have half of those fifty men assigned to stand guard the other half handle the bloated and decaying bodies."

"What should our men be doing?"

Sibley, "Have them scout the area for survivors and be on the alert for hostiles."

The convoy makes their way along the river toward the Redwood Agency. They find the remains of bodies near their burned-out cabins, along the road, and near the river. The closer they get to the destroyed agency, the more causalities they find.

The gruesome detail continues for two days. They work their way to what remains of the Redwood Agency.

Captain Grant to Captain Anderson, “What do you think? We haven’t seen any sign of the Sioux. My scouts report there are none in the area. Maybe we should split up so we can cover more ground?”

Anderson replies, “That might be a good idea, but we shouldn’t venture too far. Say within a half-hour ride of our camp."

"That sounds fine with me. I'll take the Cullen Guards with me to Little Crow's village. We will determine if the rumors are true and see if they killed any of the captives there."

Captain Anderson responds, "I'll continue in this area. It seems we have more than enough work to do here."

***

CAPTAIN GRANT AND his men approach the deserted village of Little Crow. Debris from used-up supplies is all that remains. The men search but don’t find any dead bodies of white captives in Little Crow's village. Only the scaffolds of fallen warriors and deceased Dakota villagers

A Sergeant to Captain Grant, “Can my men rummage through these remains for souvenirs.”

“I don’t see why not.”

The men all scatter to scour the former village and death scaffolds for any artifact they can keep as souvenirs.

After a few hours of scavenging, Grant announces to the bugler, “Sound the signal to mount up.” To his sergeant, “That is enough of this. Let’s head back and make camp.”

Sergeant, "Where should we make camp tonight?"

"That knoll across from the agency. Good water and large enough for us all."

Grant and his seventy-five men return to make camp first. The other detail at the burnt-out agency can be seen in the distance, digging graves and burying the dead. They make camp on a flat area near a ravine called Birch Coulee. The area is open enough to pitch tents and gather the numerous wagons in a circle. The gully provides a path for natural spring water and rain run-off from the nearby bluffs. The stream flows down Birch Coulee and empties into the Minnesota River.

***

CHIEFS, BIG EAGLE, Mankato, and Gray Bird lead a band of nearly 200 villagers south along the Minnesota River leading to New Ulm.

A scout reports, "It is true, the village of New Ulm seems to be deserted."

Big Eagle, "Good, there may be food and supplies left behind."

Mankato suggests, "Have some braves go on ahead with the wagons and see what we can use."

***

HALF WAY THERE a scout rides up to Chief Big Eagle, very excited. "We have spotted army troops making camp."

"Where and how many?"

"Near the ravine across the river from the Agency.

Big Eagle repeats, "How many?"

"Under a hundred."

Gray Bird is cautious, "We should not engage them. We should to go on to New Ulm to see what supplies we can find."

Chief Mankato is delighted, “This is a better find.”

Big Eagle adds, "If the town is deserted. It can wait."

Mankato assesses the situation, "That is a good spot. Trees and gullies surround that grassy knoll. That is a good spot."

Big Eagle asks for input, "We have wagons and women. What should we do with them?"

Mankato suggests, "They can stay here. Let's go see for ourselves."

Gray Bird is hesitant, “I don’t like this idea.”

***

CAPTAIN ANDERSON AND the Cullen Guard return to the new camp just after sunset.

***

GRAY BIRD ANNOUNCES with concern, "Damn, there are more."

Big Eagle confidently states, “More to kill.”

Mankato slaps Big Eagle on the shoulders, “The ravine will make for a good place to attack from.”

Big Eagle to Mankato, “You take your braves and surround them on the south and west." Then to Gray Bird, "You take the heavy woods. We attack at first light, before sunrise. We'll leave the women and wagons here until we pin them down. Time to get ready."

***

The Military Encampment

A LIEUTENANT ASKS Captain Grant, "What about pickets? Sir."

Captain Grant takes a moment and responds, "Yes, of course. Set them up evenly spaced around our perimeter. Make it ten placements with three men to each. Each man is to take a turn getting a little sleep while the other two keep their eyes open."

Captain Anderson responds, "You think that's necessary? We just got back from Little Crow's camp. There ain't a soul around there?"

Grant, "You're probably right. There probably ain't an Injun any closer than 30 miles of here. But we might as well be safe about it."

Grant to the Lieutenant, "Lieutenant, you have your orders."

Chapter 22

Special Place by the River

Summer of 1862

LITTLE THUNDER KEEPS a safe distance behind an unaware Chaska. Both travelers are on horseback with different missions. Chaska follows the river bank over game trails that are easy to follow. She ducks behind trees and bushes when long open areas could reveal her.

Chaska's mind wanders, and a smile comes to his face as he anticipates what's ahead.

While Little Thunder's ire increases with every clop of her painted mare. She knows what she will see when she gets there. She has made this same arduous trip many times for a few months now.

"What could he see in that child?"

Still, she follows as if drawn by a physical magnet.

"She isn't even one of us."

Little Thunder watches Chaska duck down to enter the heavily forested area. She seethes with anger as he disappears into the foliage.

She secures her mount, scales the bluff, finds the deer trail along the ridge, and works her way toward their secret hiding place.

"It is you and I, not you and her. We should be together."

***

HANNAH ARRIVES FROM the other direction a little later with a picnic basket.

Chaska hears something, and his head turns automatically.

Hannah pushes branches aside, making her way through the underbrush.

He walks up to her as she enters their special place.

Chaska, "Hi!"

"Hi, good to see ... "

The words are silenced by a kiss.

Chaska leans into Hannah, holding her tight, and the kiss continues.

Little Thunder's pursed lips are so tight they whiten. She does all she can to keep from screaming, "This is not right."

Hannah leans back and sighs, "Let me put the basket down."

"Okay. I just missed you."

"I missed you too..." She puts the picnic basket down. "Okay, where were we."

They return to their embrace. The second kiss is even longer than the first kiss.

Hannah sighs again, "Oh my, you did miss me."

"You doubted me?"

"No, no, I didn't doubt you."

Chaska, "Here, let's set up over here, under our tree."

Chaska opens their hidden, wrapped-up quilted blanket and cloth bags for pillows. Hannah helps spread the blanket and positions the pillows at the base of the tree, the basket at their feet. They lay down, Chaska on his back, Hannah on his left side, one leg over his. She touches his stomach. His hand caresses the side of her face. Hannah slides her hand to his chest, his to her shoulders. He pulls her closer. She doesn't resist. They kiss again.

Little Thunder can't watch anymore. She silently makes her way back to her horse.

Chapter 23

Birch Coulee

The Dakota Encampment

September 1st 1862

IN THE MIDDLE of the night, the Dakota make preparations in the cover of darkness. Seed-laden bromegrass surrounds their adversary's camp.

The military camp is set back under fifty yards from the edge of the Birch Coulee ravine.

Mankato sends the first braves crawling through the high grass before the sun begins to lighten the eastern horizon. The first wave of warriors creep slowly to within a few yards of the pickets. These braves are to take out the pickets silently, then creep in and take the camp while they sleep.

An alert picket yells, "Indians!"

He fires his black-powder musket, and then all hell breaks loose.

The warriors take out the pickets first.

Those soldiers who can, try to run back to the wagons. Many don't make it.

Gunfire and screaming awaken the camp in the early morning darkness, creating chaos. The troops are at a significant disadvantage. The element of surprise has worked again in the Dakota's favor.

***

IN THE CONFUSION a Lieutenant in a panic is overcome with his training.

He yells, "Men, form a line of defense."

Before the command could be rescinded, many of his soldiers fall in the early moments of the battle. Finally, the individual soldier's better judgment takes over amidst the chaos.

Grant orders his Lieutenant, "Spread your men out and cover each side of the camp."

A Sergeant implores his men, "Let's turn over the wagons for protection."

"In the process, we'll be shot."

"But if we don't, we'll be shot."

Soldier admits, "Good point."

"Who'll volunteer to turn 'em over."

"We'll need the strongest of us for that."

Sergeant, "We'll give you cover. The best we can."

While under heavy fire, one after another, they heave and push over all but one of the wagons. As quickly as the wagons are on their sides, other men race in and take positions behind the turned-over wagons. The men give cover fire by shooting at anything that moves in the trees and bushes surrounding them. As they reload their muskets, they notice in anguish that their horses slump to the ground one by one. Like their wagons, all of their horses topple over in a heap.

By daybreak, the situation is clear. They are pinned down.

Captain Grant orders a Lieutenant, "Get me an assessment of our strength."

"Yes, Sir."

When the Lieutenant returns, he reports to Grant, "Sir, there are twenty-two dead, nearly sixty in bad shape, and quite a few others hurting but still able to defend." Without those horses, we have no way out of here. The fort is over 20 miles away."

Grant assesses the situation, "This is not good. The Dakota have taken up multiple positions around our encampment. There are braves using the gullies on both sides of us."

"Yes, Sir, and others are in those trees. Some are climbing high enough to perch themselves in the upper branches."

"Those Sioux over there are using the eroded sloping banks of Birch Coulee for cover."

Lt Baldwin, "Yes, Sir. All we can see of them is when a warrior peeks over the edge. All we can do is wait for them to show themselves. This is not good, Sir."

Grant, "Damn right, it isn't good, Lieutenant… What about our ammunition?"

"Running low quickly, Sir."

"I need you to spread the word to all of the officers. If they haven't already started, have their men dig to create some cover. Besides these wagons, have them use the dead horses, whatever they can find."

Lt. Baldwin asks, "What are we going to do? Captain."

"We are going to wait them out, so make sure you tell them to make every shot counts."

"We have reserve shot and powder in the supply wagon."

Grant asks, "The only wagon not turned over?"

"Yes, Sir. It was too heavy… And they are filling it full of holes."

"Have the men give cover fire for a crew to retrieve that ammunition."

Lt. Baldwin, "There are a lot of boxes in the wagon."

"Then send some volunteers. The Sioux must know what is in it."

"That is possible."

Lieutenant adds a worrisome thought, "Thank god they haven't sent flaming arrows at that wagon."

Captain Grant cringes and dismisses the thought, "Get those men together and get what you can out of there before they think of that."

Baldwin, "Yes, Sir."

Lt. Baldwin low scurries to a group of men huddled behind a wagon. He takes cover among those gathered together.

He utters his request, “I need volunteers to run to that wagon. That one, the only one still standing. And each man will need to bring back a box of our ammunition.”

When no one answers.

“We’ll provide cover fire.”

No one volunteers.

“If we don’t get that powder and lead first, the Sioux may set the wagon a blaze.”

Promptly, four men crawl over to the Lt.

Lt. Baldwin to the messenger, “Spread the word to let the men know we are going to send them out. They'll need to be read to commence cover fire."

A sergeant responds, "Okay."

The sergeant begins to leave. Lt. Baldwin catches his shoulder.

"First. Listen to me. Tell each group to get in threes. First man fires, then the next, got it?”

"Yes, Sir."

Lt. Baldwin, “Each one needs to pick his target and be read to fire when he sees anything move over there.”

"Okay, sounds like a good idea."

"Wait. One more thing. Before the first man fires, the second man should already be aiming and getting ready to pick a target and fire.”

Sergeant, "Okay, I got it."

“The third the same way, while the other two are reloading. Keep up the continuous fire as long as you can."

“Yes, Sir.”

A few minutes later, the sergeant returns, “They are ready to go. Sir.”

Lt. Baldwin looks at his four volunteers, “Are you ready?”

Only one answers, “As ready as we are going to be.”

“Okay, on my call, signal the cover fire.”

Sergeant, “Ready.”

"Fire."

The black powder muskets explode all at once. The runners take off. Both sides of the battlefield erupt. The soldiers behind the turned-over wagons and the warriors in the trees begin firing. Black powder smoke curls from both sides of the battlefield.

***

THE FOUR RUNNERS reach the upright wagon on the soldier's side. Arrows and lead shot strike the wagon. With only minimal cover available, each soldier reaches over the side of the wagon, grabs an ammo box, and begins a slouched run back to the protection of the tipped wagons.

"We made it!" with a sigh from a young, stocky soldier.

Lt Baldwin, "Good job, men. Anyone hit?"

"Not me."

"Not me,"

A farm boy, not 16, "I'll be alright."

"Where are you hit?"

"My leg, Sir, just my leg. I'm able to help, Sir."

Baldwin orders the lad, "Take care of that. And, Yes, get back here as soon as you can."

A soldier opens an ammo box, "Damn, these are the wrong shot."

Lt. Baldwin, "What do you mean?"

"These are the wrong shot. They sent .62 when we have .58 muskets."

"Well, it is better than the other way 'round."

A soldier asks, "What are we going to do?"

"Shave or melt 'em down. Have a few men set up to downsize the lead shot. The necessary tools are all in there."

"What else could go wrong?"

Lt. Baldwin answers, "We could be dead, soldier."

"Right."

The sun continues rising in the clear blue sky, as does the scorching heat. There is no wind, not a cloud in the sky. The pinned-down soldiers are cut off from the river. The Dakota warriors occupy the ravine and have the only access to the stream. It has been three days since the soldiers left the fort, and they were told to only bring enough rations for two. Some men have a bit of jerky left, others nothing at all.

***

The Day Before the Birch Coulee Battle

BIG EAGLE TO one of his runners, "Go get the women and the wagons. Have them set up a camp and get ready to cook. We are going to be here awhile."

The Dakota laying siege are not suffering in the least. The causalities are low, only two dead and four other braves are not seriously wounded. The braves take turns keeping the soldiers pinned down.

***

Back at Fort Ridgely

SIBLEY SUGGESTS, "That burial expedition should have been back by now. I don't feel good about this."

Captain McPhail, "Shall I take a company of men with me to find them, Sir?"

"No, take five companies. I have a bad feeling about this."

"Yes, Sir."

Sibley adds, "And two howitzers. From what Lieutenants Sheehan and Gere say, they don't like cannons."

***

CHIEF MANKATO TO one of his braves, “I need fifty of your braves to set up a watch for the reinforcements from Ft Ridgely. Eventually, they will be coming. We need to know when."

“Good idea.”

“When you see them, you will send a runner back.”

“Yes.”

***

THAT AFTERNOON, ONE of McPhail and his five companies of soldiers approach a wooded area. One of his scouts returns and reports, “Indians ahead.”

Captain McPhail, “Where?”

“In the forest.”

“Sergeant, have the bugler signal a halt.”

“Lieutenant, have our men pull back to that clearing.”

The bugle sounds the directive.

McPhail states, “We were almost in the worst spot.”

“Sir?”

“That narrow passage through the heavily timbered area. The Sioux would have had excellent cover for an ambush.”

Scout asks, “What do we do now?”

“I’m not going to risk my men… We’ll pull back and wait in that clearing.”

After the men have assembled.

McPhail turns to his Lt, "Bring up the cannons."

“Cannons? Sir. Don't you want our infantry?”

McPhail answers with a directive, "No, we need those cannons up here now."

Then, to a Sergeant, "You have our cavalrymen spread out in formation, and when they see one of them, they need to announce it and give the artillery the general direction."

"Seriously?"

"Yes, seriously."

Sergeant, "Yes, Sir, right away."

"Hold on… Then send several men back to the fort to inform Colonel Sibley of our situation."

"Yes, Sir."

The infantry spread out on the perimeter of the grassy field. The artillery crews direct their horses in front of the cannons and wagons with ammunition.

A short time later, a Dakota warrior is spotted.

"Over there."

A private lowers his musket and fires.

Sergeant to the artillery crew, "Fire into the trees over there."

"Another one."

A Second private and his fellow aligned soldiers begin firing into the trees.

McPhail yells, "Bring up the second cannon."

Sergeant, "Permission to fire at will, Sir?"

"Yes, by all means. Don't hesitate."

***

THE DAKOTA AND the besieged troops at Birch Coulee hear two loud rumblings that sound like distant thunder. Mankato didn't need a runner to tell him what it was.

***

MESSENGER TO SIBLEY, "The five companies are held up just before the wooded area. Sir."

"How many hostiles are there."

"No telling. Sir, they have good cover, but McPhail says it looks like a lot. Sir."

"A lot? Well… Thank you private."

Sibley to his Captain, "Every last man, save one company, to assemble."

Bugles shriek, and men run. Horses are saddled, and supplies are loaded. Within an hour, nearly a thousand men file out of Fort Ridgely. They begin their long march to relieve the stranded troops.

***

Birch Coulee

GRANT'S MEN HAVE settled in for the long haul. Their numbers dwindling by the hour, and the wounded and survivors become thirstier by the minute. Reluctantly, the men remove the only shade they have left, their military hats. The hats make too easy a target. The sun and hostile fire continue to beat down on them relentlessly.

***

SIBLEY ARRIVES AT McPhail's position

McPhail acknowledges Sibley, "Good to see you, Sir!"

Sibley nods, "What is the situation?"

"Heavily wooded area, with brush on both sides. We are too vulnerable to march in."

“What would you do with all of these men?”

McPhail answers with a question, “Sir?”

"You are much more prepared and aware of what needs to be done. Let me know what you would do with an extra thousand soldiers?”

"Well, I'd send 300 around to the right along the river and 300 around to the left over the bluff. ... And I'd march right through the remainder when the others are in place."

Sibley to his Captain, “Okay, let’s do it. Six companies to flanking maneuvers on both sides, double time. The remainder set up in formation.”

***

THERE ARE FIFTY Dakota braves waiting along the road in the trees and underbrush. They are split evenly on both sides.

Scout to Gray Bird, “They are preparing to send hundreds of men into the woods.”

“It is time to go.”

***

AN DAKOTA SCOUT reaches the Birch Coulee siege.

He tells Big Eagle, “The troops from the fort are here.”

“How many?”

“The line goes back to the wide bend in the river.”

Big Eagle, “Spread the word for our warriors back out slowly so as not to give it away that we are leaving.”

***

SIBLEY MARCHES ARROGANTLY into Birch Coulee an hour later.

He addresses the beleaguered officer, “Captain Grant.”

Grant states his relief, "Thank god you are here, Sir."

“Time for a chat later. Let’s get these men taken care of.”

"Yes, Sir."

Sibley asks, “How many did we lose?”

“Too many, Sir. Too many!”

Sibley glances about the once war-torn grassy knoll. It is now peaceful but a complete disaster. After orders are given and followed, the horrific sight develops. The dead soldiers lay stacked alongside the splintered wagons. Many of the wagons shattered almost beyond use.

Grant to Sibley, “What should we do with the dead horses?”

Lieutenant, “They are swollen and decomposing hulks.”

Grant affirms this and adds, “Yes, many have already burst.”

Sibley cringes, "I can tell. The stench is overwhelming. Let them rot. Don’t waste time on them. We’ll be out of here soon enough.”

A Lieutenant mentions, "Many of our wounded are too seriously injured or weak to walk.”

Sibley, “Have them placed on the wagons that are usable.”

Grant asks, "Should I have the cavalrymen give up their mounts to convert to teams to pull the wagons?"

“Yes, of course. Have them get on that right away.”

A Lieutenant reports to Sibley, "I've sent details of men to the creek to fetch badly needed water.”

"Good, good. I hope you have troops securing the area for them."

"Yes, I'll seen to that already."

Grant requests, “Can I have what scarce rations your men have with them, passed around to my men?”

"Yes, of course."

Sibley turns to a Lieutenant standing nearby, "Take a note for me."

“Sir?”

“I want to leave a note for Little Crow.”

Lieutenant, “Okay, let me get a piece of paper and pencil.” He begins rummaging through his parcel.

Grant continues the report, "Some of the men are ill, Sir. They are unable to keep anything down.”

"Then don't waste any rations on them. Give them water until they feel up to eating."

“Yes, of course.”

The note-taking Lieutenant to Sibley, "Ready, Colonel."

“Okay, no need for niceties, just something along these lines, if Little Crow has any proposition to make, let him send a half-breed to me, and he shall be protected in and out of my camp.”

“Anything else?”

Sibley’s ire is beginning to peak, “No, just something like that will do.”

“Sir. How will we deliver this message?”

In frustration, he states firmly, "Take a board from one of these wagons and place the note on it."

The bewildered Lieutenant asks, "Sir, how will that work?"

With contempt, he yells, "Damn, do I have to do this myself. Make a stake out of the scraps of one of these wagons, pound it into the ground, split the top, and put the note in the split."

A humble reply from the Lieutenant, "Yes, Sir."

Sibley sighs deeply and explains, "His braves will come to retrieve it. I am sure of it. They will scour the site for anything they can salvage."

Grant to his Lieutenant, “You have your orders.”

Sibley interrupts, "One last thing, Lieutenant, have all of their arrows collected and broken."

The confused Lieutenant just stands there with a blank stare.

“They will come back to collect anything useful to them. It takes months to craft a good arrow. Without arrows, they can’t fight.”

Lieutenant, "Yes, Sir. I understand now."

Sibley to Grant, “Have you given the order to bury the dead?”

"No, Sir."

“Have the men from our relief column assigned to that detail. Your men have been through enough.”

After everyone but Grant had left, Sibley postulates, “The Minneapolis press will have a hay day with this.”

“Sir?”

"The insolent editorialists will drag me over the coals for this.”

Grant, “Sir, it was my… and Captain Anderson’s decision to camp here.”

"That won't matter to them...

Well, I won't have it."

Grant questions his statement, "Have what, Sir?"

“The blame. Captain, who recommended this location?"

"We both considered it a good location. It has good access to water, and it is away from the Lower Agency."

Sibley repeats himself, “Who chose this location?”

“Joe pointed it out, but we made the decision.”

"Joe Brown, the half-breed Indian Agent?"

Grant nods.

“Okay. That will work.”

“But…”

“Sibley, "No, it is settled."

Chapter 24

Henson continues his journey home.

August 4th, 1863

HENSON COUGHS REPEATEDLY, his body aches from the constant riding and walking. What little rest he attempts is always interrupted by thoughts of home. His children's last words before he left in the belief he would be assisting the US government in protecting his and all of the neighbor's settlements. Henson's handkerchief is soiled and almost useless.

To Wildfire, "I'll wash it when we reach the river."

He spots a decent-sized wooded area along the river and says aloud, "That is a great stand of timber."

He rides to the edge and admires the uncut timber, imagining what he could do with this variety of wood. Then, his mind returns to his home place. Back to the times when he and his sons, John, Benjamin, and Arthur, chopped down trees, which was always done in the early fall. The fallen trees are left to cure until spring, then sectioned and split in the late summer of the following year. He remembers the teamwork of hauling split wood to the river's edge to be sold to steamers. He recalls working with his sons hauling the other longer lengths to Lewis Jones' sawmill to be sold. Lewis would cut it up for lumber to build new houses, homes, businesses, and sheds. He remembers the story his wife told him one night after he returned from hauling lumber to the Lewis Jones' sawmill.

***

PHEOBE STATES ALOUD as Henson and Arthur walk through the door, "Do you know what 'your' little boys have been up to?"

Pheobe vigorously cleans crawdads at the end of the counter in the kitchen area of the main log cabin.

Arthur tosses his light jacket over the back of a chair. Henson motions for Arthur to hang up his jacket on a peg by the door, as he does the same.

"My little boys? I guess they got into something. They are only mine when they are in trouble."

Arthur laughs, takes a seat at the table, and begins grinning ear to ear, awaiting the story.

"Oh yes, they got into something alright. I swear it is going to storm."

Henson replies with a smile at Arthur, "A cloud bank is forming on the horizon."

Pheobe, "Oh, you men. You think this is so funny."

"Now, now, Pheeb, what did they do now?"

"Hannah has been busy cleaning up after those three since they got home."

Henson recalls his final question before the story begins, "Cleaning up, will I need to have them fetch a stick?"

Pheobe sighs and suppresses her laugh, "No I don't think that will be necessary. Extra chores would be in line though. They ventured over to Bow Creek."

"Oh no."

***

Earlier that day

ANDREW AND WILLIAM stand on the edge of a box elder tree-lined bank of a small creek. The watery stream flows about six feet below them. One of the many cool-flowing springs that feed the stream is nearby. They have chosen a fishing hole upstream and a good distance away from the Mighty Mo. With fishing poles and tin-bucket in hand, they make their way down the black dirt slope leading to the water's edge.

Their father whittled their poles from weeping willow branches into useable fishing equipment. The green branches are springy enough to give and not break. Henson cut a breach in the thick end, then stuck another short stick in the gap at a right angle. He then bound it firmly with a beeswax-coated string. The small stick positioned out to the side of the pole is to wrap the extra fishing line.

Their bait is leftover roasted ham slices from last night's supper.

Andrew says, "This should be a good spot."

William complains, "It's not very wide here."

"No, but none of it is very wide out here. That is what makes it a good spot."

"Let's give it a try."

The two young gents set their tin bucket behind them, higher up the bank, and their poles beside them. They each pluck the hook jammed into the top of their poles and attach a piece of ham. Each young fisherman dangles their bait over the water and drops it in, causing tiny ripples to spread from one side of the two-foot-wide creek to the other.

Now they wait.

William breaks the silence, "Think this is going to work?"

"I don't know. Arthur said he done it plenty, and he says he, John, and Benjamin caught stuff."

William's eyes brighten at the prospects.

Minutes seem like an eternity.

William pulls the bait up and out of the water to discover a crawdad dangling precariously from the ham slice. With a gentle swing of the pole and line to the bank, the shrimp, like a freshwater crustacean, falls on the bank. The prawn immediately turns to defend itself from

William's grasp. He carefully picks the crawdad up behind its snippers and drops it into the tin bucket and closes the wooden lid.

Andrew suggests, "Get a stick to pin the bucket to."

"Okay."

Andrew pulls his bait out to find a crawdad on his bait also. The two boys continue this until the crayfish in the narrow stream are nearly depleted.

When boredom sets in, Andrew has an idea, "What if we build a damn."

William, "A what?"

"We use some of these sticks and rocks and block the water to make a big pond."

"I don't know if that is a good idea. I don't think it will work."

Andrew insists, "Sure, it will work. Then we can catch fish instead of just these little crawdads. If there is more water, we could catch some big fish."

"Really, like Bullheads?"

"Sure, maybe carp like Pa and Arthur catch out of the river."

William, "Maybe even catfish."

"Yeah, them too."

"Okay, what should I do?"

Andrew stands, "Here. You use both poles while I find some more branches."

William sits there with both poles, watching his brother scavenge for sticks and tree bark.

With nothing biting, he asks, "What can I do?"

"Gather any good-sized rocks you can find."

"Okay."

Now, both boys are diligently hunting material to place in the creek. Andrew lays some sizeable branches across the water, and water flows over the branch unimpeded.

William whines, "That doesn't seem to be working."

"No, we aren't even started yet."

Andrew places more branches and bark in the water, sticking the material in the mud. He works diligently as William gathers more stuff.

William returns to say, "That's working."

"Bring me more stuff."

"Like what?"

Andrew suggests, "The water is seeping through the holes between the branches and bark."

"Can you use mud to fill the holes?"

"Sure, good idea."

Andrew scoops a handful of mud from the creek bed and slaps it into place.

Andrew, "That will work. Maybe bring grass and leaves."

"Okay."

William hustles nearby, pulling grass from the ground and gathering fallen dried leaves.

William, "Here. Will this work?"

"Let's see."

Andrew stuffs the grass and packs it with mud. The water is backing up ever so slowly, but it is working.

Andrew orders his brother, "I need more grass and leaves."

"I am doing the best I can."

William returns with an arm full of bromegrass and lays it by Andrew.

William asks, "Can I help?"

"You are gathering stuff, is helping."

"I mean building it."

Andrew relents, "Sure, I don't see why not. I'll work on this side, and you work on that side."

The two boys set to work. The dam of branches and sticks begins to grow higher and higher.

William says, "The water is coming around the edge."

"Then we have to build it wider."

William smiles and heads for more material.

Moments later, William announces, "I found this!"

He carries a rock too large to carry upright for the nine-year-old.

Andrew, "That will work great in the center to hold the branches in place… Here, give it to me."

"No, it's mine, I got it."

"Over here."

William, "Okay, here."

"Yeah, sure."

William drops the rock, splashing the two boys with mud and muck. They both begin to laugh.

Andrew, "We need more stuff."

The two boys run for more leaves, grass, and branches, wading in and out of the creek. They dig mud from the standing water side of the growing pond to pack the front of the dam's surface. Once rolled up, shirt sleeves and pant legs fall from the weight of the sludge and creek water. With filthy hands, they reroll them, as well as their pant legs, in a failed attempt at staying clean and dry.

While they toil diligently at their dam building, their poles go unattended. The water rises high enough to begin submerging both poles and almost reaches the covered tin bucket full of crawdads.

Andrew exclaims, "Our poles!"

"I'll get them."

All of a sudden, on the top of the bank, they see Boots. The canine begins to bark dismissively at the two dam builders. Loren then appears next to their family pet.

Loren asks, "What are you doing?"

Andrew snidely responds, "What's it look like?"

"I don't know."

William answers, "It's a dam."

"Can I help?"

Andrew, "No, you are too little."

"Am not!"

William, "If we don't let him, he'll tell."

"You are right."

Andrew to Loren, "Only if you help gather grass, leaves, and sticks."

Loren, "Okay."

Loren scampers down the tall bank and is off gathering material.

The two builders continue increasing the size and width of the damn till the reservoir is almost knee high and over twelve feet wide. With no regard for their clothes, they wander in the depths of their creation, pulling mud from the bottom of the new reservoir to smear over the rocks, branches, and sticks.

Andrew, "If we build the sides higher first and let the water run over the center till we have it higher."

William, "Then what?"

"Then, when the sides are done, we can close in the center and let it fill up."

"Yeah, that should work."

Andrew, "Yeah, let's do it."

Boots sits on the banks of the reservoir.

The three little boys work diligently on their creation. Ignoring their four-legged friend. He wanders into the water next to Andrew for some attention but is shooed away, "Not now, boy, I am busy."

The four-legged friend wades through the new pond, now well over belly deep on the mangy Shepherd Collie. Reaching William's side of the new pond, he steps out and shakes off the creek water.

"Ah, boy, why did you have to do that right here?"

Andrew laughs, and so does Loren.

William, "You think that's funny, do ya."

"Yeah!" says Andrew

William stoops over and digs deep down in the pond water.

Andrew, "Oh, no, you don't!"

Andrew quickly bends over and digs into the retained pond of water, only to feel the plop of slimy mud stick to his side.

Andrew, "Oh, now you are going to get it."

He tosses his hand full of mud at William, splattering him with a dark gray, smelly substance.

Loren, "Mud fight!"

Both older boys say, "No, don't!"

Too late, Loren has stepped in the pond, almost crotch-deep on the nearly four-year-old. He bends over to scoop up mud but slips and sits. The water is chest-high on Loren.

The older two begin to laugh as Loren starts to cry. The two boys look at each other, realizing what they have done.

Andrew wades over to his little brother, "Loren, it's alright."

William tries to help him stand up, reaching out his hand to his little brother. Loren takes it and tugs in an attempt to get up, but William is pulled off balance and goes face-first into the water. Loren joins Andrew with a boisterous laugh now. William stands up, soaking wet from head to toe.

Andrew tries to make his way to the creek's bank, slipping and sliding all the way still laughing hysterically.

Loren and William look at each other and nod.

Andrew's eyes get really big, "Oh no, you don't!"

William yells, "Get him!"

Double-teamed, Andrew goes back-first into the water. Now, all three are drenched and covered with mud. They wade to the creek's bank, looking at each other, covered in mud and muck. With nothing to dry off with, they stand there dripping.

Loren speaks first, "I'm cold."

Andrew suggests, "We better get home."

William, "Yeah."

With their trusted canine, the three mud ducks make their way to the creek's bank, grab their fishing poles, the bucket of crawdads, and start across the grass-covered prairie toward home.

***

HANNAH PULLS CLOTHES pins from the sheets hanging on the line. She looks over her shoulders to see the three dark figures walking slowly across the hay field.

"Oh my!"

As they get closer, she calls out in a loud whisper, "You guys are going to be in big trouble."

Andrew shivers, "We know."

"Go behind the barn and wait there. I'll go get some clothes for you. Here, wrap up in this."

She gives each shaking boy a clean towel to put over their shoulders.

The three lads waddle toward the barn.

Hannah grabs her basket and turns to go to the twin log cabins. Halfway there, Pheobe steps out of the front door of the main cabin, shaking her head.

Pheobe states in disbelief, "Boys! I swear it is going to storm."

"I'll get them a change of clothes."

"Better take 'em a bar of soap, too."

"Okay." Hannah giggles.

"Tell them to use the horse tank. I swear."

"Yes, mama. It's going to storm."

Hannah laughs to herself.

"Tell them, just wait until their father gets home."

"Oh, yes, mama. I'll tell them."

Pheobe disgust quickly disappears with a grin, "I tell ya, it must be gunna storm."

Chapter 25

Little Crow's Village

September 3rd, 1862

LITTLE CROW AND his shrinking band of warriors hold a council. The most trusted warriors sit around a roaring fire. The mood is solemn, and all are discouraged.

An anonymous warrior asks, "What are we to do now?"

Gray Bird insists, "We must attack again."

Little Crow shakes his head and answers, "We need a different plan."

Wowinape, "What else can we do?"

Gray Bird, "The barricades are too reinforced at the fort."

"At the town of New Ulm, too."

Walks Among Sacred Stones speaks up, "If we get Red Middle Voice and Shakopee to join us, we can defeat the whites."

Little Crow dismisses the suggestion, "They are too busy attacking farmhouses."

"But they are effective. The whites are leaving the valley."

"That might be, but the white man's army is assembling and getting supplies."

Walks Among Sacred Stones asks, "Then what should we do?"

Little Crow pauses for a moment, "We prevent their ability to get new supplies and soldiers."

Gray Bird asks, "How do we do that?"

"We can send some of our braves to attack steamers on the river. Walks Among Sacred Stones, "That will slow them down or completely stop their ability to get reinforcements."

Wowinape nods his head in agreement.

Gray Bird asks, "But what about the land roads?"

Little Crow's eye widens, "You are right. They can send men and supplies by dirt roads."

Walks Among Sacred Stones suggests, “We can cut those off also.”

Little Crow, “That is what we will do.”

***

LITTLE CROW AND his band venture deep into the Big Woods. They are northeast of Little Crow's village and the burnt-out Redwood agency. He and his band of nearly two hundred warriors spread out on both sides of the two-wheeled path that leads to St. Paul. It branches out to numerous villages along the way, including St Peter and the rest of the lower Minnesota River valley.

A scouting party returns to report to Little Crow, “We have discovered a group of white men.”

“How many?”

“Maybe fifty.”

Little Crow ponders and then asks, “Military?”

“They are not wearing uniforms, but they look and act like army men.”

“Where are they?”

The scout replies, “They are on the move.”

A frustrated Little Crow asks, “Then where are they headed?”

"I am not for sure. They seem to be going toward a small town the whites call Forest City.”

“But that is nearly twenty miles from there.”

Walks Among Sacred Stones inquires, “They only have fifty men?”

The scout adds, "That is a close guess. I think. We didn't want to be seen."

“We need to get to them before they get to the town.”

Little Crow considers the situation, "The sun will be setting soon. They will have to camp for the night."

Walks Among Sacred Stones, “We should attack them before they make camp.”

The scout asks, “Out in the open?”

Little Crow disagrees, “No, not this close to sunset. Let them make camp. We need a good plan and a restful night’s sleep.”

Walks Among Sacred Stones, “What are you crazy?”

“No, I am not. We don’t have a plan.”

“Why don’t we just attack now?”

Little Crow, “Because our men are tired. We have been on the move all day.”

“Okay, how do we find a good location to attack.”

“We should wait until they make camp.”

Walks Among Sacred Stones, “Why do we need to wait?”

Little Crow dismisses his question and tells the scout, “You and your men follow them. Send back word when they have made camp and where.”

He and his braves hurry off on their assignment.

Little Crow squats down to draw in the dirt. He then says to Walks Among Sacred Stones. “You will take two-thirds of our braves with you.”

“Split our forces? Why?”

"You will understand. Just listen. Once the soldiers make camp for the night, I will send you out to find a place to set up an ambush.”

Walks Among Sacred Stones asks, "And ambush? There is not much out here to hide behind. It is mostly grass and not much else."

“Their roads usually go around the hills or in between them.”

Wowinape asks, "What are you thinking?"

Little Crow explains, "The grass may be all that we need. From the path looking up on the hillside, our warriors will be out of sight."

“I’m not so sure.”

“We will do the planning tonight. It will work.”

Walks Among Sacred Stones asks again, “But where? How can we find a suitable place for a surprise attack in the dark?”

"There is nearly a full moon and no clouds in the sky. I am confident we will be able to find a location somewhere between their camp and Forest City."

"Okay, when the scouts return, we will take another party out to find a location."

Little Crow explains, "It has to be a valley with plenty of high grass."

"I don't know if that will be enough."

"Any two hills. Any two that their path goes between will be a good place."

Walks Among Sacred Stones asks, "What are you going to do with your third of the warriors?"

"I will take the rest of our warriors all the way around to get behind them."

"I see. We'll have them surrounded… How will we know when to attack?"

Little Crow contemplates his decision, "In the morning, they always sound their bugles to awaken their men to get ready. It takes them an hour or so to eat and get started. You will have our warriors get into position before the second bugle. Which is their signal to mount up, and it will be our signal to get ready for the attack. Have your men in place and ready. Split your men on both sides of a valley. Keep a small group of braves with you to block their path, not enough to concern them, but to bring them to a halt. When they come to a halt and before they sound the bugle. Attack."

Walks Among Sacred Stones, "Trapping them in the valley."

"Yes, and we will be right behind them."

"There will be no way out."

***

CAPTAIN STROUT AND his nearly fifty volunteers rest peacefully through the night. The bugle call awakens them to prepare for a short day of marching. If everything goes as planned, they should be in Forest City as early as noon. Long before daylight, they eat their slimy gruel and then saddle their horses. The second bugle call signals for the men to assemble in formation to move out. Soon, they are plodding along the unremarkable road again. Two by two, they march, some still half asleep. The sun hasn't risen above the horizon.

A corporal shouts, “Sergeant!”

“What is it?”

“Indians.”

The sergeant yells, “Captain!”

Strout announces, “Company halt!” He attempts to assess the situation. They find themselves in a narrow valley banked by tall grass-covered, gently rolling hills. A couple dozen Dakota sit on horseback, muskets and bows drawn, across the only established path through this valley.

Captain Strout to his sergeant, “They must be suicidal. There can’t be but twenty of ‘em.”

Sergeant, “Don’t be so sure.”

“What do you mean, Sergeant?”

"The tall grass, Sir. The tall grass can conceal them."

Strout, “Bugler, the assemble to form a line!”

"These are recruits. They haven't drilled for this."

"We don't have a choice. These recruits will have to figure it out."

The sergeant asks again, "Are you sure you want to do this, Captain?”

The bugler sounds his directive. The men begin to dismount.

Walks Among Sacred Stones fires his musket, and shouts in his native tongue, “Now!”

An excited Sergeant announces, "The hills, Sir, … The hills on both sides, Sir."

The musket fire is the signal his remaining warriors know is to attack. Both sides of the hill explode,

After the first volley, the Dakota warriors begin as they always do, with a high-pitched, blood-curdling scream. Arrows and lead shots fall upon the unorganized troops.

The untrained recruits attempt to return fire, but their attempt at a defensive line quickly collapses.

Little Crow's men attack the rear of the retreating formation.

The sergeant yells, "We are surrounded, Sir."

Captain Strout orders, "Have them mount up. Sound the attack. We'll have to fight our way out."

"The wagon?"

"Leave it!"

Sergeant questions in the heat of battle, "Our men, the wounded?"

"Leave them. We'll have to come back for them… Sound the charge!"

The bugler blows his horn to no one listening. Some of the men, those lucky enough, mount up on a horse, anyone's horse, and ride for any gap in the warrior's line. All others flee on foot and are quickly cut down. Both sides exchange fire as the green troops ride for their lives past the attackers.

***

WALKS AMONG SACRED Stones' warriors follow Strout and the few of his men who escape. The pursuers continue to flank the retreating militia relentlessly on both sides.

Little Crow to his braves, "Return to the battlefield. Take anything, we can use. Anything the troops left behind."

"The wagons and horses?"

"Yes, there may be munitions and food."

A Dakota brave, "What about their wounded men."

"What about them?" When the brave did not answer, Little Crow continues, "They wouldn't let us live."

***

AS THE RETREATING force approach Hutchinson, Walks On Sacred Stones calls off the pursuit. At the top of the hill, he waits for his closest warrior.

Little Crow rides up alongside and says, "They have made preparations like New Ulm."

"Yes, just like at New Ulm and Fort Ridgely."

The Hutchinson villagers have been building a stockade for the previous week. They constructed a 100-square-foot enclosure from dismantled log cabins and timber from the nearby forest. The builders of the log enclosure left four-inch holes in the walls to fire their muskets. They even dug a ditch, a moot of sorts, around the makeshift fortress, ten feet wide and nearly three feet deep.

The sun has barely escaped the treetops in the distance. Little Crow and his followers watch the village defenders rush to the security of the walled enclosure.

Walks Among Sacred Stones, "What are we going to do now?"

"Have your braves search the countryside, take what is useful, burn everything. When you are done, come back here."

"What will you do?"

Little Crow, "The same, but all around their walled fort."

Walks Among Sacred Stones and his warriors ride off on their mission.

Wowinape, "Father, what will we do?"

"Son, look before you. What do you see?"

"A white man's village."

Little Crow, "If you look closer, you'd see their farmers still in the fields."

“Yes, I see them.”

“Do you see the buildings that are not inside the walls?”

Wowinape, “Yes, of course.”

“We will burn them one by one as they watch.”

“Then we are going to attack.”

Little Crow cautions his son, "We will carefully approach, and they will see their buildings go up in flames."

Little Crow sends in a group of warriors to approach the town. "You are to stay out of the line of fire. I want you to determine if the outer buildings are vacant."

"We understand."

***

CAPTAIN STROUT TO over a dozen men hell-bent on defending the outer buildings, “It is suicide to defend those buildings. We should remain behind these walls.”

The hotel owner disagrees, "That building is all I have. I will offer any man willing to defend my property a hundred dollars apiece.

A bystander, “That is more than what I make in a year. I’ll do it.”

A crowd of men approach the hotel owner.

A farmer named Heller disagrees with Captain Strout, “Those buildings mean nothing to you, they aren’t yours. Those buildings are all we have. We have to try.”

"You are all crazy, and if we open the gates, it could jeopardize all of our safety."

“We are going whether you come with us or not.”

An inflexible Captain Strout: "I'm not putting my men in danger for your foolishness."

Heller insists, “I’m going. Who is with me.”

A group of nearly fifteen men gather at the gate.”

Captain Strout, "I order you to stand down."

Hotel owner turns away from Strout and yells, "Open the gate."

A mild-mannered villager lifts the brace and opens the gate. As planned, fifteen men scatter to different buildings. Most of the other Hutchinson citizens take up positions inside the walls.

***

THE DAKOTA WARRIORS approach with stealth. They first occupy sheds, then homes and businesses, setting fire to the town one building at a time.

As the buildings go up in flames, the men of Hutchinson gradually retreat to the hotel.

The warriors continue to close in on the stockade. They notice the musket barrels firing from the openings in the wall. As instructed by Little Crow, they stay out of musket range.

The war party approaches a nearby farm place with four outer buildings and a house.

A farmer named Heller exclaims, "They are going to burn my farm."

One of the other men held up in the hotel, "There is nothing we can do."

"I can stop them. That is what I can do."

"You'd be out in the open."

Heller insists, "Let me out of here."

The leader relents and yells, "Open the door for this fool. But only him."

Heller runs toward his farmhouse with musket in hand.

***

WALKS AMONG SACRED Stones, "We have a brave one."

A warrior takes aim, "He is mine."

Heller stops to aim.

Two shots ring out. Heller tumbles to the ground in pain. A red stain flows from his thigh. He uses his empty musket to get back on his feet and then turns back toward the stockade.

The brave who shot Heller nudges his mount forward, pulls his bow, places an arrow across the taut string, and goes after the wounded man. Heller hobbles as quickly as he can. Musket fire erupts from the hotel and walls of the stockade. The warrior halts his stead and retreats.

***

LITTLE CROW TO another warrior, "Take your warriors to the North of the walls and position half of your braves on the road to the village they call Glencoe."

"Why spread ourselves so thin?"

"When the villagers see the outer building in flames, they will certainly understand their log walls will be next. They will try to escape to that village."

***

FROM INSIDE THE wall, the citizens lament the destruction of their village. The villagers sob with fright as the black smoke rises from the schoolhouse and the steam driven sawmill.

Little Crow's men encircle the entire village.

Walks Among Sacred Stones and his warriors attempt to send flaming arrows toward the innermost buildings on the west side of the walled enclosure. But the defenders opened fire and and other put out the flames.

Red Trail, one of Little Crow's warriors, yells to the defenders, "Come out of your hiding place. Come out here in the open and fight like men."

The challenge is not answered.

***

A COLUMN OF warriors approach Little Crow's position. They bring back wagons filled with food and anything they could use before burning the outer structures. The braves have captured over a hundred horses and oxen.

A lone scout approaches swiftly from the north. He rides from those braves sent to the road to Glencoe.

He reports to Little Crow, "Soldiers are coming up the road."

"How many?"

"Not certain, but more than we have here."

"How far out are they?"

"Our braves say close."

Little Crow, "Send word to all warriors. It is time to end this."

***

Around three in the afternoon, inside the walls of the Hutchinson stockade, a picket yells, "A large number of riders are approaching coming from the north."

The women begin pulling their hair out in frustration and fear of the worst. The men start planning and cursing. Everyone is certain it is more Dakota attackers.

Minutes later, the same picket announces, "They are soldiers!"

Women faint, and men begin falling to their knees in prayer.

The Dakota attackers are long gone.

Chapter 26

Chaska's Yankton Lakota Village

Mid-Summer 1862

TWO MIDDLE-AGED Lakota men work together to carve up an already-skinned deer carcass.

Roaring Cloud cuts while the other holds the slippery meat in place. He slices repeatedly through the joint area of the leg of the deer.

Roaring Cloud asks, "Did you try to convince your son to work this out with my Little Thunder?"

Black Elk stands face to face, holding the carcass in place, "Of course I did. But he said it was not possible."

"All things are possible. Your Chaska just had to try harder."

"He said he did try, but your daughter wouldn't listen."

Roaring Cloud looks at his friend in disbelief, "Seems your son is not a man yet."

"What are you trying to say?" Black Elk stands back and glares at his friend.

"A true man would have taken control of his woman."

Black Elk repositions himself over the middle of the carcass, "Really? That is how you would want your daughter treated."

"Her mother was a strong-minded woman, too."

"She still is."

Roaring Cloud stares at Black Elk. Anger fills his eyes.

Little Thunder's father continues slicing, "She is nothing like she was as a young woman."

"And how did you tame her?"

"She learned to listen. I am the chief in our tepee."

Black Elk, "Really?."

"What is that supposed to mean?"

"If that were the case, your daughter hasn't learned the same lesson."

"She minds me. The rest was up to your son." Roaring Cloud insists

"Not anymore."

"I guess he was not up to the task."

Black Elk's face hardens, he turns his head in anger, and his ire increases. "He has proven himself over and over again, the robes, blanket, and horses. All of that was enough to prove to you he was worthy."

"I guess it wasn't enough. Your son hasn't learned how to control his woman."

"He has learned to tame horses and hunt buffalo. How to be a Lakota brave."

The leg is separated, and Black Elk lays it across their workspace.

Roaring Cloud wipes his knife, "But not so good with his woman."

"I have heard enough. You should have taught your daughter to respect her husband."

"I have heard enough also. I can handle the rest of this myself."

***

BLACK ELK THROWS back the buffalo skin flap and enters his tepee. To his wife, "Roaring Cloud is becoming more and more unreasonable."

Shining Moon mends buffalo hide for their multiple tepees, "What is it now?"

"He blames this on Chaska."

He takes a seat on one of the many hides used for blankets.

"The failed relationship between his unruly daughter and Chaska?"

Black Elk replies, "Yes, and he blames us too."

"Us?"

"Yes, he says we should have trained him on how to control his woman."

Shining Moon sarcastically replies, "Like he treated Red Dove?"

"What are you saying?"

"You probably didn't notice, but he brutalized her in the first years of their marriage."

Black Elk, "No. I didn't notice."

"I didn't think so. Many times, she would come to me to cry."

"He beat her?"

Shining Moon, "Yes, and tormented her verbally too."

"I never knew."

"You two were off hunting or fishing, I suppose. Too busy to notice us women. Until you wanted something."

Black Elk, "That is not fair. We were taking care of our village, feeding those who had no one or were not capable. Either too old or inexperienced."

"Yes, you were doing good things for our village. But many times, she would hide her bruises from the village."

"I didn't know."

Shining Moon, "He finally stopped."

"Good."

"She finally threatened him."

"What?" A surprised Black Elk asks.

"She told me she was sharpening a knife one day when he came home. And he was displeased with something again."

"An unsuccessful hunt?"

Shining Moon, "She didn't say. But she told me she told him if he touched her again in anger, he would wake up with no balls."

"Really?"

"That is what she told me."

Black Elk, "He never mentioned any of this to me. And we have been friends forever."

"Some people keep secrets."

"You would never have done that to me?"

Shining Moon, "Keep secrets?"

"Ohhhh, what?"

She laughs, "No, dear. You wouldn't have a dick either."

"You never… "

"I am joking. You have always treated me with respect. Just as we have raised Chaska to treat others."

Black Elk, “She really threatened him?”

"She is good at sharpening knives." Shining Moon pauses, then continues, "You cannot tell him you know."

“Yes, it will be a secret.”

Shining Moon, “We all have our secrets.”

“You don’t have secrets from me?”

“You will never know.”

She laughs, and he frowns.

Black Elk rolls to the side to stand and leaves the tepee. Outside, he begins readying the cooking fire by stacking kindling and wood in the fire pit.

Shining Moon comes outside to assist, "Are you two going to still be friends?"

“I’m not sure. He has insulted us and our son.”

“Our son has defamed their daughter.”

Black Elk, “That is different.”

“How so?”

“Chaska and Little Thunder were going to be married.”

Shining Moon, “And?”

“And our friendship has been since we were children.”

“Yes, that is a long time.”

Black Elk, “Their lives together were only beginning.”

“And your friendship might now end.”

“They seemed like a good match.”

Shining Moon, “Yes, but we were wrong.”

"Maybe I could have taught him how to talk to a woman."

“What do you mean?”

Black Elk, “You know, sit him down and explain how things work. How to convince her how it should be.”

“Like?”

"Oh, this is not going to work. I see that now."

Shining Moon, “We raised him to respect all things, all living and nonliving. We did a good job. They didn’t raise Little Thunder with the same values.”

“So, it is their fault.”

"Don't you go off on some high horse.

Black Elk, "I won't.

"There are many ways to raise children. We prefer our way."

"But we did good, though?"

"Yes, we did. Chaska is a fine man."

“But he is a bit of a loner.”

Shining Moon, “What is wrong with that?”

“Most men need male friends. To go hunting and fishing.”

“Chasing women?”

Black Elk, "I didn't chase any other woman. You were my parent's first choice."

“And yours?”

“My parents picked the right woman for me.”

Shining Moon, “And who would you have chosen?”

“You.”

“Good answer.”

Black Elk sighs, "But he is quite different from me. He has no problem going off alone. On his own private vision quests."

“What is wrong with that?”

"Nothing, I guess. I never did that. I always had many male friends to hunt and fish with."

Shining Moon, “And…”

"And nothing. We always hung out in large groups. It was always more productive when we hunted in groups."

“You think he has problems making friends?”

Black Elk, “I am not sure. He has Little Eagle as a good friend.”

“They go hunting and fishing together.”

“Yes, but not recently.”

Shining Moon, "That group of messengers has arrived, and many of our young braves are drawn to them."

"Strangers from a strange land. They say they live in the forests along a river. That is so different from here. There must be a lot of deer in those woods."

“But not so many buffalo.”

Black Elk, “No, not as much buffalo. They bring news of dark times for our people.”

“We have seen some of what they say is coming with Agent Burleigh.”

"We have gotten past that, I hope. We received our annuities. They say theirs never arrived."

Shining Moon, "More and more whites come here, too."

“Yes, they do, but they stay off our reservation.”

“Maybe because we are restricted to the worst ground. No farmer would want our dry sandy soil.”

Black Elk, “I know. That is true. There may be dark times ahead.”

“What will we leave our son with?”

“What do you mean?”

Shining Moon, "You and your friends were free to go wherever you wanted. He will be restricted to this reservation land that cannot support our village. He and our village will rely on what the whites provide us."

“Our chiefs made the decision for us. We must abide by their decision.”

"Even if it is the death of our people."

Black Elk, “It won’t be that bad.”

“Maybe he will become a leader and find a way to change all of this.”

“He’ll need friends to do that.”

Shining Moon, "He'll do fine. He has shown he is a skillful hunter."

“You sound like Little Thunder.”

"She was right about some things, and that was one of them."

Black Elk nods in agreement, “You know who she is chasing now?”

“Who?”

“Little Thunder.”

Shining Moon, "I knew who you meant. Who is she after?"
“Ohhhh, the leader of the messengers. Killing Ghost.”
“He seems very angry. That might not be very good for her.”
Black Elk, "He may be more like her father. The part I didn't know."

Chapter 27

Governor's Office in Minnesota

September 7th, 1862

THE GOVERNOR'S AID enters the governor's office and declares, "There are reports of an attack on Fort Abercrombie and other locations in the Northwestern part of the State."

Ramsey asks, "When did this happen?"

"I am not sure. The newspapers in St. Paul are reporting it."

"Why wasn't I informed first."

The aide replies, "I don't know, Sir... But they are asking for assistance."

"Send a telegraph for men, arms, and horses."

"From who?"

Ramsey explains, "President Lincoln of course. We need help from the Federal government."

"That will take weeks, Sir."

"Well, this won't blow over soon. We'll raise local volunteers in the meantime."

Aid asks, "Okay, what else should I ask for?"

"If we can't get supplies, request that the men we sent to fight back east return here, immediately. So, they can defend their home state."

***

PRESIDENT LINCOLN READS the dispatch and says to his military advisor, "We can't relinquish any men."

Secretary of War, Edwin M. Stanton coughs forcefully, then asks, "What is this?"

"The governor of Minnesota, Ramsey, wants his volunteers back… Are you alright?"

"Yes, just my asthma flaring up again."

He spits the phlegm into a handkerchief. He continues to wheeze. He answers, "As it is, we need every man we can get."

Lincoln asks, "What are our options?"

"Instead of sending back soldiers, how about sending General Pope out west?"

"Didn't he just lose a battle where he had the advantage?"

Stanton wheezes and humbly replies, "Yes. But Pope may be better suited to deal with poorly armed savages than these southern armies."

"That might be true. From what this telegram states, they feel they can raise enough volunteers. All they may need is someone to train them."

Stanton continues to cough but agrees, "He has good ideas and is a competent manager, just not the best leader."

"Will that be enough to quell the uprising?"

Breathing quickly through his mouth, "He would at least get them organized. With him reassigned, that would give you an opportunity to bring up a stronger leader here in the field."

Lincoln nods and asks, "Who do you have in mind?"

"We have several choices. There is General Grant out West. He has had success along the Mississippi."

"Yes, he took Fort Donelson and Fort Henry back in February as I recall."

Stanton attempts to take a deep breath, but fails. He takes short quick breaths and replies, "Yes, he has been having good success out west."

Lincoln sighs, "But the losses at Shiloh are concerning."

"War is hell, Sir. He was attacked and he stood his ground and he prevailed."

***

NEWSPAPER IN MINNEAPOLIS and St. Paul begin printing editorials calling for mass extermination of all Indians in the State of Minnesota. It doesn't matter to the owners of the white press whether or not the natives participated in the uprising.

The news of the Birch Coulee disaster fuels this appeal for revenge. These editorials also bring new calls for firing Colonel Sibley. The newspaper columnists call him an undertaker because he only sent out a burial detail instead of a fighting force against the Dakota.

***

GOVERNOR RAMSEY TO his assistant, "We need to counter these newspaper editorials before they incite a mob and try to lynch me."

He folds the newspaper back to its original shape and slams it on the desk in front of him.

The assistant gets up from his chair and approaches, asking, "Do you want me to write a letter for you to sign off on?"

Ramsey pushes the newspaper to his assistant's side of the desk. "Yes, draft up a response. Make sure to include everything is being done, that can be done. We have organized militias, and more troops are being requested and sent. Things are under control."

The assistant begins to read the article in question, "I'll word it differently, but I got the idea."

"Explain that Colonel Sibley is moving as quickly as possible under the circumstances."

"But what about the Birch Coulee incident."

Ramsey, "He rescued the detail from a total massacre."

"So, he is a hero."

"Yes, that is what they need to believe."

***

North of Yellow Medicine Agency

CHIEFS, BIG EAGLE, Mankato, and Gray Bird enter Little Crow's camp with the other Birch Coulee attackers.

Gray Bird hands Little Crow Sibley's note.

Little Crow reads it aloud,

If Little Crow has any proposition to make, let him send a half-breed to me, and he shall be protected in and out of camp.

Little Crow suggests to the other elders, "We can use this message to convince the warriors to negotiate peace. But a council would have to be called. Both peace-seeking chiefs and warring chiefs would need to attend. The response needs to come from the opinions expressed at the council."

Little Crow sends messengers to all prominent chiefs. Again, there is no sign of Red Middle Voice and Shakopee, but both send spokespersons. The council gets heated quickly.

Rdainyanka, the son-in-law of Wabasha, begins, "Ever since we began to make treaties with the white man, they have robbed and cheated us. Our people have been shot and killed by the whites.

But we get no justice.

Many of our braves have been hung without even an attempt at holding a white man's trial.

Again, we get no justice.

Others have been bound and placed on floating ice and left to drown.

And still, we get no justice.

The whites wrongfully accuse our braves of crimes, arrest them, and place them in their prisons. Only to discover they were starved to death awaiting trial.

We are not allowed to seek justice."

The elders, in attendance, nod in agreement to his statements.

Rdainyanka continues, "We have lived under these conditions for many years. We have no way of seeking justice for our people with the white man. When four of our braves told us of what they did near Acton, we all knew the whites would not give them a fair trial. We also knew the army would attack our villages without warning if we didn't give them up. And they may have even if we had given them up."

A rumbling of agreement rolls around the council tepee turns into a more vocal recognition that what he spoke was true.

Rdainyanka adds, "Our older chiefs have gotten us into this situation by signing away our land. If they could have stopped this war, they would have, they haven't. So, now we must finish it. Those chiefs who have signed away our land have lost all influence with our people. We may sit here and regret how out of hand this war has gotten, but we cannot stop now. We must continue to rid the valley of the whites, or we will all die of their diseases or from starvation in their prisons. But the prisons we die in might be our villages. If we are to die, let us die as warriors. Let the captives then die with us."

A raucous cheer erupts from most of those present.

Paul Mazakutemani from the Upper Agency speaks next, "We should seek peace. We need to end this war. The chiefs from the lower agency were wrong to encourage our young braves to join you in this unwinnable fight. They should have come to us and held a council like this one before beginning this disastrous war. You have committed a great injustice by not coming to us first. Now, we must try to end this. I have heard your braves return from committing their savagery, claiming to be warriors. You are not Dakota warriors if you kill innocent women and children. Those of you who have done these things are not brave men but only cowards. If you desire to fight the white men, do it as a Dakota Warrior."

Little Crow does not speak. He listens. After the council disperses, he writes a response to Sibley's note.

I will explain to you the reasons we are at war. It is on account of your traders, like Major Galbraith and Andrew Myrick. We have made many treaties with your government. We have honored all of them. Yet we have to beg your traders for what we have been promised in those treaties. What we do get, we don't receive until our elders, our women and children are dying from hunger and your diseases. It is the greedy traders who have commenced this war, long before this outbreak of hostilities. Your trader, Andrew Myrick, told us in a council, in front of Captain Marsh and his men, that us Indians could eat shit for all he cared. Then trader Forbes insulted our warriors when he told them, they were not men. Trader Roberts and all of the rest of the traders are working together to steal our annuities.

You must admit this isn't all our fault.

If the young braves have punished the white man, so the white man is guilty of punishing the Dakota for no cause. We all bear some of the blame. I want you to tell Governor Ramsey, we have a great number of prisoners, mostly women and children. We will return those prisoners when you declare all lands west of the Minnesota River to be off-limits to white settlers.

The Winnebago are not involved in this fight, even though two of them were killed.

I will await your answer. You can send your reply along with the bearer of this message. We have held a group council of the Yellow Medicine and Redwood agencies and all are present.

Little Crow sends two mixed bloods to take his reply to Sibley.

***

SIBLEY INTERVIEWS THE two messengers separately and discovers the Dakota were at odds, which pleases him. This knowledge of strife gives him a bit of encouragement. Sibley's reply reflects this.

Little Crow, you have started this conflict of murder without any sufficient justification. If you return the captives to me, under a flag of truce. Then we can talk, not before then. Then I will talk to you like a man.

I have sent your letter to Governor Ramsey.

Chapter 28

Closer to home

The Long Journey Home

HENSON NOTICES WILDFIRE is sweating and pats the side of her neck.

"It is time for another break girl."

He pulls the reins to the right, spotting a patch of green grass under a grove of trees along the river's edge. He coughs fiercely as he directs his steed to the shade and grass. Henson gently pulls back on the reins to come to a stop. Wildfire immediately begins to graze. With a groan, the sore rider leans forward to bring his right leg up and over his pack. Every muscle and bone in his body seems to ache. Even worse, stiffness and tingling are settling in his legs and back.

"I can use the rest myself, girl."

With a thud, he lands on the dry, packed gumbo soil. Keeping the reins in hand, he leads Wildfire to the water's edge. He checks for a good spot for her to get a drink without sinking in the muck.

"This will do, girl."

He drapes the reins over her back.

"Now, get a drink."

Henson refills his canteen and then walks along the bank to loosen up his sore backside while he looks for a place to lie down. His mind quickly goes back to home.

“What has become of my oldest son, John?”

His thoughts go back to a time before all of this. About a year earlier.

***

Village of St James

Late September 1862

HENSON AND ARTHUR pull up to the Ames General Store by the water trough with a cast iron long-handled pump. Both men jump from the barter-loaded buckboard.

Arthur notices the trough's water level is low.

"I'll take care of the water, Pa."

"Good idea. I'll be inside."

Arthur begins to pump water for the two horses.

Henson notices the smell of beeswax candles as he makes his way to Martha Ames' counter, "We have some garden produce to barter."

Mrs. Ames exclaims, "Great, we can always use fresh produce."

Arthur enters and begins to wander the store, checking out the ever-increasing variety of merchandise. The scent of horehound draws him closer.

Henson notices his son's arrival but continues with his list, "Do you have any molasses?"

"I'm not sure. That is a difficult item to keep on the shelves. I'll check. What else will you need?"

"We'll also need some curing salt, baking soda, and a few other things."

"May I?" Martha takes the list from Henson's hand, "Well, I'll see what we have."

Arthur notices the exchange and asks, "Pa, should I go to the stable?"

"Naw, we'll go together. This shouldn't take too long."

Arthur checks out the bowls of bulk items along the wall in the back of the store. The fragrance of produce reminds Arthur it is almost lunchtime. A few minutes later, the storekeeper's wife has all the items and packed them in two wooden crates.

Mrs. Ames asks, "Will that be all?"

Henson adds, "Yes, I think that will be all." Then asks, "How are we on credit?"

"You still have a credit."

"Okay, Thanks a lot."

Martha, "You are very welcome, thank you."

Henson turns toward his son as he picks up one crate and says, "Arthur, come get this other crate."

A bit distracted, Arthur responds, "Sure thing, Pa."

Henson grabs his container and turns toward the front door of the store.

Arthur grabs his crate, "Thank you, Mrs. Ames."

"You are quite welcome, Arthur."

The Wiseman men place each grate on the wagon. Henson suggests, "Maybe we should leave the wagon here. Let's walk."

"Sure thing, Pa."

Henson's gaze goes side to side as they walk down the growing little town's main street. The astonishing progress in just a few short years brings a smile to his face. New businessmen continue to arrive and build stores while other stores add more space. A few men sit on chairs along the boardwalk, just outside the barbershop. Some of the men smoke pipes, and the others cigars. They nod at the father and son walking down the street.

Arthur asks, "What are we going to get from the livery, pa?"

"Gossip."

"Huh?"

Henson laughs, "Information, there weren't any papers left at the Ames' store. We'll go to the next best place. If there is any news, Al will know. Elam usually knows more than what is in the newspapers."

"Oh!"

Alfred Elam stands behind three men seated at a table in the corner of the livery. A small wood-burning stove has a pot of coffee still steaming on top. The main table has a couple of bottles of whiskey in the center and a shot glass in front of each man.

Al greets the duo, "What brings you two to town, ole timer?"

The others at the table laugh politely.

Henson shakes Al's hand, nods to the others, and smiles wryly, "We were just over to your store, Dave. There weren't any papers left, so we figured you might still have one on ya."

"I do. Let me get it."

Mr. Ames pushes back his chair, "Good to hear, did you buy me out?"

"No, but we bought enough."

Dave laughs and makes his way out of the livery to his mount.

Elam questions his friend, "What you two been up to lately?"

"Not much, just finishing up the harvest."

Al offers, "Can I get either of you some coffee?"

Henson, "No, not this late in the day."

Arthur waves slightly to signal he'll follow his father's lead.

"Well, then pull up a chair."

Henson grabs a vacant chair while Arthur finds a barrel outside the seated group.

George Ironside, "Whiskey then?"

George raises the bottle to Henson.

Arthur grins and waits to hear that response.

Henson lifts his eyes with a grin, "Naw, better not."

George suggests, "Your boy here can handle the team."

Ironside puts the bottle down on the table with a thud.

"Yes, he can, but he can't handle my wife."

Laughter follows.

Dave returns and hands Henson the paper. Henson unfolds it and begins scanning,

Frank Freeman pipes up, "Have you heard any news from your oldest boy?"

Henson answers, "No, that's one of the reasons why we are here, to find out if anyone else has heard anything."

Frank and his two boys are new arrivals in St James. Frank is a farmer by trade and a former slave on a cotton plantation down south. He and his boys escaped before the war started. His wife and other children were sold off to an unknown owner. Not long after, he was contacted by the underground railroad operative and helped to freedom. Not wanting to keep his owner's last name, Frank chose Freeman instead. His desire to start a new life for himself and his boys has brought him west. He finds work wherever he can along the way. He has struggled to save enough money to buy a place of their own. They work the land now for hire.

Henson asks Frank, “Where are your boys?”

“They got some work stacking hay down at Brooke’s place.”

"That'll keep them busy for a few days."

Frank adds, “I hope maybe longer.”

"Brookey bottom is good land. They'll put up a lot of hay off that ground."

Elam interjects, "Gimme that." Al snatches the paper unceremoniously from Henson's fingers. He realigns the paper and continues, "If you two keep yapping, you won't read a damn thing."

Frank and Henson laugh quietly.

“I saw it in here this morning. Here it is. I’ll read it. Says here they fought a battle near Kansas City.” Al mumbles aloud.

The four men scoot to the edge of their chairs with elbows on the table.

“Pa, that’s not far from here. Could John be there?”

"Son, it is a couple hundred miles, and I'm not sure. John hasn't been forthcoming with where his company has been sent. Let's hear what Al has to read."

Al nods and continues to read, “They call it the Battle of Independence.”

Henson is shocked, "What?"

Elam laughs, “Independence, Missouri.”

Arthur sighs, "Oh."

Elam scans the article, “That was on August 11th.”

Henson responds, “That’s over a month ago.”

George adds, “News doesn’t travel very fast out here.”

Frank asks, “What was the result?”

“Rebel victory.”

A worried Henson, “Damn… They say which battalions were involved?”

“No, not from what it says here… Then there is another battle they call Lone Jack.”

Arthur nervously asks, “Where was that one?”

“Missouri also.”

“Pa! John said he was with a Missouri regiment.”

Henson waves his calloused right hand toward Arthur, "I know, son." To Elam, "The result?"

“Another Confederate victory, the Union commander was killed.”

“Pa!”

Henson tries to calm his son, then asks Al, "Where is Lone Jack?"

“It says here it is just south of Kansas City.”

Henson shakes his head, "Well, that explains a few things."

Arthur asks, “What does it explain, Pa?”

“You can’t write if you are busy fighting… Does it say anything else, casualties?”

Arthur stands and begins to pace like his father normally does.

“Nothing here, but they say the Federal troops did give up the town… but they retook it shortly after with help from additional companies of troops.”

Henson interjects, "Well, that is good news. We'll just have to wait to hear any other news."

Al starts again, “Then there is this, not near where John is, I suppose, but it’s news of what is happening back there.”

Henson, “What’s that?”

“They call it the 2nd battle of Bull Run, near a town called Manassas.”

Arthur asks, “Where is that?”

Henson responds calmly, “In Virginia.”

"Pa, whereabouts in Virginia?"

Al interrupts, “To the east of where we all are from.”

“Oh.”

Henson calmly asks, “Any details?”

“Lee’s army won this battle also.”

A concerned Frank Freeman adds, “This isn’t looking good for the North.”

Al agrees, "Sure isn't. It says here that Lee's army went up against General Pope's army. This battle was much larger than the first one."

Arthur queries, “When was the first one?”

Henson fills in the details, “Last year, if I remember right, wasn’t in July.”

Frank adds, “I think you are right.”

Al nods in agreement, "It continues, a General, they call Stonewall Jackson, captured a Union supply depot at a place called Manassas Junction, cutting off General Pope's access to Washington D.C."

Henson, Arthur, and the three men at the table listen intently as Al reads and reports what it says in the article.

"Then Jackson took up positions at a place called Stony Ridge and waited for his fellow rebel, General Longstreet, to arrive."

Al pauses to read more and continues, "Then Jackson attacked Pope's forces at a town called Gainesville, but there was no clear-cut winner in that battle. While Longstreet attacked a small column of Union soldiers near Thoroughfare Gap."

Henson, “I know where that is!”

Frank, “Me too!”

"Where is it, Pa?"

“It’s on the other side of the Appalachians.”

Al interrupts, "There's more. Says here, Pope was fooled into thinking he had Jackson trapped, and in an attempt to finish him off Jackson, he attacked with the majority of his forces with multiple attacks. Each attack was defeated. Both sides reported heavy losses. Unbeknownst to Pope, Longstreet had joined Jackson on Pope's right flank. When Pope attacked again, Longstreet opened fire with artillery, devastating Union General Porter's command."

Arthur, "Oh my god."

"There's more. General Longstreet had 25,000 men and counterattacked in mass. This attack sent the Union's left flank all the way back to a place they refer to as Bull Run."

Henson sighed heavily, "Well, thank God John's not anywhere near there. At least, we hope not."

Al announces, "Then there is the battle of Richmond!"

Frank and Henson, in unison, "What?"

"Richmond, Kentucky." Alfred then laughs.

Henson sighs, "That wasn't funny, Al."

Frank exclaims, "Oh, damn, I was hoping it was Richmond, Virginia."

Al laughs, "Yeah, if it was Richmond, Virginia, that war would probably be over. But that doesn't seem to be the case."

Frank states firmly, "But if that were so, by the sound of it, the South would be the winners."

Henson acknowledges the point with a head nod.

George asks, "So, what does it say about that battle?"

"It says here the Confederate rebels won that one, too."

A frustrated Henson exclaims, "Damn, this is not looking good."

"A Major General Smith went against a Union Major General Nelson, nicknamed Bull Nelson. Nelson was supposed to defend the town. This battle was the first big one in Kentucky, and it was near another Union Army depot."

Frank declares, "That means the rebs have a clear path to Lexington."

Al shakes his head, “It would seem!”

Alfred sets the paper down on the table.

The sole silent member of the group, Samuel Gamble, states, "I was to Yankton just the other day, but there was not much in the paper there, either."

Henson shakes his head.

Al confirms, “I heard from Henry Ashton that the uprising in Minnesota is quite a mess.”

Sam asks, “What does that mean?”

Al reports, “The savages first attacked their own Agency, then they turned on Fort Ridgely.”

Henson inquires, "Any report of casualties?"

“Henry didn’t say, but that can’t be good.”

"Where did he hear all this? There hasn't been anything in the papers."

Al speculates, "I'm not sure, but lots of settlers moving this direction, bringing news with 'em."

“Gossip and rumors mostly.”

"Sure, but he did say there were traders and a lot of settlers killed at the agency and surrounding area, but the Fort didn't fall."

George Ironside, "All of this news is weeks old. Who knows what is happening now."

Al continues, "From what I heard, they attacked the fort twice and the small town of New Ulm twice, too."

After a sip of whiskey, Sam Gamble says, "It seems like it is a lot worse than what we figured."

Sam offers to pour a shot for each person at the table.

Arthur looks at his father with a concerned stare.

Henson dismisses the offer.

He looks back to Al, “Anything else?”

Alfred states firmly, "From what he told me, they didn't take either one."

Sam, “That’s good news!”

Everyone at the table agrees with a toast followed by a quick gulp of whiskey.

Henson adds, “But that doesn’t tell me anything about where John is.”

Al, "Tell you what, ole timer. If I hear anything else, I'll personally ride out to your place."

Henson bristles and then gives Alfred an insincere smile at the ole-timer comment, "I would appreciate that, but that won't be necessary."

"I don't mind at all. Your Pheobe is a good cook. So, as long as you feed me, it's not a problem."

There is laughter from all at the table.

Chapter 29

On the 31st day of the,
Minnesota Uprising 1862

September 18th, 1862

BOTH PEACEFUL AND hostile Dakota bands decide it is better to move further away from Sibley's forces that are camped near Fort Ridgely. Little Crow's supporters move north to Lac Qui Parle, about a dozen miles north of the Yellow Medicine Agency. Some peace-seeking Dakota prepare to move west, while others remain in their villages.

Little Crow and his band encounter Chief Red Iron and his warriors at Lac qui Parle, blocking their path northward.

Red Iron begins, "That is as far as you can go. We want nothing to do with you or your war. If you come into our village, it will appear we are with you, and we are not."

"If you had joined us, we would have been able to rid this valley of the whites, but you are satisfied to take the scraps from the white man."

"We will live in peace with the whites."

Little Crow insistently answers, "You will live and die their slaves."

"Enough from you. Find another way. You cannot cross our land."

"This is Dakota land. You cannot prevent us from passing."

Red Iron responds firmly, "We can and we will."

Little Crow and his followers begin to move forward.

Red Iron's braves fire shots into the air.

Little Crow's warriors respond in kind. Warriors on both sides draw their bows and place their arrows.

Little Crow, "Don't! Put those away. They are our people."

Red Iron agrees, "We can hold a council between our elders."

***

RED IRON, “WE do not approve of your crossing our land.”

Little Crow responds, "This is the land of our ancestors. It belongs to all of us."

Wabasha answers, “You gave away our ancestor’s land to the whites.”

“We negotiated and were lied to. You were there. You should understand this more than anyone else.”

Wacouta interjects, “But today, this is Red Iron and his people’s land. He decides who can cross his land.”

Little Crow tries again, “If you are unhappy with the treaties we all signed, then join me and rid ourselves of those treaties.”

Red Iron answers, "You and your braves have attempted to do this on your own. That was foolish. If you had come to us, we might have joined you. But you didn't include us in your decision. We will not be a part of your decision now either."

Wabasha adds, “We tried to convince you this war was a mistake, but you wouldn’t listen.”

Little Crow's frustration increases, "You are unhappy with the treaties you signed with me and the other chiefs. But you are still too cowardly to stand up for your people and against the whites that have cheated us at every turn."

Both Wabasha and Red Iron become incensed by the insult.

Red Iron, "We are not fools. We hear that you understood this before you agreed to bring death and destruction to our people. You acted like the ones you called children. We heard you changed your mind when Traveling Hail arrived. You acted like children."

Little Crow replies, "The four braves that started this would have been turned over to the whites and certainly killed. They would not have been given a fair trial. There is no justice with the whites. Our only hope is to fight and take back our land. Now we will negotiate a peace."

Wabasha dismisses Little Crow's remarks, "Negotiate peace. You have not won a battle. The attack on the first day was successful because it was a surprise attack. The battle at Birch Coulee was only partially successful for the same reason. We, our people, don't have the weapons or the ammunition to fight the whites. You must face reality."

Wacouta adds, "Negotiations can only be successful with strength."

Little Crow seizes on that comment, "That is correct. Join us, and we will be stronger."

Red Iron answers, "If we join you, we'll be no longer."

Wabasha adds, "Your braves have slaughtered many innocent whites."

Little Crow rebukes that assertion, "Red Middle Voice and Shakopee's warriors are responsible for those types of attacks. I told them and their braves that was unacceptable."

Wabasha dismisses Little Crow, "They are not warriors. Warriors don't kill innocent women and children."

"I agree. I have told their messengers at our councils. Councils they refuse to attend, exactly what you said."

Wacouta adds, "But it has not stopped them."

"No, it hasn't. Some of our braves have brought in hostages. Again, it was against my instructions. But now they are here. We can use them in our negotiations."

Red Iron, "We are not going to negotiate with the whites, peace for the prisoners. They would never honor that agreement anyway."

"You admit we can not trust the whites, but you won't join us. If we come together, we can have the strength to negotiate a lasting peace."

Wabasha stands up, "You are a fool."

Little Crow stands up quickly in defiance.

Wacouta stands also and separates the two chiefs.

Red Iron slowly rises and speaks firmly, "We called this council to decide if you would be permitted to cross our land. I say no. If you cross our lands, if we allow you to cross, it will be seen as joining you. We will not."

Wacouta, "I stand with Red Iron."

Wabasha, "I stand with Red Iron."

Red Iron states clearly, "You will go around. You may not cross our land."

Little Crow glares at the three chiefs one at a time in disbelief. He turns to the lodge opening, looks back, and shakes his head in disgust.

***

AFTER THE COUNCIL, Little Crow and his people go around Red Iron's land.

Wabasha, Wacouta, and other peace-seeking chiefs bring their people into Red Iron's village and set up their tepees beside theirs in a show of support.

Little Crow's band continues to grow weaker. In an attempt to find a way to end this conflict, he sends a second letter to Sibley. He sends the same messengers as the first time. Unbeknownst to Little Crow, the peace-seeking Dakota chiefs intercept the two messengers and include a letter of their own to Sibley.

Little Crow's letter,

We have over a hundred and fifty captives, mostly women and children. We have moved our people to Lake Qui Parle. You said you sent my letter to the Governor. What was his response? As friends, I would like you to tell me what I can do to make peace. The prisoners are well. They are doing as well as we are.

The peace-seeking chief's letter to Sibley.

We are not with Little Crow and his warriors. We seek peace. Let us know what we can do to secure a lasting peace.

Sibley answers both letters.

To Little Crow,

You have not given up the prisoners as I asked. It would be better for you to do so. I have sent your letter to Governor Ramsey. But I have not received a reply as of yet. Furthermore, your people have committed more murders since you wrote your first letter. This is not the way to make peace.

Sibley's letter to the peace seekers was more conciliatory.

Secure as many prisoners as you can and bring them to me under a flag of truce. Your people will be safe in and out of the fort.

September 19, 1862, Sibley finally moves away from Fort Ridgely. It takes his troops four days to travel, what takes a regular wagon just one day. Ever cautious, he starts each day at mid-morning, camps for lunch, and then makes camp for the night at four in the afternoon.

Chapter 30

Chaska's Yankton Dakota Village

Fall of 1862

ELDERS OF THE Yankton Lakota people gather in a lodge at the center of their village. Killing Ghost and his three companions sit around a fire with these elders. The council is almost over.

Killing Ghost asks, "Where will we find the nearest village to the north? We have been to most of those to the east of here."

Smutty Bear to Killing Ghost, "You will find a large village along the river less than a casual day's ride north. They will be camped along a good-sized stream that flows into the river. There are many more villages along the river."

"Thank you. We should get some rest before we leave tomorrow."

Just as he stands to leave the council lodge, Killing Ghost is greeted by Little Thunder's father.

Roaring Cloud, "May I have a word with you?"

"Sure."

"Alone, if you will?"

Killing Ghost motions for his three followers to step outside the council lodge. The three find positions near the village's centerfire, where many villagers have gathered.

Smutty Bear nods as he exits with the other elders.

Roaring Cloud "Have a seat. I don't think this will take long."

Killing Ghost accepts the suggestion.

"In your presentation, you mentioned a lot of things."

"Yes, there is a lot to tell."

"One thing stood out to me. The contest at the farm."

Killing Ghost is taken by surprise at the bluntness of this stranger, "Yes, that was an important moment in the presentation."

"But the things that led up to it didn't justify what happened."

"Did you hear about the white men stealing our kill?"

Roaring Cloud nods, "Yes. Yes, I did. I was going to ask about that, too."

"What did you want to know?"

"Did this happen many times?"

Killing Ghost, "Yes, on a few occasions, but I, we had had enough."

"We have not had that kind of incident here."

"You will. It is only a matter of time."

Roaring Cloud, "I'm sure you believe this."

"I do. The white man will continue to come."

"We have not had the same experiences that you have."

Killing Ghost responds, "But I have talked to many elders here, and they mentioned your Indian agent, Burleigh."

"Oh, yes, him."

"How can you forget about things like that?"

Roaring Cloud, "I have not forgotten about that. It was a few years ago."

"It will happen again. They keep coming and taking our land."

"You seem very angry."

Killing Ghost, "I have every right to be. So do you. Your village was once free. You are now restricted to this desolate reservation. At least my people had land that was fertile."

"How free are you now? You are on the run."

"We are not on the run. We are on a mission."

Roaring Cloud, "Yes, I understand your mission. You are here to spread hate and death."

"We have come here to tell you the truth. The white man is out to kill us all."

"Then why do they give us land and supplies."

Killing Ghost, "They are trapping you with those things. You will forget how to hunt, fish, and fend for yourselves."

"I don't believe that."

"I have seen it with my own people and many villages we have visited."

Roaring Cloud, "You are an angry young man. I understand you lost your wife and children and blame the white man for it."

"It was their diseases that killed them. They brought those contaminated blankets to us. They had their medicine but would not give us any of it."

"So, what is your answer?"

Killing Ghost, "We must join Little Crow and the other chiefs to stand up to the whites."

"You mean go to war?"

"I mean, stop their taking our hunting grounds. Stop them from killing our people with their diseases and whiskey."

Roaring Cloud, "You are not as wise a young man as you think you are."

"I am not a fool that only wants to live off what the white man promises and doesn't deliver."

"You will lead these naïve braves to their deaths."

Killing Ghost, "If we don't stand up, they will die in their sleep from the white man's diseases. They spread these diseases to our people on purpose."

"I have heard enough. You are not to see my daughter."

"Is that what this is all about?"

Roaring Cloud, "Yes."

"Little Thunder is your daughter?"

"Yes. She is my daughter."

Killing Ghost, "Nothing has happened between your daughter and myself."

"And it won't."

"Do you understand our mission?"

Roaring Cloud, "Yes, I understand you want to die a warrior."

"You refuse to listen, so you will not understand our mission."

"I understand you care not what happens to those that follow you."

Killing Ghost, "You forget how your agent sunk a steamer with your supplies."

"I remember."

"But you forget he stole all of it for himself."

Roaring Cloud, "We got our supplies."

"Only after their military stepped in and threatened to kill every last one of you."

"I see you have talked to the elders."

Killing Ghost, "Yes, I have asked many questions."

"I'm sure you have."

"I have also answered many questions."

Roaring Cloud, "Many fools are ready to follow you to your death."

"We will stand up to the whites and prevent them from taking everything that was ours."

"You sound like them. We cannot own the land. We cannot own the buffalo."

Killing Ghost, "You still hang on the old ways."

"You should try to understand the old ways."

"Those old ways have gotten us stuck on reservations."

Roaring Cloud, "At least we are alive."

"For how long? When will you see they are out to kill every last one of us?"

"I have heard enough. You are forbidden from seeing my daughter."

Killing ghost, "I will take what I want when I want."

Roaring Cloud stands abruptly. Killing Ghost responds in the same manner.

His three companions have heard the discussion and have returned. They stand outside the council lodge.

The Dakota brave stands toe to toe with the Lakota father.

"I am warning you. Stay away from my daughter."

Killing Ghost, "You do not intimidate me."

Roaring Cloud pushes Killing Ghost with both hands in the chest.

Killing Ghost stumbles backward and recovers.

"You shouldn't have touched me."

The three companions hear the commotion. They look at each other in shock. They rush into the lodge.

Killing Ghost waves his arms to calm them.

"You have heard me. Do not go near my daughter."

"We were supposed to stay in one of your tepees tonight?"

Roaring Cloud, "I will find you a different lodge to sleep in."

***

ROARING CLOUD arrives at his tepee. Little Thunder sits on a buffalo blanket, sewing decorative designs into deerskin leggings.

Red Dove greets her husband, "Are you hungry?"

"Yes, but not right now."

She can see he is in no mood to question further. She goes about her activities.

Roaring Cloud to his daughter, "You are not to be seen with the messengers."

"Father. Why?"

"Don't you worry about why."

Little Thunder, "What happened?"

"You heard me. He is trouble."

"Killing Ghost?"

Roaring Cloud, "Yes, you know who I mean. Any of them, but especially him."

"Father. What did you do?"

"I had a face-to-face talk with him."

Little Thunder, "What?"

"I sat him down and forbade him from seeing you."

"Father. How could you?"

Roaring Cloud sheepishly states, "It is for your own good."

"I can't believe this. First Chaska, and now my father betrays me." She throws her leggings aside and stands up.

"I didn't betray you. I saved your life."

Little Thunder whines, "I don't believe this is happening. Mother?"

"It was an easy decision. He is full of anger, and he is not good for you."

Red Dove, "Dear, you should listen to your father."

"How can you say that? Mother!"

She turns from one parent to the next.

"Father. He just got here. You saw his presentation. He is a leader."

Roaring Cloud, "He will lead those ignorant enough to follow him to their deaths."

"Why are you doing this to me?"

"I am protecting you from a very troubled man."

Little Thunder, "Mama, tell him. No man in this village or any around here will have me."

Red Dove to her daughter, "I have told him."

Roaring Cloud, "You are a good woman. It may take time but you will find someone good for you. This brave is not good for you."

Little Thunder, "Didn't you listen to his story?"

"Yes, I listened, and yes, many terrible things happened to him and his family."

"He lost his wife and children."

Roaring Cloud, "I heard, and I understand."

"The whites stole from him."

"That is what he says."

Little Thunder, "You don't believe they stole from him?"

"It was his response that troubles me."

"They disrespected him and his followers."

Roaring Cloud, "I understand that too, but he didn't think ahead."

"Father, what are you saying?"

"I'm saying I understand the anger, but now look at what that decision has done to so many. Word has it that most of their villagers are fleeing to the west."

Little Thunder, "What would you have done?"

"We faced a very similar situation, and we didn't… "

"You didn't stand up to the whites and look where we are."

Roaring Cloud, "We are alive."

"So is he."

"But for how long. He has a destiny with death."

Little Thunder, "We all do."

"His will come much sooner, and he will not take you with him."

"Father, you can't stop us."

Roaring Cloud, "I will protect you, but…"

His daughter turns and throws the buffalo hide back off the opening of their main tepee, then runs out crying.

Roaring Cloud to his wife, "Oh, we'll need to find somewhere else for the messengers to sleep."

"Yes, I was giving that some thought. I'm proud of you. She might hate you now, but she will eventually realize it was for the best."

"I hope so."

"She will."

They embrace and sigh.

Chapter 31

Battle of Wood Lake

Minnesota

September 23, 1862

THREE DAKOTA WARRIORS sit around a freshly lit fire in a modest tepee on bare earth. Silence screams in their heads. The fire burns slowly. Each man stares at the growing infant flames. The orange and yellow flickering flames build, catching kindling and firewood one by one. The fire heating up, just like the tempers of the three Dakota braves, increases as they avoid discussing their dire situation.

Little Crow breaks the silence, "We are greatly outnumbered. We must use our abilities of stealth to our advantage."

Walks Among Sacred Stones responds with a question, “What are you suggesting?”

Gray Bird interrupts, “We could attack them in the morning, before they are awake, as Big Eagle and I did at Birch Coulee.”

Walks Among Sacred Stones, "That is a plan of a coward. We are Dakota warriors. We don't need tricks to fight the white man."

"But we were successful. We lost few warriors, and they lost many soldiers."

Little Crow dismisses the advice and continues to scrutinize the situation, "But we are now even more outnumbered. Our numbers are dwindling, not growing. We need a victory. If the other bands are to join us, we need a victory. We need to use our heads if we ever desire to drive the white soldiers from our valley."

Walks Among Sacred Stone, “What if we do as we did near Hutchinson, that worked.”

Gray Bird asks, “What was that?”

Walks Among Sacred Stone explains, “As the column advanced through the valley, we found a place to attack from all sides.”

Little Crow agrees, “Yes, we can place our warriors in the trees and grass again.”

Gray Bird asks, "How is that different from what I suggested?"

Little Crow stares at Gray Bird.

Walks Among Sacred Stone breaks the silence, “Our braves can wait along the road until we attack the front of their column.”

Little Crow to Gray Bird, “You attacked when they were sleeping. We will attack when they are marching past us. Just like we did near Hutchinson. Like Dakota warriors.”

"As long as the whites die in large numbers, it is all the same to me."

Little Crow turns to Walks Among Sacred Stone, “When you hear the first bugle.”

Walks Among Sacred Stone finishes, “We will have our braves ready and prepared.”

“Yes, and by the time they blow the second bugle…”

“Our warriors should be set to do battle.”

Little Crow smiles at the eagerness and to Gray Bird, “It will take them time to saddle up and march out of camp and up the road.”

Gray Bird, “What will be the signal to attack?”

“Your warriors along the road will need to be patient. They will need to be silent and not show themselves. This is very important.”

Walks Among Sacred Stone adds, "Once they are deep into our trap, past the last hidden warriors, I will… "

Little Crow interrupts, “I will attack the back of their column.”

Walks Among Sacred Stone begins again, "When the battle starts, you will hear the musket fire, and everyone on all sides will attack."

“Yes, Everyone from all sides of their column.”

Gray Bird, “Cutting off retreat.”

“Just like we did near Hutchinson.”

“Yes, and large numbers of white soldiers died.”

Gray Bird adds, “Then it is a good plan.”

Little Crow to them both, “You will take your warriors out in the middle of the night to find places to hide along the road.”

Walks Among Sacred Stone agrees and to Gray Bird, “The high grass is sufficient.”

Gray Bird nods and suggests, “And there are many trees and brush along that road.”

***

DAKOTA BRAVES SETTLE in for a long night and wait in groups. Hundreds of Dakota slumber in the tall grass of the meadows near Wood Lake.

***

MOST OF SIBLEY'S camp is sound asleep. Tents are all arranged in rows only separated by companies. The only ones awake are the cooks. Each company has at least two cooks and a couple of helpers.

The Quartermasters hands out provisions for gruel and coffee.

The first helper complains, "This is all we get?"

"That is all we have. So, yes, that is all you get. Same for all of the companies."

***

THE HELPER REPORTS to his cook, “This is all we get this morning.”

"I'll don’t see what I am supposed to do that."

In frustration, the cook removes his apron and says, "Do with it the best you can."

He marches to the head cook and says, "We need more food. We don't have enough to feed all of these men."

“I’ll take it up the chain of command.”

"To hell with that. We need something done now."

Head cook, “I’ll talk to the captain.”

An assistant cook, “Take it to Sibley. Cut the red tape.”

“Yes, that will be much quicker.”

***

AFTER HEARING THE complaints, Sibley to one of his Captains, "Send out a few details to rummage the farm sights in the area. Have them bring back whatever they can find."

“Yes, sir.”

"I guess it is time to implement General Pope's ideas. But only we’ll be scavenging from our people.”

"Sir?"

"Never mind. Go. Go."

***

BEFORE SUNRISE GROUPS of four soldiers fan out in different directions along the road and countryside, each group with a wagon and three riders begin rummaging through farm places nearby. Livestock of any kind will do. They scavenge the gardens and fields, the barns and sheds, and abandoned homes for anything edible.

The foragers continue entering farm places and returning to the road and on to the next.

***

A GROUP OF natives hiding in the grass hear the riders and wagons rubble down the dirt path.

One whispers to the others, prostrate on the ground, "Someone is coming."

***

A PRIVATE RIDING alongside one of the wagons shouts and points, "I see a farm place over there."

Like an adult Easter egg hunt, a group of men on horseback cut across the high grass field in a mad dash. They almost trample the hiding Dakota natives.

"Indians!"

The warriors are exposed and forced to defend themselves.

***

THE MUSKET FIRE alerts Sibley's camp and the other hidden warriors.

Sibley at his tent opening, "What is that?"

Sergeant, "The scavenging crews must have been attacked."

A Lieutenant asks, "Orders, Sir?"

"Sound assembly."

The orders are passed down the ranks, and the bugle blares within moments.

Chaos follows but in an orderly fashion.

***

LITTLE CROW THROWS down his knife, sticking it in the ground, "We have lost the element of surprise. Spread the word to seek cover and be ready to fight."

Walks Among Sacred Stone's eyes widen with shock, and he asks, "Cover?"

"It is all we can do. Have them find any trees, bushes, ravines, anything to take cover."

Gray Bird arrives and asks, “What happened?”

"The ambush is over. Now, we must prepare for battle."

“You know we don’t stand a chance against their muskets.”

Little Crow's face crumples with hostility. He dismisses the comment, "Spread the word. Have them prepare for battle."

***

SIBLEY TREMBLES WITH fear. Quivering, he asks, "Any word from the scavenging details?"

“Only a few from the foraging details have returned.”

"Is there any useful information?"

The captain hesitates, "They say the Sioux are hiding in the hills along the road."

“Where they were planning an ambush?”

"It seems like that, Sir."

Sibley contemplates his predicament, "Assemble all companies but two. Those two companies are to stay and protect the camp if this is a diversion."

"Yes, sir, and the other companies?"

“I’m working on a plan. Bring me those soldiers that made it back.”

Captain sighs, "Yes, Sir."

***

LITTLE CROW TO Walks Among Sacred Stone, "He won't march down the road now. He'll spread his men and clear the fields."

“We may have sufficient cover in the trees to make a stand.”

“Spread the word to the braves to not be foolish. Wait until they have a good shot and then fall back. They won’t get a second shot off once discovered.”

Walks Among Sacred Stone moans and states with certainty, “This isn’t like Hutchinson.”

"No, it isn't. We had the element of surprise, and that worked for us."

"It is more like the Fort or New Ulm but without barricades or buildings for protection."

Little Crow, "Those hiding in the grass may only get off one shot. With a limited number of arrows and very little black powder and lead. They need to make each shot count."

“I’ll spread the word.”

***

SIBLEY GIVES THE order to his captains. The first column marches out of camp in a two-by-two formation, ready to do battle. Each soldier holds his loaded musket across their chest. Once the column is near where the scavenger patrols was attacked, orders are given to break down the column. One soldier marches to the left while the other marches to the right. The second column follows the same orders until they are two deep, with hundreds of men spread across the grass fields with muskets across their chests and ready.

When they are in position, an order is given by one of the captains, "Company halt."

Orders are relayed down the line. All movement stops.

“Prepare.”

The soldiers lower their Ensign muskets and systematically prepare them.

When all soldiers are finished, and the order is given, “Ready, March.”

In an uneven line, the soldiers march toward the hidden warriors.

***

ON A NEARBY hill, Sibley sits on his horse with his field officers. He lowers his telescope and tells one of his captains, "Have them bring up the cannons."

A messenger is dispatched.

The captain asks, “Where do you want those placed?”

"We'll see where they are hiding before I make that decision."

“Those trees along the road on the west side are the most likely spot.”

Sibley responds, “I haven’t seen any movement over there. But I agree that is most likely where they are hiding.”

"A ravine on the east side of the road could make for good cover, too."

"I agree with that also. Have the cannons brought up behind the troops, flushing them out of the grass. And have them prepare to fire on those locations if it is proven correct."

“Yes, Sir.”

“Do not wait for my orders. Have all of the sergeants relay the order to fire at will.”

“Yes, Sir.”

***

WALKS AMONG SACRED Stones, “They are spreading out.”

Little Crow answers, "As I thought. They are clearing the high grass areas, and they will try to corral us in the trees or that ravine. Because of their military maneuvers, our warriors will not be able to hold their positions. They will need to retreat after their first shot."

***

BOTH SIDES EXCHANGE scattered fire for a few hours. The soldiers force the Dakota braves to relinquish the field.

***

AS THE SUN sets on the battlefield, and the black powder smoke drifts solemnly to the East. Dakota warriors sit on their ponies on a hill a mile from Wood Lake. They watch pockets of their fellow braves scattering like the drifting musket smoke in the wind.

Little Crow announces to Gray Bird, "It is over. There is no way to continue. We must leave this place."

Wowinape asks, "What do you mean? Where do we attack next?"

"There will be no more attacks. Our numbers are not enough to continue. Our warriors and their families flee to the west."

"What will we do?"

"You do not have to come with me. You are free to go where you please."

Gray Bird insists, “I will stay with you.”

"So will I, father."

***

AT WABASHA'S VILLAGE encampment, two elders sit across from each other in the council lodge. A small fire burns between them.

Wabasha, a peace-seeking chief, smugly states to Little Crow, "You wouldn't listen to me."

"No, it is you who wouldn't listen to me. You will sit there and tell me you are right. But you are still wrong."

"After all of this, you still can't see it."

With disgust in his eyes, Little Crow yells, "If you had joined us. If you had supported us, we could have taken the fort."

"You are a dreamer. Suppose you had taken the fort. You would have lost it soon after."

"We could have begun to negotiate from a position of strength. We could have gotten our valley back, our forest, our way of life."

Wabasha shakes his head in disbelief, "Enough of your foolishness. What are you going to do with the captives?"

Little Crow frowns and shakes his head in disgust. "You and your people have removed most of them. This I already know."

"It was the right thing to do!"

"It was the cowardly thing to do. If you had fought with us, we would have been successful."

Wabasha snidely states, "Don't blame me for your losses."

Little Crow stands abruptly and steps beside the fire, "We were not united. If we were, we could have our land back."

Wabasha rises and steps back for each step Little Crow takes forward.

Little Crow's raises his voice and it is filled with rage, "But you and you sniveling chiefs are content with what the white man gives you. Scraps from their table."

"We will seek peace."

"You will get starvation and disease as a reward for your cowardice."

Wabasha looks away, "What about the captives? What will you do with those you still have in your camp?"

"They are yours now. Do as you have wished."

Little Crow gathers those warriors still loyal to him and heads north, along the Minnesota River.

Some of the Dakota chiefs from the Wahpeton band send a message to Sibley asking to bury their dead.

Sibley refuses. He tells them in another letter via messenger.

I will bury them like whites. I will care for the wounded, and I will not exchange any prisoners until the white captives are released.

Wabasha replies in a letter to Sibley,

The warring Dakota have left. The only Dakota left are the peace-seeking Indians. We have most of the prisoners here waiting for you.

TO BE CONTINUED

Made in the USA
Monee, IL
09 February 2025

d3c477c2-33be-483d-b92a-95e4d029e1efR01